VIVIAN VAN TASSEL AND THE SECRET OF MIDNIGHT LAKE

MICHAEL WITWER

ALADDIN
New York ✦ London ✦ Toronto ✦ Sydney ✦ New Delhi

ALADDIN

An imprint of Simon & Schuster Children's Publishing Division

1230 Avenue of the Americas, New York, New York 10020

First Aladdin hardcover edition August 2023

Text copyright © 2023 by Michael Witwer

Jacket illustration copyright © 2023 by Raymond Sebastien

For information about special discounts for bulk purchases, please contact Simon & Schuster Special Sales at 1-866-506-1949 or business@simonandschuster.com.

The Simon & Schuster Speakers Bureau can bring authors to your live event. For more information or to book an event contact the Simon & Schuster Speakers Bureau at 1-866-248-3049 or visit our website at www.simonspeakers.com.

Designed by Tiara Iandiorio

The text of this book was set in Fournier MT Std .

Manufactured in the United States of America 0723 FFG

2 4 6 8 10 9 7 5 3 1

Library of Congress Control Number 2023932717

ISBN 9781665918190 (hc)

ISBN 9781665918213 (ebook)

For Kalysta, Vivienne, William, Arthur, and Iris

Prophecy of Thorns 1:1–9: The Song of Arborem

Three brothers born of an ageless king
One thousand years of peace they bring
To reign o'er cities, sea, and land
And uphold virtue hand in hand

But humankind, so hungry they are
To conquer lands both near and far
Felling trees to build their homes
A scourge on nature where'er they roam

The lord of forest, land, and brae
With folk lost patience and his way
He sought to end the race of men
A plan to cleanse the world again

The city lord didst not agree
"Give men a chance," he made his plea
"They should be taught, not be forsaken
Your visions of doom, these ways mistaken"

The brothers warred, a bloody clash
Men, elves, and dwarves made steel flash
'gainst woodland creatures that crawled and crept
Upon ruined towns while children wept

The forest monsters felt men's wrath
so Tree Lord took a darker path
He opened gates to other worlds
to draw out armies, flags unfurled

The sea lord finally joined the fray
to aid the cities, men and fey
The brothers banished the forest lord
To parts unknown and places untoward

Yet still a frightful vision remains
of Tree Lord's return, the world he gains
To finish work he once began
To cleanse all worlds of human span

He shall succeed except this claim
A girl who bears a special name
a silver thorn right in his side
If she returns, his plan shall die

—Fragments from the Codex Fey Historium

Prologue

"KANE, COME QUICK!" bellowed Taran.

Kane dashed through the forest, readying his longbow in a single motion. He arrived at the narrow clearing and slipped around Taran for a better look. It was only a carcass, though mangled and fleshless.

His clear, green eyes narrowed as he lowered his bow.

"What is it?" he asked as he slung the weapon around his shoulder and knelt beside his fellow woodsman.

"It *was* a deer," Taran muttered, his grimace shielded by his long, black hair.

"*Deer* Lord," mused Kane.

"This is no joke, Kane," snapped Taran, shooting an icy glare at the blond bowman. "This is the third occurrence this week . . . it's getting worse. And this time only a mile from town."

"Nonsense," said Kane. He grabbed a stick and poked the bloody remains. "Animal attacks happen all the time. It doesn't mean . . . I mean, it could've been anything. Probably just a mountain lion."

"I wish it were," sighed Taran as he turned his attention back to the carcass, using a silver dagger to inspect the wounds. "These are from large claws to be sure, but these tears here are not from claws or teeth—they're from a beak."

"A beak?" repeated Kane. "What, a bird?"

"Nay," replied Taran as he turned over the bloody remnant.

The entire bottom side of the carcass was covered in blood-soaked brown and gray feathers.

"A vulturebear," Taran said grimly.

Kane sprung up.

"Are you sure?"

"Quite," said Taran. "It must have come through in the last week or so. Let's hope it's just one."

"We'll need to redouble the watch," Kane replied as he pulled a cell phone out of his olive hunter's vest and began snapping pictures of the carnage. "At least for a little while."

He tried tapping out a message with his thumbs.

"Dang! Bad service up here."

"After losing Sylvia, we're stretched thin as it is. We don't even have the ranks to provide continuous watch at all of the entrances anymore. That's probably how our friend came through. . . ." Taran's voice trailed off. "Make sure to copy Drusen."

"Drusen? Bah! We don't want his help," spit Kane. "He gives me the creeps—a born killer. Not one to trust."

"Just the same, the underground is his domain," countered Taran. "Drusen's the only one among us who can spend any real time in those poisonous caves."

Kane sighed deeply.

"He's not *of* us or 'among us,' if you ask me, but I'll add him."

A slight breeze whistled through the thick green and yellow wood, encouraging the cicadas to speed up their rhythmic chirp—a peaceful sound that had dominated these woods every summer evening for generations.

"Let's get back to HQ and regroup with the others." Kane shuddered. "It's getting dark and I'm not anxious to try to track a vulturebear at night. Darn things can see for a mile in the dark."

"Agreed," replied Taran. "The trail runs out here anyway. There's too much fresh ground cover . . . or . . ."

A chill fell over both woodsmen as the breeze suddenly died down. The cicadas ceased their song, leaving the pair locked in tense stillness.

"Shhh!" Taran whispered. "Do you hear something?"

A low, chittering growl rumbled from the trees above. In an instant, both men had redrawn their weapons to the ready: Kane his bow strung with a silver arrow; Taran a gleaming longsword from the rifle case he had been carrying to complement the dagger in his other hand.

That's when they saw them: a pair of huge, red-rimmed vulture eyes that loomed above them, piercing through the waxy green canopy.

"Hold still," Taran hissed through his teeth. "No sudden moves."

Low, rumbling sounds emerged from the trees behind them. Taran slowly turned his head. To his horror, he saw two more sets of soulless, vulturelike eyes stabbing through the leaves.

Then, from behind a distant tree, a brown-robed figure emerged leaning upon a twisted, thorny staff.

"Who in the blazes is that?" hissed Kane.

The man stepped forward. His eyes were wild and bloodshot, bugging through a horned helmet made from the skull of a ram. A tattered gray beard hung below a jaw full of jagged, yellow teeth.

"No . . . ," sputtered Taran as he made out the large talisman around the man's neck. It bore the image of a tree with tangled, slithering snake roots. "It . . . It can't be."

"But it is," whispered the figure as he lifted his staff and cackled softly.

A chorus of tinny growling emerged from the canopy in all directions, followed by a roaring shriek that rattled the eardrums and weakened the knees of the men below.

Kane had waited long enough. In the blink of an eye, he let loose a half dozen arrows as the pack descended on their position; Taran's sword and dagger flashed with lightning speed and deadly accuracy.

Silver. Blood. Darkness. Stillness.

A gentle breeze began again. The cicadas resumed their chirping as the last rays of the summer sun abandoned the wooded hill.

The Chicken Pox

THE GIRL KNELT motionless before her saber, her eyes tightly shut. She pressed the hilt to her forehead with such force that the jagged imprint almost broke the skin.

"C'mon, Vivy, breathe," she whispered to herself, doing everything she could to control the fury that surged through her.

A whistle shrieked, ending her troubled quiet.

She stood and padded onto the fencing strip. The dimly lit gymnasium quieted as her clubmates regathered around the mat. Agitated whispers bounced off the gym's glazed-brick walls.

She slapped on her mask and toed the en-garde line, slowly lifting her eyes, piercing blue even through the mesh.

Ordinarily it wouldn't have been a good idea to pick a fight with a boy practically twice your size, but this was fencing: not a game of strength, rather an art of speed and reflex. Few had a greater measure of these talents than twelve-year-old Vivian Van Tassel.

On the other end of the strip was Johnny Matona, a high

school sophomore and the Viper Fencing Club's top dog. He was Coach Raymond Pierre's star student and the reigning state champion. He also happened to be a jerk.

Vivian grabbed the tip of her saber and straightened the thin blade, her eyes fixed unblinkingly at the boy.

Ever since Vivian joined the club four years ago, at the age of eight, Johnny had been nothing but cruel. On her very first day, he had been kind enough to "show her the ropes." This included a training exercise Johnny called "human pincushion" where he and his snickering friends stood around her and jabbed her with their blunted fencing sabers, leaving her covered in blotchy red dots and bruises. When she got home, her parents thought she had caught the chicken pox.

Maybe it was that Johnny seemed to think he was better than everyone else, and deserved whatever he wanted—a "Malfoy," Vivian called these types, named after Harry Potter's snobby rival. Or maybe it was simple jealously. To be sure, anyone who had ever watched Vivian fence marveled at her speed and grace.

Whatever the case, Johnny had it out for Vivian, but today, he had crossed the line. After witnessing Vivian twist an ankle during a practice duel next to his strip, he suggested she "run home and cry to Mommy."

Vivian's mother was dead.

"Fourteen all! Next touch wins," bellowed Coach Pierre in his thick French accent.

Vivian nodded coldly at Coach Pierre, who was playing the role of referee. A former Olympian, he had definitely lost a few steps over the years, but his pencil-thin mustache remained in top form.

Behind the coach stood a line of excited fencers awaiting the match's conclusion—many of the younger students loving every moment as one of their own challenged the house bully. Meanwhile, Johnny's gang of high-school cronies stood closely together on his side of the strip, half whispering taunts to the other side.

Vivian took another deep breath—she needed to calm down. She had already proven that she was the better fencer, Johnny only scoring using cheap tricks, which usually pushed her into a clumsy rage. Of course, that was the idea, Vivian having developed a reputation for her temper since her mother passed—a symptom of "unresolved grief," according to the school counselor.

Johnny's latest ruse had been an "injury time-out," with him claiming that Vivian's last thrust had somehow slipped under his neck guard. Vivian wished it were true. She had taken the last three points and this was another one of his tactics to get under her skin. It was working.

Vivian lifted her saber in salute. Johnny taunted her with a fake grimace and a wink before lowering his mesh mask and answering her with a cursory salute of his own.

Vivian's anger swelled.

"En garde!" bellowed Coach Pierre.

Both fencers lowered their swords to the ready. Vivian's muscles tensed and coiled.

"Fence!" yelled Coach Pierre.

Before Coach Pierre's spittle had even hit the floor, Vivian had invaded Johnny's end of the strip, charging furiously, lacking any of her usual precision and grace. Violent swipes and clicks were delivered so fast in the melee that no one could track the movements. But her maneuvers were clumsy and off-balance, and she nearly toppled over as she swiped and thrusted.

BEEEEP! blared the electronic scoring system as Vivian tumbled face-first at her opponent's feet. A combination of gasps, cheers, and jeers echoed in her ears.

Vivian lay motionless on the strip, filled with anger and disbelief. She had been aggressive; she had been reckless; she had been beaten. Vivian's temper had gotten the best of her . . . again. Her pounding heart had been pierced by her challenger, or at least it would have had this been authentic combat. How could she have let herself be played like that?

"Nice match, Vivy," Johnny drawled patronizingly as he offered his hand. "I'm sure your mom would've been *so* proud."

The flame already burning inside Vivian became an inferno. From the mat, she positioned her saber behind Johnny's heel and forcefully swept his leg forward with the hilt as she sprung up to her feet. Shaking with anger, she unleashed a volley of hard saber thrusts on the tumbling boy, instinctively targeting seams in the padded fencing suit and other uncovered areas of his body with the blunted weapon.

A new burst of gasps filled the gym.

The vicious smiles from Johnny's gang faded as they witnessed their leader under assault. All planning separate routes to rush to his aid, they became entangled in a mishmash of legs and fencing sabers and tumbled like dominoes beside the strip.

"Vivian! Viviaaaannn!" blared Coach Pierre as Vivian continued her bombardment of painful jabs.

Coach Pierre grabbed a nearby saber and lumbered onto the mat, positioning himself over Johnny. Even he struggled to parry Vivian's cobra-like strikes.

"Arrêtez, Vivian! Stop!" shouted Coach Pierre. "Stand down! This is unacceptable!"

Vivian almost lost her sword amid a forceful parry from Coach Pierre. She pulled back, confused and shaken.

What had she done?

Her stomach dropped as she saw the shocked faces of her coach and clubmates. Even worse, near the entrance stood another spectator, who may have been more horrified than all the rest: her dad.

"Allez! Out!" screamed Coach Pierre as he knelt over his favorite student, who had been reduced to a whimpering mass. "It's over! You're done! You're done for good! Allez!"

Terrified and humiliated, Vivian threw down her mask and saber and ran to the locker room, her father trailing behind.

After a moment of tense silence, the gym once again began to echo with excited whispers and chuckles.

By the time Vivian emerged, class had ended and the facility was nearly deserted. Vivian's father, Michael Van Tassel, rose from a nearby bench as soon as she came out, holding her discarded saber and mask. His tired, brown eyes gleamed with compassion.

"Hey Vivy," said Mr. Van Tassel awkwardly. "I've got your stuff . . . You okay?"

Vivian didn't answer. She pulled her backpack tight around her shoulders and stared at the floor.

"I . . . saw what happened. Do you want to talk about it?" asked her dad softly as he stepped toward her, a ceiling fan above them tousling his graying, curly hair.

If there was one thing Vivian's time in school counseling had taught her, it was this: *talking* didn't help.

"No," said Vivian coldly as she walked past him, toward the exit.

It had been a bad day for Vivian. But she took some satisfaction in knowing that it had probably been a worse day for Johnny. He'd certainly think twice before tormenting someone smaller and weaker. Even better, in the wake of the event, rumor had it that when Johnny's mother saw him the next morning dotted in red blotches, she immediately called the family doctor. She suspected that he might be coming down with the chicken pox.

2

This Old House

"ALMOST THERE, GIRLY," said Mr. Van Tassel above the hum of the Jeep's laboring engine.

His comment was as much to the automobile as it was to Vivian, who sat doubled over in the back seat pretending to sleep.

Several weeks had passed since what would come to be known in their household as "the fencing incident." Vivian had been grounded, but Mr. Van Tassel had gone easy on her given the circumstances, clearly doing it more out of principle. As a result, she had spent the waning days of summer watching eighties movies with her dad. Vivian knew her punishment could've been far worse, but today was definitely making up for it.

Her face buried in the pillow on her lap, Vivian could feel the hot afternoon sun beating down through the window.

The car stopped and noisily shifted into park.

"Hey Vivy, time to wake up. We're here," said her father lightly.

He reached into the back seat and gently stroked her long, auburn hair.

Vivian didn't move. She didn't want to face what was next.

"C'mon, sleepyhead, we're here," her dad persisted. "A new house . . . a new start."

After a few more moments, Vivian finally convinced herself to end her pretend sleep. She nuzzled her pillow and rubbed her eyes as she lifted her head.

"That's it, girly," continued Mr. Van Tassel. "So . . . there it is."

Vivian's eyes widened when she saw their new home. It was a mansion—like a massive, old-fashioned dollhouse—with sky-blue siding and white and navy trim. A beautifully manicured garden framed the walkway up to a large, covered porch. The house was unlike anything she knew in her tightly packed Chicago neighborhood, where the houses were small and the buildings blocky.

A nice house was certainly a welcome surprise, especially after losing their Chicago apartment—a casualty of her dad's layoff at the newspaper.

Maybe this won't be so bad, she thought to herself as she unbuckled her seat belt.

"Vivy," said Mr. Van Tassel, interrupting her train of thought. "Not that one. This one," he continued as he pointed to the other side of the street.

Opposite the handsome, blue dwelling that Vivian had

already approved was a dilapidated, yellow-and-white Victorian house, once grand, perhaps, but now peeling, fading, and foreboding. Dead flowers and weeds lined the crumbling walkway, which ended at a sagging, covered porch. Centered upon the crooked second story was a rickety balcony with odd, oval windows on each side. Above that, and nestled right below the eave, was an ornament that confirmed that this was indeed the right place. It was the crest of her mother's family, the Silverthorns: a crossed sword and arrow in front of a glowing gate—a solitary "all-seeing" eye hovered above it. It was like something you'd see on an ancient temple.

Vivian couldn't help but scowl as she studied the decaying structure. It was cute . . . if you were a cockroach.

"Um . . . are you sure this is it?" Vivian asked, unable to think of anything nice to say.

"Positive," said her dad. "Your mom's childhood home and the only thing the creditors couldn't take. Her family built this house one hundred and forty years ago, can you believe it? Your mom and I had always planned to fix it up before . . ." His words trailed off.

"I know," Vivian jumped in, trying to avoid any uncomfortable subjects. "Mom told me all about it."

Vivian's mother had indeed told her about her family home and her hometown of Midnight Lake, Wisconsin, many times, always with a combination of happy sentiment and puzzling apprehension. Only eighty miles from their former Chicago apartment, the woodsy fishing town was a renowned summer retreat for wealthy Chicago families, whose influence gave the place an unexpected refinement. It seemed odd to Vivian that they had never visited, especially as the house had sat vacant for years. "In time," her mom would always say wistfully when such a trip was proposed.

Mr. Van Tassel's face broke into a smile.

"Well, if you think you like it now, just wait till you see the inside."

Yep, the inside was something, all right.

The front door nearly fell off the hinges as they entered. Inside, they were greeted by a grand, mahogany staircase, its steps covered with a tattered velvet runner. The house was stiflingly hot and had the undeniable smell of age, which as far as Vivian could tell was made up of equal parts barn and swamp.

Mr. Van Tassel flipped the light switch, which caused the ornate chandelier to spark. It briefly illuminated the intense, humorless faces of family portraits that adorned the wood-paneled entrance hall, and then sputtered out.

"Whoa! Sorry about that!" exclaimed Mr. Van Tassel. He nodded to himself as if he'd just accepted an unspoken challenge. "I'll have to fix that."

Vivian threw a wry smile at her father, doing everything she could to hold her tongue. She knew full well that her dad was incapable of operating even the simplest of modern appliances, let alone fixing one-hundred-year-old wiring.

"Pretty great, huh?" said her dad as he edged deeper into the entranceway. "Boy, they sure don't make 'em like this anymore."

"Good thing," Vivian mumbled under her breath.

"How's that?" asked Mr. Van Tassel over his shoulder as he rubbed his hand along the fancy carved-wood walls.

"Oh, nothing," replied Vivian.

"Well, I'm going to check out the bedrooms upstairs," said her dad. "Hold tight, okay?"

Mr. Van Tassel started to bound up the staircase but quickly switched to light, careful steps when the loud creaking called into question the stability of the stairs.

Now that Vivian was alone in the entrance room, her heart raced. This place was creepy, but intriguing. After her father was out of sight, she decided to explore the first level. The oak floors groaned as she walked over to another panel of light switches. None of them worked and the only light came from the dimming afternoon sun shining through warped windows and jewel-toned stained glass, creating long, purple shadows. The glass panels above the front door depicted what looked like scenes from Greek mythology: griffons, satyrs, and centaurs.

She crept down the front hall into what appeared to be a study. It reeked of musty parchment and rotted leather. Hundreds of ancient-looking books filled the bookcases and covered the massive, antique desk, overseen by an ominous portrait that leered down from the wall. As she approached it, she could make out through the shadows the subject's long, stringy black hair and generous nose and chin. If not for his brilliant blue eyes, she'd think she was looking at Hogwarts's notorious potions master, Severus Snape.

She shuddered and made her way into a connected living room, where a warm, smoky wind swept in from the marble fireplace. The space was cluttered with threadbare furniture, while more frowning portraits lined the walls here. Maybe it was the disapproving looks, but something about them set Vivian's nerves on edge. As she avoided their stares, her own eyes landed on a tall grandfather clock, which loomed in the corner, creating crooked shadows on the wall. It wasn't running.

Vivian chuckled nervously. It seemed to her that in here time stood still and the clock, stuck on 11:59 p.m. from a night long ago, confirmed it.

She passed through a dining room illuminated by a trio of large stained glass windows depicting more scenes of mythology—a hydra, a dragon, and a sphinx. Cobwebs encased the low-hanging crystal chandelier and candelabras that lined the room.

She rubbed her hand along the enormous, walnut dining table, kicking up a cloud of dust en route to a heavy, swinging kitchen door.

"Yuck," she whispered to herself the moment she wandered into the kitchen, her eyes wide.

A surprisingly plain area, simple oak cabinets hung heavily on the walls while monstrously large enamel, steel, and chrome appliances dominated the counters, most of which had logos and brand plates in fancy cursive writing. Vivian had watched enough home improvement shows with her dad to know that this meant they were really old. She'd never seen anything like most of the appliances that filled the space, let alone had the first clue as to how to operate them. There was a narrow ascending stairway in the back wall, mostly hidden by cobwebbed copper pans that hung from the ceiling. There was even a potbelly stove in the corner of the room. To call the kitchen outdated would be a huge understatement. It was downright ancient.

Vivian sighed as she reentered the dining room. This place had probably once been lavish, but not anymore. Yet it wasn't the house's condition that troubled her most; it was the portraits. They were everywhere, her ancestors she supposed, watching coldly from every wall.

She padded over to the fireplace and studied the portrait that hung above it. It was a dark-haired woman and the first friendly-looking relative she had seen. As she peered more closely, her own hair stood on end. It finally struck her why all the portraits had made her so uneasy: they all had distinct features of her mother.

This one had her mom's high cheekbones; Snape in the study, her large, sapphire-blue eyes. In the hallway Vivian had spotted her mom's slender arched eyebrows; in the living room, her long, blond hair. *Reminders* of her were everywhere, but *she* wasn't there.

"Oh, there you are!" said Mr. Van Tassel, startling Vivian, who was still gazing at the portrait in the dining room. "So, none of the lights work."

"I noticed," Vivian replied smoothly, pretending not to have been startled.

KNOCK! KNOCK! KNOCK!

Both Vivian and her father shuddered as the gloomy stillness of the place was broken.

Someone was at the door.

3

Purple Walls

THERE WAS ANOTHER series of knocks on the door, this time a bit louder.

"Do you want me to get it?" Vivian asked.

"Huh? Oh, no," said Mr. Van Tassel as he headed toward the front door, "I've got it."

Craning her neck from her spot in the dining room, Vivian watched the door creak open to reveal a figure holding an enormous gift basket that covered his face and upper torso. Her curiosity piqued, Vivian crept toward the door.

"Welcome to Midnight Lake," a voice exclaimed from behind the basket.

"Thanks!" replied Mr. Van Tassel. "Um . . . who are . . . how did you—?"

"Oh, I have my sources," the muffled voice continued as the figure hobbled over the threshold and plopped the basket into Mr. Van Tassel's hands.

The basket no longer obscuring the visitor, Vivian could

see he was a distinguished-looking elderly man dressed in a tailored brown suit.

"Name's Carlisle Braemor and consider me the town's welcome committee," he said with a wink, his mouth nearly lost in his bushy, gray beard.

"Well, thanks, Mr. Braemor," said Mr. Van Tassel as he placed the basket at the foot of the stairs. He subtly wiped his sweaty palms on his jeans before offering his hand to the older man. "Really nice to meet you. I'm Michael Van Tassel and this is my daughter, Vivian."

"A pleasure to meet you both!" Mr. Braemor said as he shook Mr. Van Tassel's hand, squinting at both Vivian and her dad.

Vivian could tell he was trying to get a better look at them. A gold pocket watch chain swung lazily from his green-plaid vest.

"But how did you know we were coming?" asked her dad as he withdrew his hand and scratched his head. "I mean no one knows except—"

"The paper, old sport!" boomed Mr. Braemor as he clapped Vivian's dad on the back. "I have some friends at the paper. Word on the street is that you're starting tomorrow."

"Yeah, that's right," replied Mr. Van Tassel. "I'll be a staff reporter. So, they sent you?"

All at once, Vivian remembered why her dad made a good reporter: he couldn't seem to stop asking questions.

"No, not exactly . . ." Mr. Braemor paused, and then leaned in as if to tell a secret. "Truth is, I'm pretty new in town myself and when I arrived, I found it was a less than warm reception—small towns, ya know. So, I made it my mission to provide new arrivals with a proper welcome."

"Oh," replied Mr. Van Tassel. He opened his mouth to ask another question, but clearly thought better of it and just smiled and gave a nod.

Vivian took a seat on the stairs, enjoying the unexpected spectacle.

"Now, that basket there is chock-full of the town's best fudge, taffy, and caramel corn," declared Mr. Braemor, gesturing at the basket. "So, I'll let you get back to it, but I can only leave it with you on one condition. . . ." His eyes landed on Vivian.

"What's that?" replied Vivian curiously.

"Well, that you enjoy it, of course!" exclaimed Mr. Braemor as he grinned and clapped his wrinkled hands together.

Vivian couldn't help but smile back at him.

"I really think you'll like it here, Michael, Miss Vivian. And if you need anything . . . well, I expect you'll find me. And with that, I bid you farewell!"

Mr. Braemor grabbed his lapels and gave a slight bow, before turning and shuffling out the door whistling to himself.

"Well, he was certainly nice," remarked Mr. Van Tassel as he shut the front door. "A good sign, I think. About the town, I mean—the people."

"I guess so." Vivian shrugged, not at all ready to give the house, the town, or its people her stamp of approval.

"Oh, hey, I was just about to tell you before he came, there are *six* bedrooms upstairs," her dad boasted. He paused to see if Vivian was impressed. She wasn't. "And you can have the pick of the litter. We'll use flashlights and lanterns tonight and hopefully we can get the power sorted out tomorrow."

"Litter" seemed to sum it up nicely, Vivian thought as she inspected the second floor. While it was true that there were six bedrooms, two were already inhabited—by spiders, rodents, and roaches (and hopefully not something worse!). That left, by Vivian's estimation, four that seemed sanitary enough to avoid contracting the plague. The one Vivian picked was a corner space with large windows that overlooked an overgrown vegetable garden. It had a walk-in closet and a comfortable-looking brass bed. The thing that made the room really stand out to her, though, were the deep, purple walls— her favorite color.

Vivian and her father brought up their sleeping bags and a few other essentials as the last glimmer of sunlight faded behind the thick evergreens and twisted oaks of their yard. The crickets and katydids began their soft summer song.

Vivian had just finished changing into pajamas when there was a knock on her door.

"Yes?" she asked.

The door squeaked open and her dad's head poked in.

"You hungry?" asked Mr. Van Tassel.

"Nah," said Vivian. "Still full from the late lunch."

He nodded.

"Well, are you sure you don't want to stay in my room tonight? You can have the bed. I know it's a new place and kind of creepy . . . er . . . I mean, it might take some getting used to."

"Nope. I'm good," Vivian replied.

The truth was she was pretty anxious about spending the night in here alone, but didn't want to admit it.

"Okay, well, I'm right next door if you change your mind, or if you need anything," said her dad reassuringly. "I think things will turn around for us here, you'll see."

"Um-hmm," she mumbled.

Mr. Van Tassel gave a concerned frown. He entered the room and half sat on the dresser, gesturing for her to come next to him. She didn't.

"Listen, Vivian, I know this isn't ideal, but we really didn't have many options. After your moth— If we're going to make this work, you're going to need to come out of your shell. To trust people again—to trust me."

"I'm just tired," she said softly as she turned away.

She knew he was trying, but heart-to-hearts had always been Mom's department, and he was a poor substitute.

"Okay . . . well, I love you, girly," he replied as he rose, and then waited a moment for a reply that didn't come.

"Sleep tight," he added quietly. He walked out and gently closed the door behind him.

Vivian flipped on her electric lantern and flopped on the bed, upon which she had unrolled her sleeping bag. She sunk down, surprised by how soft the mattress was. Her thoughts were churning, back and forth between her mom and dad. Mom had always seemed to know what to say in tough situations; could help her sort through her feelings. Dad wasn't Mom, and the more he tried to be, the more frustrated Vivian got.

She stared at the ceiling and sighed. She was wound up and felt fairly certain that she wouldn't be sleeping anytime soon. Like everywhere else in the ancient house, her room was stuffy. Exploring the remainder of the house in the black of night was not going to happen, but examining her room was a different story. Thankfully, there were no creepy family portraits to watch her in here, only pleasant pastoral paintings of winding trails and scenic lakes. An old-fashioned oil lamp sat atop the large oak dresser, while a small writing desk stood near the window.

She reached into her backpack and pulled out her flashlight.

The walk-in closet was filled with tattered garment bags and old dresses covered in plastic that hung around the three sides of the space. Old high heels lined the walls along the floor, except for the center where the closet notched in a bit deeper.

Vivian moved the clothes aside to find a nook, just big

enough to sit in comfortably. She smiled. She knew instantly that this would be her new reading space.

She went back to the bed and grabbed one of the essentials that she had brought up from the car and took it back to the nook: *Harry Potter and the Sorcerer's Stone*—her favorite book. Vivian had already read it three times, but she hoped starting the series over again might help her with her own fresh start. Harry's troubles had always made her own seem less intense, although she wondered whether her problems were starting to equal those of the "boy who lived."

As she shined her flashlight around the space to find the perfect seat, she spotted something carved into a floorboard in the corner. She put down the book and rubbed her hand over the surface to clear the dust. Scratched into the hardwood were the initials CLS. Those were her mother's initials—Calissa L. Silverthorn . . . had this been her mom's room?

Goose bumps covered Vivian's skin as she leaned her book against the wall and traced the initials with her finger. Her mom's initials. She must have carved them herself. Of course she would have chosen her mother's room, they were so alike. The purple walls should've given it away—it had also been her mom's favorite color.

Tears welled up in her eyes, but she fought them back, gritting her teeth and pressing her palm to the inscription. The board shifted under her weight. It was loose.

She set the flashlight by her side and with both hands dug her fingernails into the floorboard seam, trying to pry it up. It lifted easily, exposing a dusty, gaping hole in the floor. Harry's spectacled eyes seemed to watch from the back of his flying broomstick as Vivian grabbed her light off the floor—a "torch" he would've called it—and shined it down into the mini-chasm. Resting on its own in the space was a small wooden box with her family's crest branded into the lid.

Vivian carefully removed the palm-sized box and stared at it for several moments. She took a deep breath and finally lifted the top. She was almost blinded by the shimmer of what was inside. It was a shield-shaped silver pendant engraved with the Silverthorn family crest, glimmering as if freshly polished. It hung on a fine, matching chain. It had clearly been here for some time, but remarkably it had not a scratch, speck of dust, or spot of tarnish.

Vivian was no jewelry expert, but even she could tell the piece was something special. She turned the pendant around; this side bore her mother's initials inscribed in fancy script with a date of July 14, 1997. That would have been her mom's twelfth, no thirteenth birthday, Vivian realized—it must have been a birthday present.

The pendant sparkled like a million microscopic stars as she dangled it in the artificial light. She wanted to put it on, but something stopped her: guilt. She didn't feel like she deserved it. After all, her mother would still be here if not for her.

4

The Gray Man

"I'M NOT GOING!" Vivian shouted. *"I'm not leaving, now or ever!"*

"Vivian, I know you're upset," Mrs. Van Tassel said gently. *"Change is hard, but it's part of life and something we all need to face sometimes."*

"No!" erupted Vivian as she slammed her fist down on the kitchen countertop. *"My friends are here, my school is here, my life is here! I'm not leaving!"*

"I'm sorry, Vivy, but you have to," her mother said. *"We have to. I know it will be hard at first, but I think you'll love Midnight Lake. I grew up there and it's time that I returned. Your father and I have discussed it and—"*

"I don't care!" shot back Vivian. *"I'm not going! Why do I have to go to some stupid small town in the middle of nowhere where I don't know anyone?!"*

Vivian's mother rubbed her fingers over her eyes, which lately seemed more careworn than usual.

"Because we said so, Vivy," said Mrs. Van Tassel firmly. *"When you're older you'll get to make decisions like this, but right now the decision is ours."*

"Shut up!" screamed Vivian. "Stop trying to control me—to wreck my life! I hate you! I hate you both! I'll . . . I'll run away!" she added frantically as she grabbed her backpack and darted out the door, slamming it behind her.

Vivian woke up in a cold sweat to the buzzing of power tools somewhere downstairs. She'd had the dream again. Unfortunately, this one wasn't a figment of her imagination; it was a replay of the last time she saw her mother alive.

Vivian had never threatened to run away before and she knew her mom had gotten into the car that morning looking for her. Of course, Vivian hadn't really planned to run away—she was furious and just needed some space. She had only cleared a few blocks before she turned around and began an extra-slow walk home, trying to make her threat seem less empty. She was hurt and wanted to hurt back a little.

When she got back to their apartment building, there were police and fire strobes everywhere, and then she saw it: their car had been crushed. A massive tree next to the parking lot entrance had fallen on it as her mom was pulling out. According to the "experts," she died instantly, but they couldn't explain the freakish nature of the accident—there hadn't even been a trace of wind.

Vivian and her father were utterly broken. By the time

the funeral came, Vivian had cried herself out but discovered something in the process: the more she pulled away from people and avoided connection, the better she could control her tears—and the pain. In a report that she wasn't supposed to have seen, the school therapist had written that Vivian was suffering from "social withdrawal caused by unresolved grief," which could also lead to "erratic behavior and outbursts." Whatever. *He* hadn't been through this and definitely didn't understand it. This way was definitely easier.

What wasn't easier, though, and what she couldn't forget, was that if she only could've controlled her emotions that morning, then her mom would still be here. It was all her fault. She would've done anything to take back that last moment; to change the script of the scene that had haunted her dreams these past few months.

She rubbed her eyes and sat up, still half sunken in the droopy mattress.

Beams of morning sunlight shot through the windows, illuminating the dust particles that shimmered around the room. The twitter of waking birds had taken the place of the chirping call of crickets and katydids. Vivian scanned her surroundings and sighed as she remembered where she was: her new home, her new room; *her mom's room.*

"I dunno, Harry," she remarked drowsily to the book that sat on the bed next to her. "I think I'd trade places with you."

Still in her clothes from the day before, Vivian swiveled

her legs out of her sleeping bag and stepped straight into her sunflower sandals to avoid touching the dusty floors with her bare feet. She sat and stared sadly at the closet door where she had made her discovery the night before. Guilt filled her chest and stomach.

Vivian had put the necklace back where she found it and had no plans to disturb it again. Seeing it was too painful. It would only remind Vivian of how she had failed her mom.

Vivian frowned as the stop-and-go buzzing downstairs became louder and more erratic. She trudged out of her room and down the once-grand staircase, which creaked under her weight. The ruckus was coming from the kitchen. She passed through the dining room and pushed open the thick swinging door.

There she saw her father balanced precariously on the kitchen counter, drilling on the inside of one of the cabinets. As Vivian watched in silence, he stopped drilling and grabbed a bolt, which he inserted somewhere inside. Catching sight of Vivian, he turned, nearly losing his footing, and clumsily jumped down.

"Good morning, Vivy! How did you sleep?"

"Okay," Vivian lied. "It was kinda hot up there."

"Yeah, sorry about that, girly," said Mr. Van Tassel as he grabbed a stack of dishes from a large box and placed them on the cabinet shelf he had been working on. "The good news is that the power is back on and we can get some fans going.

Called the power company first thing—they told me to tighten the fuses and voila!" he continued proudly.

Vivian was pretty sure her dad's call to the power company was like calling tech support and the service technician asking if the machine was plugged in and the power switch on—the solution to half of all tech issues.

"Then I ran to the mini-mart to pick up some essentials and lunch for you for today. And then I tackled installing these shelves. . . ."

Just then, there was a sharp crack followed by a loud, shattering crash. The shelf that Mr. Van Tassel had just secured had given way, and the dishes cascaded down in a spectacular waterfall of porcelain and glass, before exploding upon the tiled counter below. Shielding his eyes, Mr. Van Tassel rushed to the cabinet in an effort to stem the falls and managed to grab the last plate before it slid down to its doom.

"Aha!" he exclaimed in confused triumph, now standing before a massacre of shattered glassware. The ruckus finally gave way to silence, and the birds outside again resumed their carefree song.

"I, uh . . . it must've been a bad bolt," he muttered as he set down the lone remaining dish on a clear spot of counter and dusted his hands. "Yep, that must be it."

Vivian couldn't help noticing that the plate sat next to an unused nut—no doubt the nut that was meant to secure the "bad bolt" her father mentioned.

"Sure, Dad," agreed Vivian, subtly rolling her eyes. "Where's the broom? Let's get this cleaned up."

"Nah, leave it for now. At least it wasn't the good stuff. I'll take care of it. It was my fault anyway."

Vivian could tell her dad was flustered, so she resisted the urge to rub it in.

Almost.

"You mean the bolt's fault, right, Dad?" Vivian smirked.

"Right, the bolt," Mr. Van Tassel laughed. "What do you say we run into town and get some breakfast before school?"

School. She had almost forgotten. As if things weren't bad enough already, today would be the first day at her new school.

"Okay," sighed Vivian, only now realizing that she was starving.

"Don't worry, girly, school is going to be fine," her dad replied tenderly. "Hey, that reminds me. Did you hear the one about the hungry fish?"

She just stared at him.

"They were looking for *school* lunch!"

She grunted lightly and headed back upstairs to get ready.

It turned out that their house was only a few blocks from Midnight Lake's downtown, and Vivian had to admit the area was really scenic compared to her old Chicago neighborhood. Charming wood and brick homes with generous green lawns adorned streets lined with thick trees, some of which had just begun to burn with the reds, yellows, and browns of late summer, reminding her that fall was around the corner.

They drove to the center of town, which was riddled with fancy, one-hundred-year-old buildings that housed upscale shops on the ground level and apartments on upper floors. But not everything was fancy, as the elegant downtown was occasionally interrupted by tired local holdovers: a pizza parlor with the glow of 1980s arcade games through the window; a mom-and-pop bakery with a faded, handwritten price list taped to the door.

Even from the inside of the car Vivian could smell the bakery's fresh-baked bread, and it made her stomach growl.

They parked in front of a corner game store called the Catacombs, which Vivian could see through the shop window was practically overflowing with boxes and books, and crossed the street toward a vintage diner. A tired neon sign buzzed noisily above the door. It read MIDNIGHT GRILL.

It was still early—only seven thirty—but the place was already bustling. Businesspeople disguised in golf shirts checked their phones, while elderly couples sat quietly with newspapers and crossword puzzles. At the counter sat plaid-adorned locals drinking coffee, gearing up for a day of fishing on the lake or farmwork outside of town.

Vivian and her father made their way over to a mint-green corner booth with a faux woodgrain table. She began inspecting her oversized menu, which featured the term "homestyle" before virtually every dish. The diner reeked of bacon grease and maple syrup.

Mr. Van Tassel's eyes quickly scanned the menu and he looked up to speak, but his attention was drawn to something across the restaurant.

"What is it?" asked Vivian as she turned her head around to try to catch sight of what he was looking at.

"Dang," mumbled Mr. Van Tassel. "That's the editor-in-chief over there—my new boss. He was my final-round interview and not an easy one. He probably saw us on the way in. I should go over and say hi. Hold tight, okay?"

"Okay." Vivian shrugged.

Her dad slapped a manufactured smile on his face and walked over to a pallid and serious-looking man who held up the newspaper as he read, as if promoting its front page. ANOTHER LIVESTOCK MASSACRE! read the headline, while a secondary header declared, ABANDONED STONE MANOR PURCHASED BY ANONYMOUS BUYER. But Vivian thought the real headline was the man's terrible, brown toupee that rested crookedly on his head, fooling absolutely no one.

As Vivian watched, the man in the bad toupee lowered the paper and nodded coolly at her father. He didn't seem thrilled about being interrupted. Mr. Van Tassel made overly animated expressions and gestures, signaling to Vivian a forced conversation if ever she saw one. It looked to her like this might take a while, so she returned her attention to her menu. She decided she'd order one of the ten variations of "homestyle" eggs and toast.

After finally making a selection, she checked back on her dad, who was now nodding and furiously scribbling notes on the pocket notepad he always kept on him—it looked like he was taking the man's order.

"He was absolutely devastated," blared an elderly female voice in the booth next to Vivian's. "I've never seen him so down. Said he'd have to sell the farm!"

"But what could've caused it?" replied a man's voice. "They keep saying animal attack, but how could one animal take out an entire stable like that—carnage everywhere and no one heard or saw a thing."

The way-too-loud private conversation got Vivian's attention and made her Spidey-sense tingle. Animal attacks? Carnage? Behind the cover of her massive menu, she leaned in and tried to catch all the juicy details.

"I know . . . And did you hear what he found when he inspected the carcasses—"

"Hey girly!" said Mr. Van Tassel, startling Vivian and interrupting her eavesdropping. "I'm back. Sorry about that."

"No problem," replied Vivian with a fake smile, disappointed that she would miss the best part of the gossip from the next booth over.

Over the rest of breakfast, Mr. Van Tassel filled Vivian in on his meeting with Mr. Rex Bellowman, AKA the man in the bad toupee and the head of the *Midnight Lake Bugle*. It sounded like Mr. Bellowman had skipped all welcomes and pleasantries and already assigned her father a laundry list of stories before the workday even started. Vivian's dad may have been a terrible handyman, but he *was* a great reporter. Over the years, he had taught her all about getting to the bottom of a story, so much so that she thought she might want to be a reporter herself someday. Still, she couldn't help thinking her father's new position was a huge step down for someone who had once been a bureau chief and award-winning journalist, but he seemed to be making the best of it—or at least he pretended to be.

"C'mon back now, ya hear," said the frilly-aproned waitress as they rose to leave—seemingly aware she was being hokey.

Vivian gave a polite smile as she followed her father toward the door, but her grin vanished as a man entered the diner. The hood of his sweatshirt was pulled tightly over his hair, and dark sunglasses hid his eyes. Vivian felt a chill run down her spine as he removed his hood and glasses in one swift motion, revealing unnaturally pale hair, pallid gray skin—almost purple—and large gray eyes. His face was scarred and rugged, his expression bitter.

Time stopped. Vivian stood still and gawked, paralyzed by both curiosity and dread. His cold gray eyes seemed to pierce through her as he passed and disappeared into a dimly lit corner booth.

She stayed rooted to the spot.

"Vivian . . . Vivian," repeated her father. "C'mon, let's go."

"Huh?" said Vivian thickly as her senses returned. "Oh, yeah. Coming."

A rush of embarrassment swept over her. In Chicago, she was used to all kinds of people—what made this man any different? So what if he looked a little unusual? No one else seemed to pay him any mind. Maybe he was just another friendly local.

She scurried over to join her father, forcing herself not to look back as she left the diner.

The encounter had only been a moment, but everything about it—about him—haunted Vivian. She knew better than to judge a book by its cover, but that still didn't stop the questions. Who was he? Why did he look so . . . so different? Maybe some type of rare disease or illness? What's more, why did he affect her so?

Whatever the answers, Vivian knew that she was in for a long day.

Murkwood Middle School

VIVIAN COULDN'T BREATHE, at least not very well, as she watched Midnight Lake's quaint downtown pass by from the back seat of her father's Jeep. Her heart pounded in her ears, while her stomach grew queasy, but she knew it wasn't the heavy diner breakfast nor her father's herky-jerky driving that had caused the symptoms. It was the prospect of starting seventh grade at a new school. New teachers, new classmates, cliques, clubs, sports—the list of things to be worried about was overwhelming.

She wished the drive would last forever, but less than five minutes had passed when they began the short climb up Murkwood Hill on the edge of downtown—the highest point in Midnight Lake. A large stone sign reading MURKWOOD MIDDLE SCHOOL greeted them as they entered the wooded campus. Emerging from either side of the two stone pillars that bordered the drive was a rusted chain-link fence topped with barbed wire, which enclosed the woods and the campus above.

"Dad, what's with the barbed wire?" Vivian asked. "Are they that worried about students staying in?" she added jokingly.

"Well . . ." Mr. Van Tassel hesitated. "Based on what I've read, this wasn't always a school."

Vivian sensed her father's discomfort.

"What was it, a jail?" she pressed, a knot forming in her stomach.

"A sanitarium," he replied. "Murkwood Sanitarium."

"What's a sanitarium?" Vivian asked.

"It's a . . . uh . . . an . . ."

As her father struggled to find his next words, the car emerged from the winding, wooded driveway into a large clearing on the top of the hill. A massive stone building stood in the center, its gothic chimneys and turrets pointing up to the heavens like the tower of a mad sorcerer. It was only five stories high, but Vivian thought it might as well have been a thousand feet tall the way it loomed ominously over them as they approached, its stone-rimmed windows frowning at them from every floor.

"It's a psychiatric hospital," her dad said finally. "This was one of a half dozen in town, built around the turn of the twentieth century."

Vivian froze. She finally understood her father's hesitation. A psychiatric hospital—but clearly not the kind they have today. Based on the look of it, this was the kind that kept its patients under lock and key and what they used to callously call an "insane asylum." A closer look at the windows revealed thick, rusted steel bars, some of which had been forcefully bent over time.

Clearing his throat, Mr. Van Tassel continued, "Yeah, for some reason, there was a ton of mental health institutions around here in the old days—they probably thought the fresh air and scenery could help. This one was the largest. And now . . . it's your school," he finished, clearly not knowing where to go from there.

Vivian concluded that she now had one more thing to worry about: the school itself. This place was scary and almost certainly haunted by the souls of its former patients. Between the house, the creepy guy at the diner, and now this, Vivian was becoming more and more convinced that she was living in a horror movie. She just hoped that she was the main character, who usually survived.

Mr. Van Tassel pulled his Jeep into the rounded drop-off and stopped the car, which groaned as he put it into park. They sat for a moment and listened to the distressed hum of the engine. Mr. Van Tassel cleared his throat again. Vivian could tell he was choosing his next words carefully.

"Hey Vivy, I know it's a lot right now . . . I, uh . . ."

"I'm good," Vivian said quickly, not eager to have a heart-to-heart here and now.

"Okay . . . well, I love you, girly. I hope you have a great first day. And remember—"

"Dad, I'll be fine," Vivian interrupted. "I'll see you tonight," she mumbled nervously as she zipped out of the car and stood defiantly in the shadow of her newest challenger: Murkwood Middle School.

Dozens of unfamiliar sixth- through eighth-grade students congregated outside the doors, all engaged in excited conversations. Vivian stood there, trying to slow her breath, until she heard the whine of the passenger-side power window.

"Vivy!" yelled her dad. "Don't forget your schedule and your lunch! It's your favorite: egg salad."

Mr. Van Tassel stretched his arm out of the passenger window and handed Vivian a slip of paper and a brown lunch bag that may as well have been a highway billboard. He had drawn a huge heart on the side with the inscription: *Daddy loves you!* Vivian felt her face flush, absolutely certain that the entire student body had witnessed this mortifying display.

Vivian's chest tightened.

"Dad!" she hissed as she swiftly grabbed the bag out of her father's hand.

She quickly distanced herself from the vehicle in hopes that he would leave, but the maroon monstrosity didn't move. She turned to see her father grinning and waving goodbye.

She rolled her eyes and waved him away as subtly as possible to avoid drawing any more attention to herself. Finally she heard the car shift into gear and begin its labored departure out of the drop-off circle.

Vivian took a deep breath, pulled the straps of her hippogriff backpack tight around her shoulders, and trudged up the stairs on her matching Gryffindor sneakers to the school's first floor. She swore that conversations stopped and excited eyes studied her as she passed every pair or trio that was seated on the grand stone railings and stairs. Vivian kept her eyes firmly on the entrance, not daring to return the glances of her new classmates. For the first time in her life, she was the new kid at school and she definitely felt like it.

The carved oak doors looked as thick as they were tall, and were fitted with heavy antique locks that looked to be as good at keeping people in as keeping them out. The door creaked as she slowly pushed it open, filling the entrance hall with beams of sunlight. The room looked like something out of Dracula's castle, with its cracked marble floors, stone walls, and two-story-high, wood-beamed ceiling. Spacious staircases to the right and left ran along the perimeter of the room and up to the second-floor landing, which overlooked the entrance floor. Hanging from the ornate spindles was a red and gray banner that read WELCOME BACK, MURKWOOD STUDENTS!

Centered in the back wall was a huge wooden reception desk, with little rear cubbies like the ones they had at old-fashioned hotels. A stern-looking woman with dark eyes behind thick, cat-eye spectacles sat behind the desk, studying the students. On each side of the desk were steel doors with wire-reinforced view portals in each—Vivian shuddered as she imagined patients being carted off through them in restraints. One thing was for sure: this place was no Hogwarts!

Moving out of the entranceway and huddling into the nearest corner, Vivian swung around her backpack and pulled out her tattered copy of *Harry Potter* along with a pencil she had tucked into its pages. She opened the front cover, which revealed a hand-drawn, two-column comparison chart. One side was topped with an "H" for Harry; the other a "V" for Vivian. She added a row on the left that read "School," then smirked and put a check mark in the "H" column—Harry definitely had the advantage here.

BRRRIIIINNNNGGGG! rang an antique alarm bell that was tucked into a corner of the room. Students frantically crisscrossed the entrance floor as dozens more flooded in from the front door and swarmed the stairways or beelined to the steel doors. Vivian looked at her schedule: *Algebra I / Mr. Putrim / Room 502.*

Vivian glanced around the hall in search of a sign or map that might help, but none was present, so she darted up to the reception desk.

"Can I help you?" the woman asked sweetly, peering down at Vivian over her glasses.

Vivian relaxed a little.

"Hi, yes. I'm new here and I'm looking for Mr. Putrim's room, room 502," said Vivian as she presented her crumpled schedule.

"Ah, welcome to Murkwood," said the woman. "I'm Mrs. Wickams, the hall and yard monitor." She nodded as she inspected the document—apparently, it met with her approval.

"Ah, yes," she agreed in a conversation she was having with herself. "Mr. Putrim, a fine teacher for a fine subject. He's on the fifth floor. You'll need to take the main stairs to the second floor and then walk down the center hall until you come to a stairwell that will lead you up to the remaining floors," she continued as she casually gestured behind and above her. "Oh, and one more thing, dear."

"What's that?" asked Vivian pleasantly.

"You're going to be late," declared Mrs. Wickams flatly as the smile vanished from her face.

Vivian was huffing and puffing by the time she arrived at room 502. She had taken a wrong turn on the fifth floor and gotten an undesired tour of the top level. The hallways were long, dim, and narrow, with high crumbling ceilings and peeling puke-green walls. The baffling maze of halls was lined with rusty blue lockers, which rested uneasily on warped hardwood floors. Thick doors with observation windows dotted the hallway every twenty or so feet, while long fluorescent light fixtures buzzed and flickered above. Between the observation windows and the lockers that cramped the hallways, it was easy to remember that this facility had not originally been built as a school.

Peering through the window in the classroom door, Vivian saw a group of nervous-looking students, some already feverishly taking notes. To her horror she realized that the only open desk was front row, center.

Vivian took a deep breath and slowly edged the door open, hoping to slip in as inconspicuously as possible. The door opened quietly enough at first, but after about four inches in it began to creak loudly. Vivian changed course, now hastily pushing the door open a few more inches, just enough to pass through. She rushed to the open desk, hanging her head low and using her long hair as a shield against scores of judging eyes.

"Good morning!" bellowed the imposing Mr. Putrim, who glared at her through thick, black-rimmed glasses. "So glad you could join us! You are?"

Vivian slunk low in the doodle-covered desk.

"Vivian," her voice cracked. "Vivian Van Tassel."

Mr. Putrim stormed over to his desk at the front of the room and scanned the attendance book on top.

"Ah yes, Vivian S. Van Tassel, the new girl," he proclaimed as he nodded to himself. "So glad you could finally join us. Class, now that Miss Van Tassel has decided to grace us with her presence, can anyone tell me the answer to the following equation?" Mr. Putrim continued as he returned to the chalkboard and began noisily scratching out symbols. "It's eight forty-three and this class starts at eight thirty. Vivian would be on time for this class if she arrived x minutes earlier. Solve for x."

Vivian dared not look back at her classmates, but sensed a combination of fearful tension paired with a few jeers and snickers. Vivian understood that Mr. Putrim was being spiteful at her expense and probably didn't expect anyone to actually answer him, so she was surprised when, out of the corner of her eye, she saw a raised hand.

Her head still lowered, she peered through her screen of hair to see who owned the hand. Sitting in the front row, two seats to her right, was a girl with big blue eyes and long blond hair secured with a tartan headband that matched her skirt. Vivian couldn't help noticing the new-looking, white leather backpack at her feet, and the fancy gold heart anklet draped around her ankle.

Mr. Putrim turned back to the class. "Yes, Ms. Grausam?"

"Thirteen. Vivian would've been on time if she had arrived thirteen minutes earlier," explained the girl haughtily.

Half-confused that someone had bothered answering his question, Mr. Putrim continued, "Very good, Amber, you can do basic math."

The girl's confident smirk disappeared and her face flushed red.

Even through her own embarrassment, Vivian couldn't help feeling sorry for this girl, who had failed miserably to read the teacher and the room.

Mr. Putrim turned around and began erasing the equation meant to humiliate Vivian.

"Well, she probably just didn't want anyone to see those hideous shoes," Amber mumbled under her breath to a girl in the next desk, who began to giggle. "Like what are you, six years old?"

A few other students around her joined in the snickering.

So much for pity. Vivian felt blood rush up into her own face. She was caught completely off guard. In her old school, Vivian never had to worry much about her clothes or appearance. She certainly wouldn't have been accused of being a baby for wearing stuff she was into. Vivian's embarrassment quickly flared to anger.

"So, Vivian," continued Mr. Putrim, who had now finished clearing the board and hadn't heard Amber's comment. "What time are you going to show up tomorrow?"

"Ask Amber, she's the math whiz," Vivian responded coolly.

Several snickers accompanied startled gasps throughout the classroom, which quickly went silent.

"That's a warning, Miss Van Tassel!" shot back Mr. Putrim. "One more, and you've got a detention. And remember, don't come late to my class!"

"Sorry," Vivian muttered as she slumped down into her desk. She sensed that a wrathful stare was now coming from the direction of Amber Grausam. "It won't happen again."

Vivian knew then that it was definitely going to be a very long day.

Stairwells & Stooges

BY THE TIME the lunch bell rang, Vivian had been laughed at, heckled, and generally berated—and that was just by the teachers.

How can lunch be worse, Vivian thought glumly as she wandered the halls in search of the lunchroom. As she walked, she reflected on her miserable morning and tried to decide which class had been the worst. It was hard to choose.

Mrs. Vultura, her language arts teacher, hadn't seemed to like literature or children, as she spent nearly the whole class ranting about the degradation of the language arts at the hands of texting, social media, and Harry Potter (after Vivian made the mistake of mentioning it as her favorite book series during introductions). She seemed incapable of smiling and over-enunciated every word like she was reciting Shakespeare. Vivian, who again had struggled to find the classroom in the maze of halls, was blessed with a front-row seat, drawing more than her fair share of scowls and spittle.

Science class had not been much better. Mr. Drabner, the teacher, spent the entire lesson droning at the chalkboard about the anatomy of a plant. He didn't seem to notice that his classroom didn't have enough desks for all of the students, and Vivian, who was late to this class also due to another wrong turn, spent the entire lesson standing in the back, leaning against a broken radiator.

Her stomach growled just then and Vivian picked up her pace, catching on to the flow of students and finally finding the lunchroom. She looked around the space, taking in the mint-green walls that had been retrofitted with foldout lunch tables, and realized it was also the school's gymnasium. It reeked of sweaty socks and old Wisconsin cheese, probably due to the room's two main functions: exercising and eating. She wrinkled her nose at both the thought and the smell.

The room echoed with a jumble of excited conversations, all bouncing off the graying gym floor. As Vivian scanned the room to find an inconspicuous seat for herself, she saw that most kids were standing in place with their steaming trays or brown paper bags, seemingly looking around for someone else or trying to scope out the best table. Even though she was new to Murkwood, Vivian fully understood that where you sat and who you sat with on the first day of school could have significant repercussions on the whole school year—not to mention your life beyond it.

Her eyes landed on an empty table near the door and she

decided this was as good a place as any for her to plop down. As she settled onto the bench, she felt relieved and grateful that she had brought her lunch and didn't have to walk all the way to the lunch window and through the hordes of students jockeying for table positions.

Vivian sighed as she pulled the brown bag out of her backpack and saw once again what her dad had written across the front: *Daddy Loves You!*

Ugh.

Vivian's mom used to put little Post-it Notes with jokes into her lunch bags. This must've been her dad trying to re-create the effect, but without success.

She hastily poured the contents on the table and flattened the bag, message side down, using it as a placemat. An egg-salad sandwich and an enormous, family-size fruit cup—both clearly from her dad's trip to the mini-mart this morning. However, there was one addition: a fancy silver dinner fork her dad must've rescued from the drawers of their ancient kitchen. Vivian took a big bite of her sandwich and chewed as quickly as she could, determined to make this the swiftest lunch she had ever eaten and slip away before she could be identified as an outcast.

The noise in the room eased as students found their seats— some happy and excited, others disappointed and sulky. Vivian raced through her lunch and had wolfed down everything but the fruit cup, but then made a critical mistake. Without a napkin, Vivian used the bag to wipe her egg-salad-smeared hands and face, exposing its message to the student body. No one was really watching or paying any attention to Vivian—except for Amber Grausam, who at that moment caught Vivian with an icy glare. Vivian crumpled up the bag and returned her eyes to the lunch table.

She was nearly through her fruit cup and ready to make a break for it when three fancy pairs of shoes entered her sightline. Vivian raised her eyes to meet the cruel stares of Amber Grausam flanked by two unfriendly-looking accomplices, who appeared as if they walked out of the same high-end clothing store as Amber. These must be the "cool girls," Vivian realized. She also realized that she had already crossed their leader.

"Hi Vivian, how's your first day going?" Amber asked.

"Great," Vivian lied, her heart beginning to pound.

"I'm really glad," Amber replied, her tone hinting she was not. "You know, you embarrassed me in algebra today."

Vivian couldn't believe her ears. "*I* embarrassed *you?*"

"Yep. And that won't happen again," said Amber sharply.

Without warning, Amber snatched Vivian's crumpled lunch bag and quickly began unfolding it as she stepped back from the table.

"No, stop!" Vivian cried. "That's mine—give it back!"

"It looks like garbage to me," mocked Amber as she returned the bag to its full size. "Awww, look at this! How cute," she continued as her voice shifted into a babyish whine. Her friends giggled cruelly. "'Daddy Loves You!'"

Vivian felt a familiar flame ignite inside her.

By this time, the lunchroom's other outcasts, as well as everyone at nearby tables, had stopped eating their lunches and taken notice of the scene. Some smiled, some laughed, but most kept their heads down, no doubt to avoid being a subsequent target. But Vivian could feel that they were all judging in one way or another.

More on instinct than thought, Vivian sprung up onto the bench and across the table in one smooth movement, spearing the paper bag with her fancy fork and snatching it away from Amber.

"It's mine, Amber! Buzz off and mind your own business," seethed Vivian as she straightened, now face-to-face with a wide-eyed Amber. At this range Vivian realized that Amber was a half head taller.

"Hey, you!" bellowed a vaguely familiar voice.

Vivian turned to see Mrs. Wickams rushing over from a chair she had camped in near the gym entrance. She did not look pleased.

"We do not jump around in here! You or one of your classmates could've been killed! What, do you think this is a zoo?"

"No, but it is a *gym*," Vivian muttered.

She knew she had crossed the line the moment she said it.

"How dare you!" screeched Mrs. Wickams. "Detention!" she continued, her voice lifting to the rafters on the last syllable.

The room quieted as more and more students became aware of the spectacle. Vivian was mortified and could only hang her head, studying Mrs. Wickams's shiny black shoes.

Mrs. Wickams had evidently expected to be issuing detentions today as she instantly pulled out a stack of pink slips from a pocket in her dress and tore one off the top and slapped it on the table next to Vivian.

DETENTION: Time: 3:30–4:30 p.m. / Supervisor: Ms. Greenleaf / Room: 501

Vivian was now certain that all eyes (and a few phones) were on her. Her throat tightened, and tears welled deep behind her eyes—she'd rather explode than let even one tear out in here.

Before anyone could get a better look at her, Vivian snatched up the detention slip and darted out of the lunchroom, searching for a place to hide out in the halls. Finally she found what appeared to be an empty stairwell. But when she pushed through the doors, she heard voices and realized that even this space had already been taken.

"You walk up a narrow, stone causeway," echoed the disembodied voice of a boy. "As you get farther up the mountain, high walls of sheer rock begin to surround you on the right and left. There is a clearing ahead, where you can make out the main gate of the fortress. As you arrive, you see two fully armored guards at the entrance. One shouts, 'State your name and business!' All along the gate and battlements you see heavily armed soldiers summing you up—eager to welcome enemies with bows and swords. What do you do?"

"I am Venna!" dramatically exclaimed the voice of a girl. "A mage of goodness and light. We are but humble adventurers that seek to rid the world of filth and evil and we request entrance to the fortress."

What is this, play practice? Vivian thought. *Does the drama club meet in stairwells at Murkwood Middle School?*

Vivian took a deep breath before peeking under the stairs, where she believed the voices were coming from. To her surprise, there were four students sitting cross-legged in the dark nook. Three of them had paper, pencils, and dice in front of them, and one was sitting with several books behind a dragon-adorned cardboard screen he had propped up. They were illuminated by small electric candles, which flickered orange like authentic flames, creating otherworldly shadows in the cramped, but oddly comfortable space.

Heads turned and four sets of eyes fixed themselves on Vivian, who was still flushed and breathing deeply.

"Hey, are you okay?" asked the wiry, curly-haired boy behind the cardboard screen. Vivian could barely make out his big brown eyes through the mop of sandy brown hair that hung down on his forehead.

"Huh," Vivian choked out.

"Are you okay?" the boy repeated. "It's okay if you're not. There are lots of jackasses at Murkwood."

"William!" grumbled the girl to his right as she swatted him on the knee. "I'm sure there are nicer ways to put it! Sorry about him—he lacks subtlety." The petite Black girl rolled her eyes and grinned at Vivian. "What he meant to say was, it's okay to be upset—we've all been there. I'm Mary, by the way. So, are you?"

"Am I what?"

"Are you okay?" continued Mary. "You seem—"

"Yeah, I'm fine," said Vivian defensively. "And it's none of your—"

"I know, I know," Mary interrupted. "None of my business. And you're right. If you don't wanna talk, don't talk. We're just concerned."

Vivian felt some of the tension drain out of her body. Was it possible these kids were actually *friendly?*

"Sorry," said Vivian sheepishly. "I'm okay. I just got a detention. Kinda got into it with that Amber Grausam girl."

"Ha! I knew I liked her," Mary exclaimed to her friends. "So, what did you do? Did you get in her face for making fun of your backpack?"

"My backpack? No . . . What's wrong with my backpack?"

"Nothing. Nothing at all—I love your backpack," said a pale girl with long, jet-black hair. "Hippogriffs are my favorite animal."

"Favorite *fictional* animal," corrected William.

"Says who? My great-grandma swears that she once saw one in the woods up near Silver Springs."

"Violet, I love your great-grandma, but she's kooky," shot back William. "She once told me she saw a group of mermaids on Harmon Bay. Another time, she said she rode a unicorn on the trails of the Midnight Lake Resort."

"Can we get back to the game, please?" interrupted the fourth member of the pack, a boy with wavy dark hair wearing a tie-dye tank top.

"Arturo, can you hold your horses," Mary laughed. "We're trying to be polite to . . . uh . . . what's your name again?"

"Vivian. Vivian Van Tassel."

"Well, nice to meet you Vivian. I'm Mary Sparks. This unrefined boy here is William Traumer; that's Violet Black, and this other rude boy is Arturo Fuerte."

Vivian didn't quite know what to make of this group. They certainly were peculiar. Mary reminded Vivian of her best friend back home, Jackie Walsh, who shared her witty, direct style.

Vivian's heart ached at the thought of home . . . but it was also the first time today she felt even remotely at ease.

"So, uh, what are you playing?" Vivian asked.

"B and B. Wanna play?" said William eagerly.

"B and B?" repeated Vivian.

"Beasts and Battlements," clarified Mary. "It's a role-playing game."

"The *first* role-playing game," added Violet. "Invented and published right here in Midnight Lake."

Beasts & Battlements certainly sounded familiar to Vivian. But not all the associations seemed like positive ones. Then suddenly, it came to her.

"Wait, isn't this game for—"

"Geeks?" interrupted Arturo.

"Definitely!" confirmed William as the others chuckled.

"No, not geeks," Vivian stumbled. "Like mind control or hypnotism or something?"

The four gamers shared tense, wide-eyed looks, then began to chuckle. Vivian's blood pressure rose as she turned bright red. She'd had quite enough of being laughed at today, and now even self-proclaimed geeks were joining in. She slung her backpack around her shoulder to leave.

"No, no, no! Please don't go," pleaded Violet. "We're not laughing at you—promise! It's just that rumor. It was believed by a lot of people in the old days, but totally ridiculous and disproven years ago. No, it's just a game where you create a make-believe character with certain traits, like strength and dexterity, and go through dungeons and stuff together with other adventurers."

"Yeah," added Arturo, "and you're led through the adventure by the gamemaster—that's William here—and you declare actions for your character; speak for your character; and when you want to try something, you roll for it based on your abilities."

"Sounds kinda like *Minecraft Dungeons?*" remarked Vivian.

"Not exactly, although it's certainly more *Minecraft* than mind control," answered William lightly. "But this game is done in person and all the stuff the computer does in online games is done on paper here—stats, health points and stuff. We also roll real dice," he added as he held up a sapphire-colored twenty-sided die. "Without B and B, there is no *Minecraft*, no *Zelda*, no nothin' as far as fantasy games go."

"So, do you wanna play?" chimed in Mary.

Maybe it was because these were the first friendly faces she had seen today, maybe it was that this group seemed kind of fun and strange, but the offer was tempting. Vivian almost said yes, but then she stopped herself. Visions of her mom's funeral cycled through her head followed by her last goodbye to her friends back home.

No . . . she didn't need friends—she didn't need anyone. Besides, the last thing she needed today was to jump in with a group of loud and proud geeks, setting her on a potentially fatal social course at the school. She would stay a free agent.

"Sorry, maybe another time," Vivian said finally. "Thanks, though."

"Anytime, see you later," said Mary as the others waved goodbye.

Vivian zipped up a few flights of stairs and drew out *Harry Potter*, where she made a new line on her chart, this one called "Classmates." As she put another check in the Harry column (these kids seemed okay, but they were no Ron and Hermione), she heard a collective groan from the group below, followed by a swell of clapping and laughter. Whatever happened in their game, it sounded like they were having fun. At least someone was. She couldn't help but crack a tiny smile realizing that her odd stairwell meeting had been the brightest spot of her day so far.

7

Ms. Greenleaf

VIVIAN SAT IN the locker room stall, her face buried in her hands. The sounds of running water and excited whispers echoed around her.

This stinks, she thought. And she meant it. Everything stunk in this locker room . . . and so did everything else about her day.

Just when Vivian had started to think her day was on the upswing after her encounter with the kids in the stairwell, French class happened. Madame Stern insisted on teaching the entry level French class entirely in French. "En français," she would say any time a student asked a question or made a statement in the only language they knew (not French, thus the need for French class). Vivian was sure there must have been something to the method, but she really hadn't been in the mood to figure it out. By the end of class, Vivian had placed another check in the Harry column of her comparison chart, this one for "Teachers."

Then there was PE. The gym still smelled like lunch, and the uniforms looked like they had fallen off a truck in 1980. Today's class had focused on fitness testing, which included all the bizarre athletic activities one only does in gym class and never again: flexed arm hang, shuttle run, and rope climb—not exactly Olympic sports.

Vivian had drawn top scores in the first two events amid the approving nods of Coach Savage—a tall, gray-haired man with a wheezy voice. But then it was time for rope climb. When Vivian was halfway up, she heard giggling below and looked down to see Amber Grausam huddled with a few other students pointing at her and laughing. Was it the shoes again? Hard to know when dangling fifteen feet above doing the most embarrassing of all gym activities. Vivian was humiliated and descended hurriedly without finishing. By the time she reached the locker room, she was furious and hid in a stall to cool down.

Vivian waited for the locker room to empty before she emerged from the stall and changed back into her regular clothes.

As Vivian shuffled her feet in fatigue and dread on her way to her last class, she wondered, *Is this my new life?* Sure, maybe it had just been a bad day, but was it really going to get better? Would Mr. Putrim suddenly become friendly? Would Mrs. Vultura cease her complaining while showering students in her spittle? Would Amber Grausam and her friends move away? She felt pretty certain the answer was "no" across the board and that led Vivian to a dismal forecast for the year. She looked down at her crumpled schedule:

Ms. Greenleaf / History / Room 501

Well, at least she knew where it was—right next to Mr. Putrim's room. Even better, she could just stay there for detention.

When she entered the classroom, she immediately felt something different. The quiet conversations of students waiting for class to begin didn't seem so strained; the room had a fresh airiness to it, heavily decorated with large palm plants in the corners. On the walls hung reproductions of antique maps of ancient cities. There was a shelf full of oversized books on art and architecture next to a neat stack of classic board games, from Monopoly to Scrabble. Instead of a dusty blackboard, there was a shiny whiteboard decorated with flower decals in the corners and colorful dry erase markers on the ledge. It was the first welcoming room Vivian had been in at Murkwood.

Then, the door swung open and in walked a tall, athletic-looking woman with long, jet-black hair. She looked pretty enough to be on TV, with thick eyebrows and bright green eyes. She strode across the room and stood behind the teacher's desk, smiling. Not a fake, "nice to meet you" smile, but a genuine smile full of warmth. Vivian realized this must be Ms. Greenleaf.

The unseated students quickly scattered to their desks,

and Vivian saw the class included two already familiar faces, one she was pleased to see and one not so much: quirky Mary Sparks from the stairwell a few seats back and bully Amber Grausam in a corner.

"Good afternoon, class," the teacher said as she moved to the front of the room. "I'm Ms. Greenleaf. Welcome to American history. The study of what was, what is, and, if you ask some, what will be again."

Vivian was intrigued by the teacher as she glided around the room, spreading an aura of positivity and warmth. A quick scan of her classmates told Vivian that they all were as curious as she was.

Ms. Greenleaf pushed the sliding whiteboard to one side to reveal another one behind it. This one was filled with taped-up pictures of various buildings and locations.

"This year, we have a lot of ground to cover, but I'm a firm believer that history starts at home, so today you'll be assigned your special project. You are to prepare a research paper and presentation on the history of a local building—not just when, why, and how it was built, but what went on there, who ran it, and what did it mean to society at the time. Midnight Lake is a pretty remarkable place, and you'll find that just about everything that was happening in the country—and even the world—was happening here in some way or another."

She padded over to her desk and grabbed what looked like a witch's hat—long, pointed, and green.

Vivian smiled. It looked like the Sorting Hat's Irish cousin. Maybe it would put Amber in Slytherin where she belonged!

"You'll each draw a location from the hat and that will be your project. The paper will be due the Monday before Halloween and the presentations will begin that same day," continued Ms. Greenleaf, which was met with a collective groan by classmates less than thrilled about the timing.

Vivian scanned the board and immediately recognized a few locations from their drive through town that morning, including Murkwood Middle School. Ms. Greenleaf drifted from desk to desk and called out a location after each was drawn. First it was the Midnight Lake Public Library; then the history museum; Mary got the old Midnight Theatre; then there was something called "Darkham Observatory"; Amber drew the Midnight Lake Resort, and she made sure to point out that her family were year-round members. As the locations dwindled, Vivian noticed that Murkwood School still went unpicked, and her spirits began to sink. The last thing in the world she wanted to do was think more about this awful place.

She closed her eyes and prayed: *Not the school, not the school, not the school.* When she opened them, Ms. Greenleaf stood right above her, looking down on her with thoughtful eyes.

"Vivian?" she said while holding out the hat.

Vivian wondered how Ms. Greenleaf already knew her name—maybe word had already gotten around about the ill-behaved, dorky new girl? Had the other teachers been complaining about her?

Vivian nervously reached into the hat and flicked through the remaining entries with her fingers, hoping their touch alone might differentiate the good from the bad. She plucked out what she thought might be a lucky pick. It was not.

"Murkwood Middle School!" announced Ms. Greenleaf, as she gave Vivian a knowing look before departing.

Thanks a lot, Sorting Hat's cousin!

When the bell rang, the other students began to gather their things, but Vivian stayed put. Ms. Greenleaf noticed and walked over as the classroom emptied, holding the unlucky green hat in her hand.

"Hey Vivian, class is over," she said sweetly.

"Not for me," Vivian replied as she unfolded the pink detention slip and handed it to Ms. Greenleaf.

"I see," said the teacher with an amused smile. "What happened?"

Vivian didn't know why, but for some reason she felt strangely at ease talking to Ms. Greenleaf, so instead of just recounting the lunchroom incident, she unpacked her entire school day for the attentive teacher. She finished with how unlucky she felt to have drawn the school, on the off chance that Ms. Greenleaf might switch things around.

"Sounds like it's been a hard day," Ms. Greenleaf said when Vivian stopped talking. "You know, I had a similar experience with Mrs. Wickams when I was a student here." Then, funneling her hands around her mouth, she whispered, "She's older than she looks."

"You were a student at Murkwood?" Vivian asked, the surprise evident in her voice.

"I was," she replied wistfully. Ms. Greenleaf considered Vivian for several moments. "In fact . . . I knew your mother."

Vivian was paralyzed by the remark as a flood of emotions welled up and swirled in her chest.

"My . . . my mother?" she repeated. "You knew my mom?"

"Mmm-hmmm."

"What . . . what was she like when she was young?" Vivian asked before she could stop herself.

Ms. Greenleaf smiled as she appeared to be lost in thought.

"Calissa was an amazing girl. Talented and sensitive; stubborn and curious; temperamental and beautiful." Ms. Greenleaf paused for a moment before continuing. "She was like . . . like you, I gather. And when I saw you, I knew instantly that you must be Calissa's girl—you are so much alike."

Vivian's heart began to ache. As she fought to suppress her emotions, a pained memory crossed Ms. Greenleaf's face, which seemed to snap her out of her warm reflections and made her clear her throat.

"In fact, I think she—"

"Gwendolyn, a word," interrupted a stern voice from behind them.

There in the doorway stood a tall, frowning man.

"Principal Thornwood, of course," Ms. Greenleaf said as she sprung up nervously. "I'll just be a second," she whispered.

Vivian watched through the door window as the two engaged in a tense-looking conversation. Vivian thought a few of the glances and gestures were made in her direction. Had her antics with Mrs. Wickams (or others) already reached the principal?

Moments later, Ms. Greenleaf returned. She seemed agitated.

"I'm sorry about that," she said. "Where were we?"

"You were saying something else about my mom?" Vivian prompted.

"Oh—oh yes," stammered Ms. Greenleaf. Vivian followed her gaze, meeting the cold stare of Mr. Thornwood, who continued to watch from the door. "No, it was nothing."

Mr. Thornwood turned and left slowly, his fancy dress shoes clacking on the maple floors. A bit of warmth returned to Ms. Greenleaf's face.

"Now, with regard to that assignment, I'm sorry you weren't happy with the pick," she said while looking around the classroom. "It's a creepy place, no question, and its history perhaps better left buried than unearthed. But fate knows better than we do, and I have a feeling you'll learn more than you think."

Disappointed that both the talk about her mom was cut

short and that she'd been stuck with the assignment, Vivian only nodded and smiled tightly.

"It was truly a pleasure to meet you, Vivian S. Van Tassel. You may go. I'll see you tomorrow."

"But what about that?" Vivian asked pointing to the detention slip in Ms. Greenleaf's hand.

Ms. Greenleaf dropped the slip into the green hat, waved her slender fingers with a flourish, and then showed the inside again to Vivian. It was empty.

"What detention?" she said with a smile.

That was a heck of a trick, Vivian thought as she walked home. But the real trick had been the way Mrs. Greenleaf had turned Vivian's day around.

8

The Lake

BZZZ! BZZZZZZ! BZZZZZZZZZZZZ!

Vivian flipped one eye open and then the other. It was the third time this week that she had awoken to the sound of power tools. She lay motionless on the saggy mattress, not wanting to move. She studied the pale, overcast light breaking through the window and suddenly realized that today would be different. Today was Saturday . . . finally!

Vivian sat up and rubbed the sleep out of her eyes. She shifted over to the edge of her bed and stepped straight into her flower sandals—an art she had mastered during the week.

She glanced over at her backpack slumped against the dresser—it looked almost as tired as she was. Her first week of school had been awful. Each day had been like the first day on repeat, but somehow worse each time. The school, the classes, the teachers, and, of course, Amber—nothing had improved. Not even close.

A Ravenclaw pin affixed to the front of her backpack

glinted in the bright morning light. Vivian smiled, remembering that there had been some bright spots of her week too.

The pin had been a gift from Mary Sparks, who had noticed how much Vivian liked the Wizarding World and said she had "an extra." Vivian had always considered herself a Gryffindor, like Harry . . . but Ravenclaw was a close second and she really liked the pin. Beyond the first day of school, Vivian had spent every lunch period watching Mary and her friends playing Beasts & Battlements under the stairs. She had even started calling them "the stairwell misfits," a term they had proudly adopted. Every day they invited Vivian to play, but she always declined. She enjoyed watching them play and all, but her time there had more to do with avoiding cafeteria confrontations with Amber and Mrs. Wickams.

The other bright spots in Vivian's week all had to do with Ms. Greenleaf and last-period history class. Her warm smile and "good afternoon, class" greeting would somehow instantly lift Vivian's spirits a bit at the end of each day.

Vivian's stomach fluttered when she arrived downstairs and found her father in the middle of another ambitious (at least for him) home project. This time it involved mounting bookshelves on the wall above the couch in the living room, where he had set up their TV. Unfortunately, the house wasn't wired for internet or cable, so the TV was incapable of showing anything but DVDs for the time being. Fortunately, even the best streaming services had nothing on Mr. Van Tassel's collection of retro hits—from *Care Bears* to *Star Wars*.

It only took a glance at the exhausted-looking Mr. Van Tassel to know that he'd had a stressful week of his own. He had begun his new reporting position for the *Midnight Lake Bugle*, which included the challenges of coming in as an outsider and working for the tyrannical Rex Bellowman. In fact, both Vivian and her dad were so drained at the end of each day that they hardly spoke in the evenings over their take-out dinners.

"Good morning, girly!" exclaimed Mr. Van Tassel. He proudly gestured to the shelves. "Now we'll have somewhere to put our movies!"

Mr. Van Tassel grabbed a large stack of DVDs from a box on the couch and placed them on the upper shelf, which Vivian noticed was horribly askew—right above another equally crooked shelf he had installed earlier. The shelf shifted just as soon as it bore weight, making it even more crooked. And then, as Vivian watched with wide eyes, her dad's precious DVDs slowly slid and tumbled from the shelf.

They stood in silence for several moments looking down at the jumble of movies on the couch.

"Hmmm," said Mr. Van Tassel finally. "The level must be broken. Yep, that must be it," he continued while nodding to himself. "What do ya say we go out on the lake today?"

Vivian scanned the crumbling house that had somehow gotten even worse-looking since her father had begun his improvement projects. The thought of getting away from the house—of being anywhere but here—sounded good to Vivian.

"Okay," she said, nodding. "Should we clean up first?"

"Nope!" replied Mr. Van Tassel. "My fault. I'll get it later."

"You mean the level's fault," Vivian joked.

"Let's go," he answered back with a chuckle.

The pair lugged their fishing gear the few blocks to the downtown marina, stopping by a convenience store on the way to pick up some essentials: potato chips, cream soda, and nightcrawlers—the store carried both the gummy candy version and the real version they were based on: live worms. Evidently, in lake towns like Midnight Lake one could buy live bait in the refrigerator aisle at convenience stores right next to the soda and ice cream. Vivian wasn't particularly squeamish, but something about snacks next to insects made her skin crawl.

Serving as the gateway to the marina was a huge and ornate building labeled "The Paradise," which hosted arcade shops on the ground level and a big-band ballroom on top. Vivian had learned in Ms. Greenleaf's class that the place was so renowned during its heyday in the 1940s, it drew world-famous musical acts. It must've taken some big bucks to get those groups to come all the way out here, Vivian thought.

Once at the docks, Mr. Van Tassel "got a deal" on their fishing boat rental and led them down a long pier.

Vivian's eyebrows rose in surprise when they stopped at

a slick-looking speedboat with a lightning bolt painted on the side.

This might actually be fun, she thought as she set down her things to descend into it.

"Vivy," said Mr. Van Tassel, interrupting her train of thought. "Not that one. This one," he continued as he gestured to the next boat down.

It was a tired-looking, rusty green boat, which rested lopsidedly in the water. The boat's name, THE ORCA, was written in block letters on the side. The boat did seem to float, however, so that was something.

"Figures," she muttered to herself as she changed course.

Vivian had never been a huge fan of fishing, but between the snacks and the fact that she had brought her book, she felt prepared for all possible scenarios. Some time on the lake didn't sound so bad.

It took a few moments for Mr. Van Tassel to get the hang of the lever steering mechanism attached to the antique motor in back, and he nearly plowed into a passing boat as they navigated out of the tightly packed marina. Fortunately, they were still intact and afloat as they made it out to open waters, which she could tell were quite deep by the way the boat bobbed up and down as they sputtered along.

Unfortunately, it was a cloudy day, making Midnight Lake look dull, gray, and even a little ominous. Despite the so-so weather, dozens of other boats dotted the lake trying to capture the last few precious days of warmth and good fishing. From this vantage point, Vivian could now see the true scale of wealth present in the strange lake town. Her eyes widened as they passed mansion after glorious mansion, some with their own multistory boathouses and mini marinas.

The pair watched the impressive scenery in silence, zoning out to the loud buzz and burble of the boat engine. After several minutes, Mr. Van Tassel navigated the boat to the right (or the starboard, Vivian remembered) into a narrower part of the lake, passing a sign on shore that read HARMON BAY. This area hosted an equally impressive collection of spectacular houses, resorts, and complexes. When he finally cut the engine, they were well within sight of what appeared to be a camp or college facility as well as a humungous silver-domed structure that peeked out above the thick tree line, overlooking the lake and forested terrain for miles.

"Well, this is where they said the best fishing was," said Mr. Van Tassel, the first words that had been spoken in nearly a half hour. "Do you want me to prepare you a line?"

"Nah," replied Vivian. She was more interested in the scenery. "Not right now. Hey Dad, what's with the R2-D2– looking thing?" she continued as she pointed to the strange dome that protruded from the canopy.

Mr. Van Tassel almost lost his balance as he turned around to see what she was pointing at.

"R2-D2? Oh, that's Darkham Observatory!" he said with

a grin. "Used to be a big-deal astronomy center with a huge telescope, but not so much anymore. Now it's just sort of a landmark. Yeah, I guess it does sort of look like R2."

"Oh!" replied Vivian eagerly, as she remembered some details from school. "We learned about this in history class— Ms. Greenleaf told us about it. She said that it was one of the most important observatories in the world and even Einstein once visited, but over the years they started building them far away on mountains to avoid light pollution and stuff."

Her dad looked at her curiously.

"Yes, that's right," he said distractedly. "Did you say Ms. Greenleaf? Gwendolyn Greenleaf?"

"Yeah?" replied Vivian puzzled, wondering if she had said something wrong.

"She's your history teacher?" Mr. Van Tassel flipped open the tackle box. "Wow! Small world! Your mother grew up with her—they were best friends when your mom and I first met. I got to know her a bit."

Best friends? Vivian thought. Ms. Greenleaf mentioned that she knew Mom when they were young, but she never said anything about being best friends.

"Really?" Vivian asked.

"Yeah . . . they were. Unfortunately, they had some sort of falling-out after your mother and I got married and moved to Chicago," he continued as he started rummaging through the box full of lures, lines, and bobbers. "Your mom wouldn't talk about it, so I left it alone. Wow, though. Gwendolyn Greenleaf is your teacher."

For reasons she didn't understand, Vivian's heart sank; her mind began to race. This unexpected connection to Ms. Greenleaf created for her far more questions than answers. Why hadn't Ms. Greenleaf mentioned how close she and Vivian's mom had been? What had caused their falling-out?

"Well, here's one Ms. Greenleaf probably didn't tell you about—the *Lucius Sunberry*," said Mr. Van Tassel as he dug his fingers into the tub of nightcrawler soil and plucked out a long, plump worm.

"The *Lucius* who?" she asked. "Sunberry" sounded like a jam, and the only Lucius she had ever heard of was *Harry Potter* villain Lucius Malfoy, but she felt pretty certain he had never been to Midnight Lake.

"The *Lucius Sunberry* was a grand nineteenth-century side-wheeler—a paddleboat—that used to do tours of the lake for early residents and visitors," he said with his eyebrows lifted and voice firmly in storyteller mode. "It was super luxurious inside and out and supposedly boasted a large silver bell imported from a medieval cathedral in Europe. According to legend, 1891 had been a difficult year for the locals—all of the fish began disappearing with thousands floating up dead near shore; lots of weird sightings in the water. Then one night there was a huge storm on the lake and a mist descended while the *Sunberry* was out. No one knows exactly what happened, but the ship sank, taking with it one hundred and twenty passengers and crew. It's said it went down right about where we are now, which is why they say there is good fishing here—lots of great places for fish to call home."

Goose bumps swept over Vivian's arms and legs. She really didn't like the idea of floating over the remains of a sunken ship with over one hundred skeletons probably still clinging to railings and wheels. Instead of asking any more questions, the answers to which were bound to give her nightmares, she decided to give an affirmative "hmmm," and then dip her nose into her book to take her mind off things—a "Do Not Disturb" notice to her oversharing father.

Mr. Van Tassel took the hint and finished preparing his fishhook. Vivian watched discreetly over the book as her dad tried time and time again to cast out into the water, but he couldn't seem to coordinate when to press the release button on the reel while casting. The line kept falling limply into the boat before he could make the throwing motion. Eventually he quit trying and dropped his line right next to the vessel.

They sat in peaceful silence for a long while. One thing that had already been disproven among the local tall tales, Vivian decided, was that this was a good fishing spot. Not a bite, not a tickle, or a ripple in the cool, gray water. The only activity was the occasional gentle wake caused by the passing of other motorboats. Vivian finished the first *Harry Potter* (again) and began wondering what she might do now. She lazily leaned over the bow and began stirring the water with her hand, trying to hypnotize herself in the green and gray swirls.

"Hey Vivy," interrupted Mr. Van Tassel. "What do you say we pack up and head home? The fish aren't biting anyway."

"Ya think?" Vivian teased.

Mr. Van Tassel packed up the fishing gear and started the engine, which gave a defeated drone that Vivian realized matched her dad's disposition. The ride back seemed slow and solemn—like a funeral procession—as the sad *Orca* slowly made its way back to harbor without a catch.

As they approached the Paradise, Vivian noticed there seemed to be a traffic jam on the way back into the marina. A sheriff's boat bobbed near the entrance, flashing its strobe. Mr. Van Tassel had also taken notice of the scene.

"What is it, Dad?" asked Vivian.

"Dunno," he replied distractedly. "But there's something going on at the marina."

As they neared, they saw a crowd gathering on the shore and docks, including several members of the sheriff's department and a photographer her father said he recognized from the local paper. Everyone seemed fixated on something right along the shore, within the marina. Mr. Van Tassel navigated to the pier farthest away to an area where they could hitch and get off.

As they climbed out of the boat and approached the nervous-looking spectators on shore, they were assaulted by the unmistakable stench of decaying fish and sea life. And they now knew why they hadn't gotten any bites today. Every square inch of the mostly enclosed area of the marina was now occupied by fish floating lifelessly on the surface. There were thousands of dead fish, all clumped up right along the shore.

Though technically off duty, Vivian could tell that her dad smelled a story here (literally) as he pulled her by the hand through the crowd toward the sheriff, whom he had met the week before. Vivian held her nose with her free hand and tried not to complain, her curiosity just outweighing her offended sense of smell.

"Hey, Sheriff Pridemore!" her dad called. "What have we got here?"

The sheriff's ruddy face stared up blankly at Mr. Van Tassel.

"Sorry!" Mr. Van Tassel said, realizing that the sheriff didn't remember him. "It's Michael Van Tassel . . . with the *Midnight Lake Bugle*?"

"Oh yeah, you . . . ," grunted Sheriff Pridemore. He grabbed his belt and puffed out his chest with an air of authority. "We're in the middle of an investigation, Von Tossel. What do you want?"

"It's Van Tass— never mind. Just want to know what you think could have caused this?" Vivian's dad asked as he put his sleeve up to his nose and mouth to mask the stench.

"Well, if I knew that, then we wouldn't need an

investigation, now would we?" drawled Sheriff Pridemore. "Now if you'll excuse me."

"Oh yes, of course," Mr. Van Tassel said as the sheriff walked away. "Well, let me know if you find something!"

Vivian was tasked with gathering their gear from the boat as her dad stuck around taking statements from witnesses and spectators, most of whom looked like local townsfolk who didn't seem interested in talking. As Vivian rejoined her father, he was approached by a clean-shaven blond man wearing a golf visor and holding a fancy tablet. Vivian noticed he was wearing a white leather glove on one hand—he must've come straight from the golf course.

"Well, well, well," droned the man. "If it isn't the new guy looking for a hot story."

"Hi Troy," mumbled Mr. Van Tassel. "Yeah, I happened to be—"

"You happened to be stepping on my story," snarled Troy. "Back off it, Van Tassel, or you'll find your days at the newspaper numbered!"

As Vivian watched, her dad's cheeks turned red, his ears purple. He opened his mouth but stopped and glanced over to Vivian, who quickly pretended to not be paying attention. She hoped her dad was going to tell this guy off, but he didn't. Instead, he simply took a deep breath and exhaled loudly.

"My apologies, Troy," he said with a tight jaw. "I didn't know you were on this one. Be my guest."

"Don't worry, Van Tassel—plenty of good stories to go around. I think there's a grand opening of a new candle store in town—maybe you could cover that?" Troy said with a chuckle.

"C'mon, Vivy," growled Mr. Van Tassel as he grabbed his fishing gear and stormed away, stopping for just a moment to see if Vivian was following.

Vivian and her father walked in silence and slowed as they trudged up Broad Street toward home.

"Dad, who was that?" asked Vivian, who was starting to wonder if her father had some of the same bully problems that she had.

"Troy Grausam," muttered Mr. Van Tassel. "He's the 'star reporter' at the paper and . . ." Her dad paused as if he were choosing his words very carefully. "He's a bit hard to work with. He inherited a ton of money from his parents, who owned one of the big factories nearby and a pretty good share of the paper, so he basically plays reporter for fun. . . . Actually, I think he has a daughter your age."

Grausam. Amber Grausam—this was her father.

"Yep," said Vivian stiffly. "Like father, like daughter. I know Amber from school and let's just say . . . she's as pleasant as he is."

"Well, don't sweat her, or him for that matter," he replied. "Just imagine, we only have to *deal* with them—they have to *be* them. C'mon, let's get home."

Vivian couldn't decide whether she was impressed or disappointed with her dad's restraint. Maybe it was both.

Just as they were almost out of eyeshot, Vivian suddenly got a strange feeling and felt compelled to turn around for one last look. Standing in the midst of the remaining onlookers and bustling officials was the creepy, gray man from the diner. He was wearing sunglasses, but Vivian could feel that his gaze was fixed firmly on her.

Vivian's heart began to pound in her chest. She turned and locked arms with her father, practically dragging him up the street.

"Hey girly!" her dad said, thinking Vivian was trying to cheer him up. "Thanks. I needed that!"

Vivian decided not to explain as she tightened her grip around his arm. She just wanted to get home.

Detention

VIVIAN SLAMMED HER locker, sighed, and leaned her back into the rusted blue door. It had been another draining day at Murkwood.

She shuffled through the halls amid the bustle that always followed the dismissal bell, her classmates eagerly putting away their things and racing to their afterschool activities. It had been a month now and Vivian still didn't have an activity, or rather, as she preferred to think of it, the town didn't have one for her. She hadn't had the heart to pick up a fencing saber since the "fencing incident," and there wasn't a club within fifty miles anyway; the dance studio in town had long since closed; and the antique spinet piano at home was in disrepair and desperately out of tune. Local-oriented activities, on the other hand, were abundant but entirely uninteresting to her: school sports, fishing, hunting, embroidery, and bird watching. She liked hiking and all but didn't really consider it a hobby—it seemed to her that hiking was just walking around outside.

As the halls cleared out and she prepared to descend the final set of stairs toward the lobby, she noticed a commotion at the end of the hall. When she got closer, she was not surprised to see Amber Grausam and her two pals, Kelly Frimer and Madison Bose, circling a locker like rabid hyenas. In the middle of the commotion, gripping her books tightly to her chest, was Violet Black, one of the stairwell misfits.

"Oh, c'mon, can we play Beasts and Battlements with you so we can also *pretend* to have a life?" jeered Amber.

Kelly and Madison cackled savagely.

Violet looked paralyzed in place, her back firmly pressed against her locker. Vivian could tell she was terrified. Seeing this type of cruelty made Vivian's heart ache and, without a second thought, she dropped her backpack and swiftly shot down the hall.

"Buzz off, Amber!" Vivian said firmly as she inserted herself between Violet and the bully.

"Oh, look. It's Vivian Van Tassel, the fork fencer," spat Amber as she stepped closer to Vivian, towering over her. "You don't scare me, you freak."

Vivian cringed inwardly at the "fork fencer" nickname. It wasn't the first time she had heard it. Last week, she had heard the term whispered by giggling classmates, and she came to realize the nickname was referring to her, based on the cafeteria incident with the paper bag and Amber. What did take her a little longer to piece together was how the entire school seemed to have found out about it. But Mary had helped her solve that mystery by showing her the video of the encounter that was circulating online. It was there that the "fork fencer" nickname had been born. Vivian was pretty sure Amber had been the one who had come up with it.

Vivian's adrenaline surged; she squeezed her fists and toes, frantically searching for places in her body to send her tension.

"I'm warning you, Amber," Vivian said through clenched teeth. "Back off or you'll be sorry."

"Awww. Do you play B and B with Violet here to pretend you have a life too?" mocked Amber.

As Violet sniffled behind her, still rooted to the spot, Vivian's mind raced, searching for Amber's emotional weak spots. What could she say to shut this girl up? She'd have to make some calculated guesses.

"Yes," Vivian declared. "Yes, I do. In B and B I play an *obnoxious* rich girl from Midnight Lake, whose *only* friends hang out with her because of her *money* and her parents throw her into as many activities as they can so they never need to *see* her!"

Something Vivian said had obviously struck a chord. Amber's large blue eyes narrowed to angry slits. The cruel cackles of the mean girls faded into strained, nervous laughter. Amber's body tensed—Vivian could feel that she was about to strike.

"What is this?" bellowed Mrs. Wickams as she hurried

down the hall. "What! Is! This?! Do I need to separate you two again? Deten-tion! Deten-tion!" she yelled with her familiar last-syllable emphasis, while tearing off pink slips for each of them.

It appeared that this already long school day was just about to get longer.

"You two, follow me!" Mrs. Wickams bellowed, sharply gesturing to Vivian and Amber. "And the rest of you, disperse or it'll be detentions for you also!"

Kelly and Madison scurried away like rats before Mrs. Wickams could even finish her threats. Violet nodded and hastily mouthed the words "thank you" to Vivian as Amber and Mrs. Wickams turned to leave.

Vivian smiled and gave a single nod back. The trouble had been worth it.

"Vivian!" pressed Mrs. Wickams. "Let's go, or we'll see you in detention tomorrow as well!"

"Coming," replied Vivian as she dashed to catch up, now with a slight spring in her step.

"We've got to stop meeting like this," whispered Ms. Greenleaf as she passed by Vivian's desk during detention. Vivian couldn't help but smile even though fire and fury still flowed through her veins. After receiving the handoff from Mrs. Wickams, Ms. Greenleaf had seated Vivian and Amber in opposite corners of the room, buffered by a half dozen other unfortunate students who were also serving their sentences.

Vivian had now served a handful of detentions, but she never minded the ones with Ms. Greenleaf on Mondays. The problem was that Ms. Greenleaf didn't supervise seventh-grade detention every day; it rotated between Mr. Putrim, Mrs. Vultura, Mr. Drabner, and Mrs. Wickams—and Vivian had a hard time deciding which one she liked the least. With that in mind, Vivian was especially careful which day she decided to cause trouble, or at least which days she would let herself be caught.

Silence was required during detention, which always made the hour-long session seem longer. Students could either do homework or read, but they couldn't use screens (even if it was homework related). Vivian always chose to read and she was again deep into the second book of *Harry Potter*, but kept the original in her backpack to maintain her Harry vs. Vivian life-comparison chart.

"Okay, students, time's up," announced Ms. Greenleaf. "You can all go. Vivian, a word?"

The group rushed to gather their things and cleared out in just seconds, as if Ms. Greenleaf might somehow change her mind. The last to leave was Amber Grausam, who sneered at Vivian as she exited, mouthing at her the words "You're dead," to which Vivian responded with a cocky, tight-lipped smile.

Vivian slowly gathered her own things and approached Ms. Greenleaf's desk.

"Hey Vivian, everything going okay?" Ms. Greenleaf asked.

Vivian hated questions like this. For one, they forced her to think about all the things that were going wrong; second, things weren't really "okay." Her situation hadn't improved much since she arrived in Midnight Lake; the only difference now was that she had grown more accustomed to the daily torments and challenges.

"Yeah, I guess," she lied, unable to meet Ms. Greenleaf's eyes.

"Really?" Ms. Greenleaf asked, raising her eyebrows.

Vivian's throat tightened. Realizing that Ms. Greenleaf was intent on pressing her, she decided she would turn the tables.

"Ms. Greenleaf, were you close to my mom?"

Now it was the teacher's turn to avoid Vivian's gaze—the first time Vivian had ever seen Ms. Greenleaf look at a loss for words. She opened her mouth to reply but closed it again as if she were reconsidering saying something.

"Yes," she said finally. "Yes, we were close . . . but that is a story for another day." She cleared her throat. "Have you started your paper yet?"

Checkmate, Vivian thought as she watched Ms. Greenleaf regain control of the conversation.

"Yes . . . I mean . . . uh . . . no," replied Vivian, unable to fib to her favorite teacher. "But we still have almost a month, and I'm still kinda getting used to everything."

"I understand," Ms. Greenleaf said, smiling. "But I really think you should get started. I think it might take your mind off

some of those 'okay' things and may even give you some . . .
perspective. Why don't you head over to the history museum
today before it closes?"

Vivian couldn't imagine how studying the creepiest building in town would make anything better or provide her helpful
perspective, but she understood that it had to be done and pro-
crastination never helped—something her mother had rein-
forced to her many times.

"Okay," Vivian sighed.

"Okay," repeated Ms. Greenleaf, looking pleased. "Ask to
talk to Mr. Arrowsmith. He'll be able to help you."

Case Files

IT WAS NEARING dusk when Vivian finally left school and began her slow trek down the forested Murkwood Hill. It was a gray and gloomy fall day—a perfect reflection of Vivian's mood. Yet the woods that surrounded her were ablaze with the vibrant yellows, browns, and reds of autumn, and she couldn't deny their beauty, even on a day like this.

The Midnight Lake Museum was only a few blocks from school, located on Main Street next to the Green River bridge in a former public waterworks—there was even some type of old-fashioned waterwheel still intact. A sign out front read: NEW EXHIBIT COMING SOON: MINING IN MIDNIGHT LAKE.

"Sorry, kid, we're closing," said a grumpy-looking man at the counter who was reading the newspaper. He had a thick, gray beard and even thicker glasses.

"Oh," said Vivian, surprised by how late it already was. "Sorry . . . I just . . . Is Mr. Arrowsmith here?"

Without needing to be summoned, a tall man emerged

from the back office. He had long white hair and a serious but surprisingly youthful face.

"Aha. You must be Vivian," said the man in a deep, booming voice. "Yes, Gwen Greenleaf mentioned you might be coming by. I'm Mr. Arrowsmith, the museum director. We really don't have much in the main collection on Murkwood . . . but Gwen did donate a number of things some years ago that haven't yet been curated. They're in the storage loft and you can borrow what you need for your assignment. We're about to close, but there's a private tour still going in the exhibit hall, so I'll be here awhile longer. Jim, can you show Vivian to the loft?"

"Uh . . . sure," replied the desk attendant, clearly surprised at the access Vivian was being granted.

The stairs creaked with every slow step up to the loft, which was hidden in the back of the museum above the cramped administrative offices and archives.

"There are no lights up here—it's pitch-black—so you'll need this," said Jim gruffly as he handed Vivian his flashlight at the top of the steps. "And be careful. Some of the floorboards are loose, so watch your step."

Without another word, Jim descended the creaky stairs and went out of sight, leaving Vivian in the dark and dusty stillness of the loft. She didn't find the space quite as dark as the man had suggested as she could make out the rough outline of most of the objects. She shined the flashlight and looked around. Every square inch of the space was filled up to the low, wood-beamed ceiling with random relics: framed pictures and maps, antique trunks, taxidermied animals, leather-bound books, and old science equipment that looked like it came from Dr. Frankenstein's laboratory.

Nothing weird in here? she nervously joked to herself as she slowly made her way down an aisle carved through the mess, looking for anything that might be Murkwood Middle School–related.

She passed an antique telephone switchboard next to a clothes rack full of old military uniforms. The ceiling lowered as she approached the end of the aisle, which terminated at the eave, forcing her to duck her head as she walked. Another short aisle ran along the eave. As she turned the corner, the beam of her flashlight caught a pale face that smiled coldly right at her.

Vivian's heart nearly jumped out of her chest. She gasped and turned to run but stepped on a loose floorboard that seesawed down into the floor, making her stumble backward, dropping the flashlight and slamming into a large trunk behind her.

She scrambled on hands and knees to pick up the flashlight and sprung up to make her escape, only to stub her toe on the now protruding floorboard, sending her reeling back to the ground. The figure's outline clearly visible to her naked eye, she shined the flashlight back up at the assailant from her seat, hoping to gain some sort of advantage in her cornered position. The pale face continued to smile coldly. In fact, he hadn't moved an inch. He was dressed oddly, Vivian realized, in tanned leather skins, moccasins, and a fur hat, while he gripped a musket in his motionless hands.

It was a mannequin.

Vivian giggled in relief as she buried her face in her hands.

She sat for several moments trying to catch her breath, then turned and rose from the floor to dust herself off. Written in black marker atop the chest she had been sitting against was *Murkwood Sanitarium*. She had literally stumbled right onto what she was looking for.

The lid squeaked as she lifted it, releasing a thick cloud of dust. Inside were stacks and stacks of black-and-white photographs, papers, brochures, and old books on psychology with titles like *The Benefits of Electroshock Therapy*; *Committal and Lobotomy Protocols for the Dangerous and Criminally Insane*; and *Quick Cures for Delusions, Fainting Spells, and Nervous Disorders*. Vivian skimmed the contents as she began to empty the trunk. The photos were without a doubt the most interesting find. The first few stacks were images of the Murkwood Sanitarium facility and its distinguished-looking staff, but as she continued flipping through the photos, they began showing more and more disturbing images of things like patients in straitjackets and strange-looking medical devices.

Soon the chest was empty, with only the moldy paisley lining visible. Vivian scanned the interior with her flashlight to make sure she hadn't missed anything and noticed the bottom of the trunk looked bulky and uneven. She ran her hand along the lining and discovered that there was definitely something lodged beneath the fabric.

Vivian found a loose corner of the cloth and began to peel it back—it easily pulled free of the ancient staples, kicking up a fresh cloud of dust. Vivian's eyes widened as she cast the beam of light inside. There, laid neatly and evenly across the bottom of the trunk, were dozens of folders, each labeled "Case Files."

The folders were yellowed and dusty, each marked with a year in the upper right-hand corner. At a glance the dates seemed to go as far back as 1885 and as recently as 1925. It was clear that these had been undisturbed for a long time. For a moment Vivian felt inclined to replace the moldy fabric over them; to forget them. Wouldn't it be wrong to look? These were medical records, after all, highly sensitive and confidential information.

But Vivian was curious, and the faded year written atop each folder reminded her that these would not be *living* patients. She took a deep breath and decided to start at the beginning.

DATE: June 28, 1885

PATIENT: Ethyl Wilkins

AGE: 32; EYES: Blue; HAIR: Brown

DIAGNOSIS: Delusional Psychosis

CASE NOTES: Ethyl disappeared on Friday, June 23, 1885, and was found three days later wandering in the Green River ravine, famished and confused. She claims that she had been abducted by a slimy green man with hollow, black eyes; and razor-sharp teeth—a troll, she insists—and was held captive in its cave until she was rescued by a group of huntsmen armed with bows and swords.

TREATMENT RECOMMENDATIONS: Fever induction through sulfur injections; Patient should be held in confinement under supervision, as necessary, until delusions subside.

The next page was someone named James Snyder. According to the report, he had also suffered from "delusions," these around claims that he had been attacked while hiking by a "bear with the feathers and face of a vulture."

What stories, Vivian thought. These files were already proving far more interesting than she would have expected.

Next was Suzanne Stewart. One morning, she went to the barn to tend to her family's livestock only to find that they had been massacred. There standing above the bloody wreckage was a wolf, she claimed, with long tentacles coming out of its back, but it fled as she entered. Again, "Delusional Psychosis" was the diagnosis. One from 1890 was an

account of a giant pill bug–looking creature that had supposedly wandered into a farmer's kitchen and eaten all of
his pots and pans. Then there was the outrageous tale of a
two-legged sharklike creature that walked along the shores
of Midnight Lake! But the one that Vivian found to be the
most outlandish was the 1896 report of a woman walking in
the woods who claimed she encountered a giant hovering
sphere covered with spikes, a dozen eyes, and a mouth full of
razor-sharp teeth.

Vivian didn't know why, but she distinctly had the feeling
that she had stumbled onto something really important. She
flipped through the files, skipping years at a time. Year after
year, page after page, the stories were all different yet almost
always the same. Visions of fantastical beasts, encounters with
fairies, wizards, and elves, always diagnosed as "delusions" or
"hallucinations." Why so many "delusions"? Why so many
similar accounts? Maybe a health crisis? Vivian had read that
chemicals like lead in the water could make people see things
that weren't there. That could possibly explain why the town
had so many sanitariums in the old days. But over so many
years and in different parts of town? Or was there something
more to these strange accounts?

Vivian's skin sprung goose bumps at the thought.

"Vivian!" called Mr. Arrowsmith from the bottom of the
loft stairs, startling her so much that she dropped the flashlight. "The tour is ending. I need to lock up."

Vivian stared at the extraordinary mess she had made of the trunk's contents and the trunk itself.

"Coming!" she squeaked as she frantically sorted out the key pieces she thought she might need for her project and began shoving the remainder back into the trunk.

She crammed a stack of photos, a couple of old brochures, and a file that contained original deeds and charter information into her backpack. She grabbed a stack of the case file folders and moved to put them back in, but hesitated. She certainly didn't *need* the aged case files for her project, nor would she be expected to report on these kinds of details. But there was something strange here that demanded investigation.

She took a deep breath and made the call: she hurriedly snatched as many files as would fit in her backpack and stuffed them in—a few thick folders each from the beginning, middle, and final years.

"Vivian, are you coming?" Mr. Arrowsmith called as the stairs to the loft began to creak with footsteps.

Vivian, now thoroughly in a panic, pulled the fabric back across the false bottom to cover the remaining case files and finished piling things in. The footsteps seemed to cease when they reached the top of the stairs. She closed the trunk, snatched her bag, and turned to go. She nearly ran into Mr. Arrowsmith, who had appeared right behind her.

"Ready?" he asked.

"Yep," said Vivian as casually as possible. He had

approached so silently and without the benefit of a flashlight, she wondered how much of her activity he had seen. "Got what I needed."

At that moment, the sound of thunder rumbled in the distance.

"You best be getting home, young one," suggested Mr. Arrowsmith. "There's a storm coming in."

Vivian didn't need to be told twice. She thanked Mr. Arrowsmith, zipped out of the museum, and ran all the way home, not just to beat the storm, but also because she was eager to get back to work.

When she arrived home, the house was dark.

Dad must be working late again, Vivian thought.

She grabbed some cold cuts, cheese, and an apple and flew up the steps to her room.

Tonight Hogwarts would have to wait. Vivian had her own chamber of secrets to open, and she spent the rest of the night in her cozy reading nook studying each file, while the thunderstorm took hold outside and shook the ancient house.

The pattern she had stumbled on before at the museum was now unmistakable. Hundreds of cases of fantastical delusions, visions, and encounters over forty years at Murkwood Sanitarium, but what did it mean? There was definitely a mystery to be uncovered here, and Vivian decided she was the one to solve it. She smiled as she realized that she had found herself an extracurricular activity after all.

Beasts & Battlements

BY THE END of the school week, Vivian knew just about everything there was to know about Murkwood Sanitarium, or at least as much as she could learn from the archival materials she had borrowed from the history museum. It had been founded in 1885 by a leading neurologist as a serious, full-service mental health institution, but it was also a lavish place. Several of the rooms on the lower floors had been dedicated to voluntary stays and less severe conditions—almost a spa for those who suffered from "nervous temperament," "hysteria," "fainting spells," and similar ailments. But the upper floors and basement hosted the more serious cases, and many of those rooms featured restraints, double-bolted steel doors, and strange equipment to conduct treatments that Vivian was pretty sure were no longer practiced today. It was in these rooms that they kept those who suffered from "psychotic episodes," strange visions, and "delusions."

After another late night studying case files, it was almost

noon when Vivian woke with a start. The high sun beaming through her bedroom window warned her that her precious Saturday was quickly passing by.

She hastily threw on jeans and a sweatshirt, put her hair in a ponytail, and quietly padded down the back stairs to the kitchen in hopes of going undetected. Her father was nowhere to be found, which was just as well because she had other plans. Today she hoped to stop by the Midnight Lake Public Library to see if she could learn anything else about the mysterious Murkwood Sanitarium.

Throwing a bagel, banana, and granola bar into her backpack, she tiptoed through the dim, stained glass–lit entrance hall—her only observers the scowling wall portraits—and quietly slipped out the front door. Leaving nothing to chance, she carefully pulled the door shut behind her as she stepped out onto the porch.

"Mornin', Vivy!" called a voice behind her loudly, making her jump.

It was her dad, who was vigorously mixing paint.

"How'd you sleep?"

"Fine," replied Vivian, catching her breath.

"Good, good," said Mr. Van Tassel, nodding. "So, what do you wanna do today? Maybe help me paint?"

"Sorry," she replied. "I need to go to the library to do some research for a school project."

"What's it about?" her dad asked. "Do you need any help?"

Vivian could tell he wanted to spend time together today and, as a reporter, her dad certainly knew a thing or two about getting to the bottom of something. But after her exciting discoveries of the week, Vivian really wanted to solve this one on her own.

"No, I'm good," she answered. "It's actually a history report about my school."

"Eesh, that place," her dad said, and shuddered, before catching himself and clearing his throat. "I mean, very interesting."

"Yeah, if by interesting you mean creepy," she teased. "It's okay, Dad, we both know it is. Anyway, I tried to look it up online but there was nothing, so I figured I'd try the library."

"That's my girl," her dad said proudly. "Old-school research. Well, if you change your mind, you know where to find me. And not too late, okay?"

Vivian decided to ride her bike even though the library was just a few blocks away, located on the lakefront just past the Paradise ballroom and marina. She had gotten such a late start on the day she figured that there wasn't any time to lose. It was the first time she had pulled out the bike since she arrived in Midnight Lake . . . for good reason. It was her childhood bike and she wasn't exactly keen to be seen on the undersized pink-and-purple monstrosity with frilly white handle tassels. She didn't bother locking it up when she arrived, half hoping that someone might steal it, but she probably wasn't that lucky.

Vivian peered into the library's huge front windows, which looked all the way through to the lake, making her wonder where they kept all the books. A wide, single-story building with a peaked, cathedral-like entrance, its generous windows and warm redbrick exterior somehow blended into the lakeside scenery.

Inside, the building was equally distinctive. Every surface was adorned with custom woodwork, fancy brick, stained glass accents, and cozy nooks and fireplaces. The books were placed upon freestanding bookshelves that ran through the center of the structure, which allowed tons of natural light and gave visitors a nearly continuous view of the lake. With such limited space, it didn't take Vivian long to discover a shelf labeled "Local History." It was chock-full of old atlases, Wisconsin history books, almanacs, and local histories. She grabbed as many books as she could carry, including one specifically on Midnight Lake mental health institutions, and set up camp at an ornately carved table placed near a lakeside window of the library.

Beneath the warm glow of the stained glass table lamp, Vivian excitedly flipped through the pages of the book, certain she'd find her next clue. She was wrong. It was dry and detached, and lacked any of the detail she was looking for— who founded what, where, and how, but never a why.

Next she turned to the Wisconsin history books and

there was even less there, although she did find reference to the fish drought of 1891 and the subsequent disappearance of the *Lucius Sunberry* her father had told her about. As she continued to pore through book after book, she was disappointed to discover that most of what she could find on the town's history revolved around it being a lavish summer retreat to wealthy Chicago and Milwaukee families. Glorious mansions, upscale venues, and lots of natural beauty, but why so many delusions and asylums, Vivian wondered. Hours passed, and Vivian lost more and more steam with every dry detail that appeared in each new book she perused. Tired and frustrated, she rubbed her eyes and rested her forehead atop her arms on the table, listening to the relentless tick of a nearby wall clock. There was really nothing new here and certainly nothing very interesting. She closed her eyes—all of this research had made her drowsy and she just needed a few moments rest.

"When you're older you'll get to make decisions like this, but right now the decision is ours," said Mrs. *Van Tassel firmly.*

"Shut up!" screamed Vivian. "Stop trying to control me—to wreck my life! I hate you! I hate you both! I'll . . . I'll run away!" she added frantically as she grabbed her backpack and darted out the door, slamming it behind her.

She ran down the long, dimly lit hallway toward the lobby, which glowed with daylight. She could hear their door open behind her, no doubt her mother in pursuit. She stepped into the lobby and—

Vivian woke with a start, her head popping up from an especially large and musty Wisconsin history book. She didn't remember falling asleep, but she must have, for she'd had the dream again. As usual, her heart raced and ached at the same time.

There was a collection of loud and oddly familiar voices coming from a lofted area in the library's corner nearby— probably what had woken her up. These were unmistakably the excited voices of the stairwell misfits, Vivian now remembering that the library was one of their weekend hangouts.

"Vivian!" exclaimed William from the loft through scattered cheers and a few distant shushes. "Are you going to join us for Beasts and Battlements today?"

Vivian paused. She really didn't want to see anyone today, but she had already struck out gloriously on her primary objective, so she didn't see any harm in heading over and saying hi.

"Hey Vivian, are you comin' on board?" inquired Mary as she trudged up the stairs.

"Huh? Oh, no, I'm here working on my history project for Ms. Greenleaf's class."

"Oh, c'mon," Arturo goaded her. "It'll be fun. . . ."

"Vivian, please . . ." Violet stepped forward and smiled shyly. "After all, you told Amber you played the other day— sort of—and we'd hate to make a liar of you."

Now she was getting somewhere. If Vivian still held

any reservations about playing, the only motivation she would need was doing something that Amber Grausam thought was stupid.

"Fair enough," replied Vivian resolutely. "You've convinced me."

"Great!" bellowed William, who was visibly excited to be introducing new blood into the game.

"So, do you prefer to negotiate or fight?" he asked as he quickly drew out a notepad and pencil.

"Uh . . . in real life?" mumbled Vivian.

"Sorry Viv, he's not explaining anything, as usual," answered Mary, shooting a look at William. "He means, for the character that you want to play. Do you want your hero to be more brains or brawn?"

"Oh, okay," Vivian said, nodding. "Fight, I guess. Brawn."

"I think Amber would agree," Violet said, making Vivian chuckle.

"Cool," continued William as he scribbled something on the paper. "Do you prefer the city or the woods?"

Vivian's mind shot to her old home in Chicago—her old life.

"The city," she said without hesitation.

"Awesome. Do you follow the rules or walk your own path?" he continued.

Vivian looked at him sassily and then smiled.

"What do you think?" she quipped.

"I think I know the answer to that one," Arturo said, turning to Vivian. He gave her a long, appraising look and then his face broke into a grin. "She hasn't found a rule yet that she couldn't break."

Vivian and the others laughed as William scribbled.

William went on with his questioning for a couple of minutes, furiously making notes on his notepad after each reply: "Are you talkative or shy? Do you prefer magic or hand-to-hand combat?" and so on. Then, after a few rolls of the dice, William did some more quick scribery and Vivian had a character. Her name was Alissa Sunstorm, a half-elven ranger (which was like a woodsperson and warrior, William explained) from a mystical place called Raven Haven. Vivian really liked the idea of being an elf—a species of people who could keep their emotions in check, she was told, were highly dexterous, and they could even see in the dark. Perhaps best of all, they could live hundreds of years, ensuring their relationships were not unexpectedly cut short by age.

Evidently, being a half elf instead of a full elf in this game made you kind of caught between two cultures, so Alissa, according to William's narration, had taken to the road in search of meaning and adventure and had landed at a fortress in a desolate and dangerous area known as the "frontierlands." There she had come into the acquaintance of a number of new arrivals to the fortress, a human wizard named Venna, a roguish gnome named Snarfette, and an ornery dwarven warrior called Durin—the characters played by Mary, Violet, and Arturo, respectively.

"You ready to go?" William asked Vivian.

"I guess so," Vivian replied nervously.

"Everyone else?"

"Yup," said Mary.

"Let's go!" cried Arturo.

William nodded and began narrating. "Okay, so it's just after dawn and you are back on the trail from the fortress heading east. It's warm and the sun is shining. You round a familiar bend, which opens up into a huge canyon dotted with caves: you've returned to the Tunnels of Torment!" he finished dramatically.

Even though Vivian had watched this group play for weeks, now that she was in the game, she found herself confused as to how it worked, at least for the first hour. But she had to admit, it *was* fun. Violet, who played as a gnome, would talk in a small and anxious voice, expressing worry about every sound and sign they found near the caves. Meanwhile, Mary and Arturo were locked in an ongoing debate whether dwarven mining was environmentally friendly or not (to say nothing of their safety standards). "Mind your own business, you bloody street magician," blustered Arturo in the cockney voice of his character, Durin, to finally end the conversation. Vivian couldn't remember the last time she had laughed so hard.

Before she knew it, hours had passed, and Vivian had

almost forgotten why she had come to the library in the first place. The group had just entered a cavern in the back of the gorge, hidden by the thick cover of trees. Alissa had already proved her worth with a saber and bow as she helped the team dispatch a group of nasty hobgoblins—according to William, a much larger and stouter version of a traditional goblin.

"As you enter the cavern, the first thing that strikes you is the odor—it's absolutely awful, the smell of death," explained William. "The cavern's passages branch off in two directions, left and right. What do you do?"

"Well, what do you think?" Mary asked the group.

"There's an ol' sayin' of me people," replied Arturo in the distinct voice of Durin. "Right is wrong and lef' is right."

"Great. The vast wisdom of the dwarves summed up in a single saying," scoffed Mary in the haughty, slightly English-accented voice of her own character. "What do you think, Alissa?"

Vivian didn't really have a voice yet for her character, so she basically just talked as herself, but she was sort of getting the hang of this, quickly realizing she didn't need to preface every statement with "Alissa says."

"Well . . . I guess one way's as good as another," answered Vivian. "After all, dwarven wisdom is better than no wisdom at all."

Arturo nodded in confused approval.

"I have a bad feeling about this," sniveled Violet in her peevish character's voice.

"Okay," continued William, "you make your way along the cavern, which opens up to a clearing that branches in two directions, the direction you are going and one tunnel to the right. At this point the odor is almost unbearable and now you can see why. The torchlight reveals bones and rotting corpses strewn about the cavern amid different types of refuse, dead branches, and leaves.

"Gross," said Violet reflexively in her own voice.

"Which way do you want to go?" said William.

"Let's keep straight along the tunnel we were going, unless our dwarven intuition tells us otherwise," said Mary, needling Arturo with her last comment.

"No objections 'ere, you blimey wizard," snapped Arturo.

"All right," continued William excitedly. "You follow the cavern around another twenty or thirty yards until it bends around to the left and you walk right into a den, in the middle of which is . . . a vulturebear eagerly feasting on the carcass of a deer! It glares at you through its terrible, red-rimmed eyes and rears up on its hind legs, now standing at an ominous nine feet high. It stretches its powerful feathered arms, and opens its beak to make a screech the likes of which sends chills up and down each of your spines. Roll for initiative!"

The group gave a collective moan as everyone reluctantly

rolled a twenty-sided die to see who would act when. Mary began scanning her character sheet in search of a spell that might help; Violet covered her eyes; Arturo just crossed his arms and shook his head in disbelief with a bit of an "I told you so" flare. But Vivian sat motionless. Something about this passage had struck Vivian as strangely familiar.

"A vulturebear?" Vivian asked.

"Oh, sorry," said William. "A vulturebear is a B and B monster with the body of a bear, but with feathers and the face of a vulture. They're pretty nasty."

The body of a bear and the face of a vulture. The phrase struck Vivian like lightning—but where had she heard it before?

"I rolled a two for the vulturebear, so you'll all go before it. So, what do you do?" repeated William.

Vivian bit her lip in thought. Vulturebear . . . why did this seem so familiar? Then she realized . . . she hadn't *heard* it; she had *read* about it. It was from the case files of Murkwood Sanitarium!

"Uh . . . when did you say this game was made?" Vivian asked.

"It was created by a local guy, Garrison Arnold—and published right here in Midnight Lake in 1975. It was a huge breakthrough in gaming. In fact, according to most gaming historians—"

"Oh, great!" Mary interrupted. "You've got him on his gaming history rant."

"William, can we save it for later?" Arturo chimed in. "We've got a bloody vulturebear to fight!"

"Okay, okay," William sighed. "So, what do you do?"

The voices of the misfits faded into the background as Vivian looked down at the colorful Beasts & Battlements rule books strewn across the table, each adorned with fantastic and terrible images: one called the *Player's Guide* with a group of unfortunate-looking adventurers battling a dragon; one titled the *Gamemaster's Guide* with of a bearded wizard unleashing some sort of terrible spell; and the last called the *Book of Beasts* with some type of . . . of round floating-eye creature with spikes and razor-sharp teeth terrorizing adventurers in the woods. It had one, two, three, four . . . six eyes scattered across its front!

Vivian was stunned. It was another exact match to the patient accounts at Murkwood. If the vulturebear had been some type of strange coincidence, this peculiar eye creature couldn't possibly be another—there had to be some type of connection here.

Vivian had come to the library today looking for clues and answers about Murkwood Sanitarium and she had clearly just found some. Her heart began to pound so loudly that she was convinced that her tablemates must have heard it.

"Uh . . . sorry!" Vivian blurted out. "I just remembered, I've got something I need to do at home tonight—my dad's expecting me. I've got to go," she continued, almost out of breath as she hurriedly packed up her backpack.

"Aw, come on," protested William. "Can't you stay for the battle?"

"Bloody elves!" remarked Arturo, still in character. "Never can count on 'em."

"It's okay, Viv," said Mary reassuringly. "Don't mind them. When you have to go, you have to go."

"Seconded," agreed Violet warmly. "I hope you had fun, though."

"I did," Vivian replied as she edged away from the table. And she meant it. "That was cool . . . we'll do it again sometime," she said, adding a shrug at the end, just so she didn't seem too eager.

"Awesome!" William nodded. "I'm glad you had fun. Now, if you don't mind, I've a game to run."

12

The Book of Beasts

VIVIAN'S VISIT TO the library had been an unexpected, but undeniable success. She shot out of the building only moments after leaving the misfits, shocked to discover the pink-and-turquoise sky of dusk already upon her. How long had she been there? It didn't matter, for she had definitely made progress on her objective—her new hobby and a developing obsession with Murkwood Sanitarium.

Vivian's first instinct had been to race home and start cross-checking her files, but what might those tell her that she didn't already know? As she hastily peddled to the corner of Broad and Main Street, she suddenly came up with a new plan: the Catacombs Game Shop!

A jolly-looking bald man with a white goatee was just about to turn the lock on the front door when Vivian burst in. She hadn't been inside this store yet, but she could tell from the crowded window displays that this was an old-school type of game shop that carried a combination of new and antique stuff.

Vivian looked around the store. Every inch of the interior was crammed with board games, card games, role-playing games, fancy dice, and hundreds of miniatures hanging in rows nearly to the ceiling of the store's pegboard walls. Posters for popular game franchises filled the remainder of the wall space, while a huge miniature castle dominated the retail floor.

"Greetings, Gen Zer!" said the shopkeeper in a jolly tone as he resumed his position behind the counter, stepping over a huge, snoring bloodhound. "I'm Merle. What brings you to this fine establishment this evening?"

"Beasts and Battlements," Vivian blurted out breathlessly.

"No problemo," said Merle as he gestured to a large display up front. "Tenth edition, I assume. That's been all the rage lately."

Vivian shook her head.

"No, the old stuff . . . the original stuff by . . . Garrison Arnold?"

A pleased look spread across Merle's face; his eyebrows rose in surprise.

"Aha! An old schooler!" Merle replied as he rubbed his hands together. He seemed to find a new spring in his footsteps as he headed for the back of the store, talking over his shoulder. "Yep, can do. You know Arnold was from Midnight Lake; he published the game here. He lived right around the corner, in fact! So, what are you looking for exactly? *Tomb of Doom? Silverhawk? Fortress on the Frontier?*"

Vivian realized that she really had no idea what exactly she was looking for.

"Uh . . . do you have, like, something he did with monsters?" Vivian asked finally.

"Monsters?" Merle repeated. "Hmmm. Well, there's the original *Book of Beasts*, his iconic catalogue of monsters. Will that do?"

The *Book of Beasts*—that was the name of the book with the floating sphere of spikes and eyes on the cover, but the one she had seen was definitely a new book and illustration. Merle must be talking about the original.

"Yeah," replied Vivian. She nodded with pretend confidence. "The *Book of Beasts*, definitely that one."

"Groovy," shot back Merle as he disappeared into a stack of books at the rear of the store, emerging moments later with an oversized, thin hardcover book with *Book of Beasts* printed in bold red letters on top right beneath the Beasts & Battlements logo.

"There she is," continued Merle proudly as he handed it to her. "The first-edition *Book of Beasts*—a classic."

Vivian eagerly scanned the tattered book. Its colorful but somewhat crude cover illustration featured a hydra, harpy, and unicorn on the front as well as some weird-looking subterranean creatures that Vivian couldn't identify. It kind of looked like a monster terrarium.

"Now, that's an earlier printing but the condition's not

great, so I can do this one for say . . . fifty bucks."

Vivian's heart stopped. Fifty dollars! She thought used books would be cheap like they were at garage sales, but fifty dollars? Disappointment began to set in as she lovingly examined the battered tome. This was a book of secrets and possibly answers; answers to questions that had begun to dominate every aspect of her being. She was so very close to solving something, she just knew it, and yet now it seemed so far away. Another forty bucks away.

"Uh . . . I'm really sorry, but I didn't realize it would be so expensive," Vivian said sheepishly as she reluctantly handed the book back to Merle. "I don't have that kind of money right now."

"Yeah, the darn things are collectors' items these days," Merle sighed. "Tell you what—"

Just then, the bell on the door jingled as a familiar older gentlemen walked in. It was Mr. Braemor. Merle's bloodhound woke with a start and became alert.

"Excuse me," began Mr. Braemor. "Are you the owner of this establishment?"

"Sure am," replied Merle lightly. "Will be with you in a second—just helping this young lady here."

"Hi Mr. Braemor," said Vivian with a polite wave. "No, it's all right, I was just leaving. Thanks anyway, Merle."

Merle opened his mouth to respond but Braemor cut in first, "Leaving empty-handed, are we? Not on my watch."

He hobbled up to where Vivian and Merle were standing and looked down at the book.

"The *Book of Beasts*, eh?" he continued with playful curiosity. "Go ahead and take it and run along, Vivian. It's on me. I have some business here anyway—a proposition—for this fine gentleman, Merle, is it?"

Vivian could hardly believe her ears. Merle smiled and handed her the book and then looked curiously at Mr. Braemor.

"Thank you," she squeaked. She felt a little bit overwhelmed by the kindness of this relative stranger. Not sure what else to say or do, she trained her eyes on the antique treasure in her hand.

"I'll pay you back," she said as she carefully put the book into her backpack. "Thanks so much. Thank you both."

"No need," said Mr. Braemor.

"Always happy to help the next generation," Merle added cheerfully.

Vivian rode her bike home so fast that she had two close calls—one with a pickup truck, one with a four-wheeler—an off-road, recreational motorbike that some locals from the countryside actually rode around town as if they were street vehicles. When she arrived, she found her father standing on a ladder on the porch, hastily slapping paint on the house's peeling trim. It looked to Vivian like he might have more paint on his clothes than on the house. But she had to give him some credit; he had managed to cover the majority of the first floor today. Vivian couldn't help but notice that the paint had been applied so thickly that much of it had dripped down to the ground and pooled around the house's foundation . . . but she still figured her dad deserved some points for trying.

Vivian swiftly discarded her bike on the front lawn behind an overgrown pricker bush and bounded up the front stairs and onto an unpainted part of the porch.

"Hey Dad," she called as she flew past him and ran into the house.

"Hey Vivy! How was the—?" The slamming of the front door cut off his last sentence.

As Vivian took the stairs two at a time toward her room, she heard the crash of falling ladders and clanging paint cans outside, which made her halt at the landing at the top of the stairs.

"I'm okay!" she heard the muffled voice of Mr. Van Tassel announce. "Yep, just a small spill—must've been a bad step."

Vivian gave a sigh of relief and hurried into the privacy of her room, wasting no time retiring to her closet nook for evening study. Outside, night descended rapidly, once again alive with the calls of the season's last few crickets and cicadas.

Sitting in the cool, unnatural glow of her electric lantern, she arranged the case files on the floor next to her new treasure. She rubbed her fingertips across the title and subtitle:

Beasts & Battlements: Book of Beasts—An alphabetical compendium of all of the dangerous, grotesque, and terrible monsters found in Beasts & Battlements. Taking a deep breath, she cracked the book open.

Garrison Arnold

VIVIAN'S EYES STUNG from exhaustion as she scanned the local history shelf of the Midnight Lake Library for the second straight day.

After spending a sleepless night studying the *Book of Beasts* in her closet nook, Vivian had returned to the library first thing Sunday morning when it opened. This time, she wasn't looking for books or information on the sanitariums; she was excitedly digging for information on Beasts & Battlements creator Garrison Arnold.

As her tired eyes darted back and forth, she clasped her hands together to prevent herself from fidgeting. Her head was still spinning from the night before and her nervous energy was off the charts.

The *Book of Beasts* had proven to be a treasure trove of information. It was a catalogue of monsters—a bestiary—written by Garrison Arnold in the mid-1970s for use with his B&B game. Each monster featured in the book included a brief summary, a small, black-and-white illustration, and some statistics that allowed them to be used in the game. Vivian gathered that early gamemasters would use this tome to sic these terrible monsters on their would-be players. It was a game book, nothing more.

The wall clock ticked loudly in the otherwise silent building. She nervously rocked back and forth to its rhythm while searching, but still nothing on Garrison Arnold or Beasts & Battlements. She glanced over at the lofted area where she had played the game with the misfits the day before.

Vivian had really enjoyed her first session of Beasts & Battlements, but her current interest in the *Book of Beasts* and its author had nothing to do with the game. It was all about how it connected to the Murkwood Sanitarium. Of the book's more than two hundred monster entries, roughly half were strange and obscure monsters that had shown up in the delusional accounts of the Murkwood patient case files. To be sure, some of the monsters that overlapped between the *Book of Beasts* and the Murkwood accounts were standard-variety dragons, goblins, fairies, and unicorns, no doubt inspired by real-world mythology and well-known fairy tales. But a majority of the creatures featured here were far too weird and obscure to show up by chance in these two different sources—in fact, she had never heard of most of them. A spiked, floating ball covered in eyes with a mouth full of sharp teeth—in B&B that was called a leer sphere; a wolf with tentacles coming out of its back, a worm wolf according to the game; a sharklike creature with legs that can come onto land, the beach shark; a bear with the face and feathers of a vulture: a vulturebear.

How could there be so much overlap? she thought. It was unbelievable. How could these accounts match so closely with the creatures and characters from these books, and why? Could this Garrison Arnold have seen the Murkwood case files just as she had? Did he know about these same delusions or was there something more to it? The answer, she thought, must lie with Garrison Arnold.

Convinced there was nothing helpful on the local history shelf, she headed to the reference computer up front to look up what they might have. And there, prominently located right next to the desk, was a tabletop display of books about the mysterious B&B creator and the game itself.

"Real sharp, Vivy," she muttered to herself. "Hidden in plain sight."

Vivian grabbed as many books as she could carry and heaved them over to a research table located near the front desk, dropping them with a loud thud.

The desk librarian's head popped up.

"Sorry," she mouthed, her hands up apologetically.

The librarian nodded and dropped his eyes back down to his book.

Vivian settled in and cracked the first title. In no time, she was scribbling furiously on her notepad:

Garrison Arnold

— Born 1939; Died 2010
— Grew up on Ford Street (just a block away
from my house!)
— Loved reading fantasy and science-fiction
"pulp magazines," written in the 1920s–1940s
— Ditched school A LOT! Lots of pranks and
practical jokes
— Blew up boulders for fun with dynamite at
a 50-acre family plot called the "Outskirts."
Dynamite provided by friend whose dad worked
as a local miner (um, ok? That's normal.)
— The "Outskirts" - Natural area next to the
current Midnight Lake Resort on the edge of
town (make sure to copy map)
— Created the game Beasts & Battlements
(B&B) in 1975
— Published B&B through his own gaming
company called Real Gaming Ltd. (RGL) -
headquartered on Silver Springs Road

Hours passed. Unlike her experience with the local histories that put her to sleep the day before, her heart beat faster and her eyes grew wider with every new page; every new detail leading her closer to answers.

Vivian's knee bounced up and down nervously. She distinctly had the feeling that this was all going somewhere, that the missing pieces were close.

Then suddenly, her heart leaped—she found it! Halfway down the page, deep within the fourth book she had pored over, there was the information she had been searching for:

"... Of course, it's well known that Arnold also drew inspiration for Beasts & Battlements from his frequent trips to the abandoned ruins of Murkwood Sanitarium as a young boy. ..."

According to the book, the facility was abandoned in 1925 and had been vacant during Arnold's childhood in the 1940s and '50s before it was converted into Murkwood Middle School in 1960.

This is it! Vivian thought. *This must be the missing link.*

She smiled and made a final note:

Jackpot!

Case Closed

> Vivian: Are u free?

> William: At dinner with fam at
> Little Sicily. Violet's fam here 2.
> What's up?

> Vivian: Need to talk right away.

> William: Everything ok?

> Vivian: Yup. Something
> amazing.

> William: Come by. Here for a
> while.

"Let me get this straight," said William above the ding, zip, and whoop of the 1980s *Tron* arcade game he was playing, his gaze fixed unblinkingly upon the glowing screen. "You think that Garrison Arnold got all of the Beasts and Battlements monsters from old case files he found at Murkwood Sanitarium as a kid?"

"Well, what else could it be?" asked Vivian as she stood next to the towering arcade cabinet. "He couldn't have coincidentally come up with all of the same stuff!"

"Hmmm." William bit his lip. His shoulders and arms shifted, while his eyes stayed squarely fixed on the screen. Vivian couldn't tell if he was processing what she had just said, or simply engrossed in his game.

Waiting for an answer, Vivian anxiously scanned the faux-wood-paneled restaurant called Little Sicily. The place had a tired but comfortable vibe; its checkered linoleum flooring shined bright amid the cheap red, brown, and green stained glass shades that hung over every table. A neon juke box glowed warmly, as did a handful of classic arcade games like *Tron* and *Ms. Pac-Man* that filled the corners and nooks. Thanks to her father, Vivian knew all these games well and she wondered whether her dad knew about this place— pizza and *Pac-Man* was his definition of heaven.

"Why couldn't it be a coincidence?" asked Violet from

her spot on the other side of the arcade cabinet. "I mean, you said yourself, some of the monsters in the accounts are just from mythology; the others maybe just have some similarities—"

"No way," insisted Vivian. "I mean a spiky, floating sphere with twelve eyes and a mouth; a bear with the face of a vulture with red-rimmed eyes? You're telling me that's all a coincidence?" Vivian crossed her arms. "Impossible!"

"Well, maybe he was reading the same books that the Murkwood patients were reading," reasoned Violet.

"Not likely," mumbled William, still thoroughly engrossed in his game. "The monsters Vivian is talking about are known to be original to B and B. Even the pulp magazines and books that Arnold used to talk about as his inspirations didn't come out until the 1920s and 30s, well after most of the Murkwood accounts Vivian mentioned."

"Thank you, William!" cheered Vivian, excited that he seemed to understand her point. "Yes, the case files are the only logical explanation. He sure as heck didn't see this stuff himself."

"Well, what makes you say that?" asked a soft, gravelly voice from behind them.

The voice had come from a gray-haired and mostly toothless old woman sitting in a wheelchair at the table nearest the game. Vivian had noticed her earlier, but she had seemed completely zoned out, staring blankly at the checkered linoleum floor. Apparently, she had been eaves-dropping on their conversation.

"What makes you think he wasn't writin' what he was seein'?"

"Grandma! This is a private conversation!" Violet cried as her face flushed in embarrassment.

"I'm just sayin', funny folk around here in Midnight Lake, don't you think? Lots of hallucinations, lots of asylums. Or maybe it's somethin' . . . in the water?" she continued with a gummy smile and a soft, raspy laugh.

Vivian looked at the old woman. So, this was Violet's great-grandma; the one who claimed to have seen hippogriffs and unicorns in her earlier days. Was she serious?

Meanwhile, William's jerky movements at the arcade cabinet became more intense while beads of sweat began to form on his brow. The glowing blue point tracker at the top of the screen continued to skyrocket. In fact, it was nearing the "HI SCORE," as William's *Tron* avatar fought through a screen full of grid bugs. Other patrons of the establishment began to take notice.

"Hey everybody, he's gonna break the record!" yelled a diner in a green tractor hat who had stopped by for a look.

Breaking local arcade game records must have been a bigger deal in Midnight Lake than Vivian would've thought, because a flurry of interested pizza parlor patrons, including several older folks, began to hurry over and crowd around the ancient *Tron* machine, pushing Vivian off to the side.

By the time Vivian had fought her way through the crowd and back to Mrs. Black, the old woman was again staring at the floor.

"Mrs. Black," Vivian said as she crouched down to get in her line of sight. "What did you mean about Garrison Arnold writing what he was seeing; about something in the water?"

Mrs. Black didn't answer, but just rocked slightly in her wheelchair, staring peacefully at the floor tiles.

"Mrs. Black," Vivian repeated as she waved her hand in front of the woman's vacant eyes.

Vivian shrugged, becoming more and more convinced that these were probably just the rantings of a confused old woman and that her case file theory was indeed airtight. By now, the substantial crowd that had formed around William was clapping and whooping. Vivian couldn't help but smile at the odd spectacle—this must've been the original version of Twitch, she thought.

Her eyes scanned the parlor as she studied the group of onlookers, until she spotted something that made her smile vanish. Illuminated by the warm jewel tones of the stained glass was the mysterious gray man, sitting alone at a dimly lit table in the back of the restaurant. He was the only one in the place that didn't seem interested in *Tron*; his steely gray eyes were fixed squarely upon her.

A chill rushed up Vivian's spine.

The excited *Tron* spectators erupted in cheers and applause, curing Vivian of her shock and fear just long enough to break his gaze. She quickly slipped out the front door, glad for once that no one had stolen the bike she had haphazardly left out front. She jumped on and pedaled as fast as she could without looking back, thoughts of Garrison Arnold, Mrs. Black, and the gray man haunting her every thought.

When she arrived home, she left her bike on the lawn, burst in the front door, and headed for the stairs. Before she got there, she noticed her father in the living room scrambling to set aside whatever he was looking at and hastily grabbing the newspaper.

"Hey Vivy," said Mr. Van Tassel over the paper he pretended to have been scanning. The headline read: LOCAL FARMERS HIRING SECURITY AMID ANIMAL ATTACKS; WOLVES SUSPECTED. "You hungry?"

Vivian should've been starving, but her stomach was so sour with excitement that she didn't know if she could eat. As she stepped into the room, she noticed her dad's eyes were moist. She could see her parents' wedding album behind him on the couch. He had clearly been looking at it when she walked in.

"Nah," she replied offhandedly, pretending not to notice the album or the tears. "I'll have something later. Um . . . is everything okay?"

"Huh? Oh, yeah, fine," he said casually as he wiped his eyes with his sleeve. "Just some dust left over from the sanding I was doing." He sniffed deeply. "Yep, everything's right as rain."

He clearly didn't want to talk about it, and Vivian didn't think she could handle it either. She looked for an escape route for both of them.

"Hey, have you been to this place Little Sicily? I think you'd like it—pizza and arcade games."

"Been there?" replied Mr. Van Tassel with a smirk. "I've been going there for lunch a couple times a week—I've got the high score in *Tron*," he continued with a proud smile.

"Oh . . . cool" was all Vivian could force out as she looked away. She didn't have the heart to tell him that he didn't have the high score anymore.

"Anyway, if you get hungry, there's a bucket of chicken in the kitchen and I left you the drumsticks," continued Mr. Van Tassel. "I've hardly seen you lately—is everything okay?"

"Um-hmm," Vivian said, nodding, worried that saying more might give her away. She wondered if she should tell her father about all that she had found out about Murkwood and B&B; one part of her was dying to tell him, another afraid that she may have done something wrong when she looked at (and borrowed) the case files. There were bound to be at least one or two infractions of "journalistic ethics." She chewed her lip as she thought about it, finally deciding that she'd wait and tell him once she had sorted it all out.

"I thought maybe we could watch *The Princess Bride* tonight," her dad suggested. He smiled hopefully. "Whaddya say?"

The Princess Bride was definitely a favorite, but Vivian knew there was no way she could concentrate on the movie with the B&B story looming over her head.

"Sorry, Dad, I can't tonight," she said apologetically. "I've got this paper to write. . . ."

Vivian noticed his smile fading.

"But another time soon?" she added quickly.

"'As you wish,'" he replied warmly, quoting the film.

Vivian nodded and slipped out of the living room. She felt guilty—she knew how badly her dad wanted to spend some time with her, but getting to the bottom of this B&B story was all she could think about at the moment.

He'd understand, she thought. *He's a reporter.*

She figured she'd likely get hungry as she worked, so she dropped by the kitchen and grabbed a plate of drumsticks, some coleslaw, and a few paper towels before padding up the back stairs toward her room.

For the rest of the evening, the rapid, gentle clicks of her laptop keyboard could be heard through her bedroom door. Vivian hadn't figured out why the town had hosted so many sanitariums, but she had discovered something better. Something that would make her project stand out and was sure to impress Ms. Greenleaf. She thought it might even be front page material for the town paper and fast-track her career in reporting! *Murkwood Student Solves Mystery of Beasts and Battlements Monsters!* she thought to herself, smiling.

She was going to blow the cover off this story!

Vivian lay sunken in her way-too-soft-bed staring at her phone and biting her lip. The morning had come far too soon and the glare stung her eyes.

She stared at the new texts on her phone from last night and wondered, what she should say?

Violet: What happened to u?

William: Yeah, where did u go? I broke the record in Tron btw 😊

Mary: Wait, what did I miss?

Violet: We were at Little Sicily. Vivian discovered something really cool . . .

Arturo: What was it?

William: Did I mention I broke the record in Tron? 😉

Mary: Yeah, I think you mentioned that. Violet, spill!

Violet: Vivian found a bunch of old files from Murkwood Sanitarium. People had delusions about B&B monsters 50+ years before the game came out. She thinks Arnold must have seen the files and then put them in his game.

Arturo: 😲

William: Well . . . it's a little more complicated than that . . .

Mary: Oh, shut it WT!

William: 😳 Speaking of, who's in for B&B on Friday at Arturo's?

Violet: In.

Mary: Yup.

Arturo: Obviously. Congrats on Tron btw—will name my next lamb after you in honor of this incredible achievement. 😁 Vivian, what's ↑?

Vivian had spent almost the whole night working on her project. She had even made an at-a-glance chart to illustrate the overwhelming overlap: all of the rows were monsters from the Murkwood accounts and the corresponding B&B monsters in the columns—an "X" indicating a match for each account. The chart was nearly full. She thought that this visual would help prove her thesis.

She glanced over at the poster-board exhibit she created on her desk titled "The History of Murkwood Sanitarium and the Birth of Beasts & Battlements." Her heart raced. Violet was right—she *had* discovered something really cool.

She grinned and began tapping out a message.

Vivian: Sorry, had to run. Yep, solved the mystery of B&B monsters! Juicy details at lunch.

She put the phone down on her nightstand and sat up, her eyes still fixed on the phone. She nibbled on her fingernails. Before she could change her mind, she picked the phone back up and began tapping:

Vivian: In for B&B Friday btw.

Friday Night Frights

IT WAS FRIDAY and Vivian's legs bounced in nervous anticipation as she sat in Ms. Greenleaf's class. She was anxious for the school bell to ring.

The last few days had flown by for Vivian as autumn took hold outside. Her school days were spent doing her best to drown out her teachers' voices as her mind worked to connect the dots; her evenings spent in the lantern-lit comfort of her closet nook drafting her class project and journalistic masterpiece.

Vivian had recently considered going back to the history museum to dig through the remaining files, but given that she had already borrowed the case files she had under debatable permission, she didn't want to risk it. Besides, while she was certain she would uncover dozens more accounts and new monsters, she felt comfortable that the foundational concept would be the same: Murkwood played host to lots of folks who had delusions about fantasy monsters; Garrison

Arnold saw the files and incorporated them into his game—case closed!

She looked around the classroom. Amber Grausam glared at her, but Vivian pretended not to see her. Two seats behind Amber, she caught Mary's eye. Mary smiled, looking as anxious as she was to get out of class.

Seeing Mary reminded her of her other research: Beasts & Battlements itself. Every day this week, she had joined the stairwell misfits for their lunchtime sessions at the dreaded Tunnels of Torment and her half-elf ranger, Alissa Sunstorm, had even "leveled up" and gained some new abilities. Given the impending deadline, Vivian justified the time spent with the misfits as "research," and even told them as much, but secretly enjoyed the time more than she let on. Not for fun or friendship, of course, she told herself, but purely for research.

The misfits rotated the venue of their games, which occurred a couple times a week outside their stairwell activities. A weekend evening at the library or Mary's house; an occasional weekday at William's; Fridays at Arturo's farm—that was tonight.

Finally the bell rang.

The students of Ms. Greenleaf's class hastily gathered their materials and made for the door, Vivian among them, with the promise of an evening of adventure, root beer, and laughter with her friends— acquaintances, rather—ahead.

"See you in a bit?" asked Mary as she passed by Vivian.

"Yep, be there soon," Vivian replied as she caught Ms. Greenleaf watching out of the corner of her eye.

"Vivian," called Ms. Greenleaf from her desk. "Do you have a second?"

"Sure," Vivian replied as she approached the desk. She felt a pang of guilt and wondered if Ms. Greenleaf had noticed how distracted she had been in class these last several days.

"So, how are you doing?" Ms. Greenleaf asked.

"Fine," Vivian said carefully.

"And how's your project coming along?"

"Good . . . great, actually!" Vivian replied, unable to contain her enthusiasm. Realizing that she might be showing too many cards, she straightened up and cleared her throat. "I mean, it's going better than I expected. I've had some interesting discoveries. . . ."

Ms. Greenleaf smiled.

"It's okay to be excited, Vivian, even if it's just a school project," Ms. Greenleaf said lightly. "I have no doubt you'll surprise us when you present next week. . . . It also seems that you've made a friend along the way."

"Oh, her . . . ?" Vivian gestured to where Mary had stood a few moments earlier. "No, not really, she and her crew are more just acquaintances, really. They're helping me with my research is all."

"Research? On Murkwood?" asked Ms. Greenleaf.

"It's kind of a long story," Vivian replied. "It'll make more sense next week, I promise."

"Well, I'll be excited to hear your presentation on Monday," Ms. Greenleaf said. She paused a moment and tapped her fingers on the desk, a thoughtful expression on her face. Vivian shifted uncomfortably, wondering what her teacher might say next. "And Vivian, it's okay to have friends, to let people in. It's what makes us human."

Vivian's cheeks grew hot. Was Ms. Greenleaf criticizing her?

No, she thought as she looked at the warmth in Ms. Greenleaf's eyes. Her teacher definitely cared, but she didn't understand.

"Yeah, but people go away," Vivian said finally, unable to keep the bitterness out of her voice. "They go away and you can't do anything about it."

Ms. Greenleaf furrowed her brow in concern.

"Vivian, you have a choice to make, we all do. You can put yourself out there and be vulnerable—you can connect, but risk the pain of being hurt, or you can guard yourself and retreat to the deepest, darkest, and most remote places within, where you might not find much pain, but also no joy. You might say it's our dual nature—you can choose one way or the other."

Visions of her last encounter with her mother filled her mind. The painful things she had said and done; the guilt that went along with them. Vivian looked sadly back at Ms. Greenleaf.

"I think it's already too late, Ms. Greenleaf." Vivian's voice was calm even though many feelings swirled inside her. "I think I've already chosen."

Before Ms. Greenleaf could respond, Vivian moved toward the door and said, "See you on Monday."

That evening, as Vivian biked over to Arturo's farm on the edges of town near the Midnight Lake Resort, she thought about Ms. Greenleaf's words—they stung. Ms. Greenleaf didn't understand; no one could. Losing her mother was the most painful thing she'd ever been through. The fact that it was her fault was unbearable. As these memories crept back into her thoughts, she stopped her bike, just as she reached the perimeter of Arturo's family's property. She breathed heavily.

What's the point of loving someone if you have to lose them in the long run? Why should I ever connect to anyone?

"It's not worth it," she whispered to herself. She had decided to leave and began to turn her bike around.

Getting too close to the misfits is a mistake. It's better to distance myself than . . .

Just then she noticed the flashing strobes of police cars lining the long gravel driveway.

Forgetting her decision moments ago to head back home, Vivian sped up the driveway past police cars and officers looking around with flashlights, and their agitated search dogs straining on their leashes. She dropped her bike in front of the farmhouse and zipped onto the porch where she found William, Violet, and Mary huddled around Arturo on the porch swing. There were tears in his eyes.

"Sorry I'm late," Vivian panted. She gestured to the police cars around them. "What happened? Arturo, is your family okay?"

"It's my . . . my sheep," Arturo responded, fighting to speak through his tears. He took a shaky breath. "The ones I raised. They were grazing near the edge of our property near the woods. I went to check on them before dinner and they were . . . they were . . ."

"Another animal attack," Mary said grimly, finishing Arturo's thought when he struggled to continue. "Whatever it was, it got them all."

Vivian went to put a hand on Arturo's shoulder, but stopped herself and awkwardly shoved it in her pocket. She knew this pain—the pain of loss—and she realized she was afraid to go near it.

Just then, a young-looking police deputy with the name tag "Brookfield" walked over to Vivian and her friends. "Sorry, kids. You should all go home. It's not safe out here and we've got an investigation to do."

As the group disbanded and Vivian went to retrieve her bike, she overheard Arturo's father, Mr. Fuerte, giving his statement to Sheriff Pridemore.

"Approximately how many sheep and how many turkeys did you lose?" Sheriff Pridemore asked.

"No turkeys, just sheep. We lost all twenty of them."

"No turkeys?" the sheriff repeated. "Are you sure?"

"Yes, I'm sure," replied Mr. Fuerte. "We don't raise turkeys. Why do you ask?"

Sheriff Pridemore scratched his head. Vivian could see the confused expression on his face.

"It's just we found an awful lot of brown, gray, and red feathers among the carnage."

How strange, Vivian thought to herself as she climbed on her bike and headed home. She pedaled faster and harder than usual, as if trying to outrun a chilling feeling that had little to do with the cool evening air.

16

Missing

VIVIAN'S HEART POUNDED; sweat beaded on her forehead. It was down to just her. Across the line, Amber Grausam, Kelly Frimer, and Madison Bose lined up like hungry wolves armed with bright red, green, and blue rubber spheres in their hands. It was dodgeball day in gym class.

Vivian retreated to the back of the gym on her side of the line to grab a ball of her own, keeping her eyes fixed on her opponents. Amber and her lackeys had developed a coordinated strategy where they would throw simultaneously, Amber directly at the would-be victim, her accomplices immediately to their left and right, giving the opponent nowhere to dodge. They had systematically knocked off Vivian's team members using this strategy, but Vivian had proven too elusive and now she was the only one left. She tensed her body in anticipation of another round of attacks, somehow sensing each throw coming just before they were released.

"Ready!" Amber exclaimed.

The girls cocked their arms back in unison.

"Throw!"

A flurry of colorful dodgeballs came flying at Vivian from three directions, all seemingly thrown with intent to harm. Vivian barely ducked out of the way of Amber's missile, while the two others whizzed by her right and left, all hitting the back wall of the gym with a dull thud. It would take perfect throws to trap and hit Vivian today, and these throws, while strong, weren't perfect. Vivian noticed that Madison's throws were a bit weaker than the others, hers often coming up short and low. This gave her an idea.

"Ready!" Amber said again as they prepared a new assault.

Vivian grabbed a blue dodgeball of her own.

"Throw!" screamed Amber.

Even before the words came out of her mouth, Vivian had begun her charge, straight at the unsuspecting Madison, jumping in anticipation of another low throw. Vivian was right. Madison's throw bounced harmlessly below her while the two others screamed by behind, leaving her nearly face-to-face with the now unarmed Madison at the line. Vivian's accuracy with the dodgeball almost matched her dodging ability and at point blank, Madison had no chance. A light heave at her shins would do it.

"You're out!" yelled Coach Savage. Vivian was pretty sure she heard a hint of amusement in the coach's voice.

Bright red and stunned, Madison stomped over to the side

wall, while Amber and Kelly ran to get more ammunition. Vivian retreated to her own back wall for safety and more ammunition of her own. Now it was two on one.

"Ready!" Amber yelled again, her voice growing hoarse with rage. "Throw!"

Vivian charged again, this time at Kelly, her plan to deflect the throw with her own ball. It worked, and Amber's ball again whizzed right by her. But Kelly had learned from Madison's failure and had retreated as soon as she threw, giving Vivian a harder target—but not too hard. Vivian's laserlike fling caught her off her foot.

"And you're out!" bellowed Coach Savage. "Take a seat!"

Now it was just Vivian and Amber left.

Kelly ran up to Coach Savage to appeal. "It totally bounced off the floor before it got me!"

Amber sneered as she grabbed a new dodgeball and approached the center line.

"You're dead meat!" spit Amber as she readied her throw. She glanced at the sideline to see Coach Savage still debating with Kelly and turned her glare back to Vivian. "You're a born loser, just like your dad!"

Vivian, who had already retreated to the safety of her own side and grabbed a fresh ball, froze in her tracks. Her dad? What did she know about him? Then it struck her: this must be something from Amber's father. Insulting Vivian was one thing; trashing her father was another.

Vivian forgot all about her dodgeball strategy as rage took over. Without another thought, Vivian bounded toward Amber at full speed, her arm cocked like a catapult.

The class watched in amazement, witnessing Vivian's grace, speed, and anger.

Amber's eyes grew wide as she realized, too late, that she had crossed the proverbial line. She didn't even have time to raise her own dodgeball in defense as Vivian's missile zapped her in the stomach so hard that it knocked her over.

The only problem was Vivian had crossed the line too, literally.

"Vivian, you're offsides! You're out!" yelled Coach Savage, who was again watching the match. "Red team wins!"

Vivian looked down in a furious daze and saw that she was standing squarely on the bottom fangs of the wildcat head painted in the center of the floor—she was indeed on the wrong side.

"Damn it!" she screamed as she bolted toward the locker room, the sound of Amber's mocking laughter ringing in her ears.

"Language, Vivian! That's a deten—" Coach Savage's final syllable cut off as the locker room door closed.

Her temper had gotten the best of her again.

After class, Vivian sat quietly on a locker room bench with a towel draped over her head, disappointed that she had not been able to keep her cool. How could she allow herself to be goaded like that? The game had been all but won—unfortunately "all but won" and "won" weren't quite the same thing.

The sounds of running water, excited conversations, and the slamming of lockers finally began to subside as she fumed. When the locker room seemed mostly empty, she finally removed the towel and stood in front of her locker. The hair on her arms stiffened, telling her that danger was afoot, but the warning came too late.

The next she knew, she was pushed against her gym locker, bumping her nose against the cold, blue steel. Vivian turned just as two sets of strong arms, one on each side of her, grabbed and held her. Facing her was Amber Grausam, assisted by her mean girl minions.

"This is my school, Van Tassel," sneered Amber. "Here, there are winners and losers—I'll always be a winner and you'll always be a loser. The sooner you get that, the sooner you can stop this from happening!"

Amber grabbed Vivian's Gryffindor sneakers off the floor and calmly walked over to a stall, where she smiled and dropped them into a toilet.

"No!" Vivian screamed, still held in place by Madison and Kelly.

"Oops. My hand slipped," Amber said mockingly as she motioned to her friends. "C'mon, girls."

Madison and Kelly pushed her back into her locker before letting go and hightailing it behind Amber out of the humid space. Vivian slammed a locker shut in anger and slid down to the floor, wounded more on the inside than she was on the outside.

She squeezed her knees into her chest, so angry she could barely see straight.

Finally she pulled herself up and fished her shoes out of the toilet, where she got some much-needed good news: clear water. She put her sneakers over a turned-up hand dryer and began putting herself back together, hoping the worst was behind her. The moment she squished out of the locker room in her still wet shoes, she was greeted by Coach Savage, who held out a pink detention slip, clearly unaware of what Vivian had just endured.

"You're a heck of an athlete and I could really use you on the basketball team, Van Tassel, if you could just keep your head about you."

Vivian shot him an icy glance, snatched the slip from his hand, and stormed off.

The afternoon was proving no better than the morning, when Mr. Putrim had administered a pop quiz, which Vivian knew she had barely passed. Then, Mrs. Vultura returned nasty comments on her book analysis report. "*Harry Potter* is NOT literature," it read on top in bold, red marker. And now this.

But Vivian knew that things were bound to change during next-period history. Today was the day that she was to present her Murkwood project to Ms. Greenleaf and the class. She was convinced that her findings were so extraordinary that the presentation was certain to be a triumph—nothing could stop her today.

Her excitement grew as she bounded up the stairs to the fifth floor. She even caught herself smiling as she arrived at the classroom, but when she entered, a short woman with a tight pencil skirt and even tighter hair bun stood in her place.

"Where's Ms. Greenleaf?" Vivian asked nervously.

"Please, have a seat," replied the woman in a serious tone.

Across the room, Mary met her eyes and shrugged. Vivian's other classmates seemed equally puzzled as they arrived, most quickly taking their seats, eager to hear what was going on—even Amber took a break from gossiping and sat. Finally the entire class was seated with only the gentle murmur of a few waning conversations.

"Good afternoon class, I'm Mrs. Zilch, your substitute for today," the woman began.

Vivian's stomach sank. She had been so excited to present her paper to the class, but most of all to Ms. Greenleaf. Where was she?

"But where's Ms. Greenleaf?" asked one of Vivian's usually quiet classmates, Milton Murrows, voicing the exact question that was on Vivian's mind.

The manufactured smile on Mrs. Zilch's face faded instantly. She tried to speak but only an airy gasp emerged. She cleared her throat and tried again.

"Ms. Greenleaf?" Her voice seemed to go up an octave. "Oh . . . she's not here."

"We know. But is she sick?" asked Mary.

"Uh . . . no. She's not sick . . . she's . . . uh . . . she's missing."

The entire class sat and stared in stunned silence; only the hiss and clink of the radiator was audible.

"Missing?" Vivian repeated. "As in, the school doesn't know where she is today?"

Mrs. Zilch shot Vivian a look that suggested she didn't want to answer any more questions.

"No," she replied finally. "As in no one knows where she is. Now, I'm only telling you this because it will, no doubt, be in the news soon anyway, but she hasn't been seen since Friday night; the police visited her house this morning and there's no sign of her."

That news set off a flurry of whispers around the classroom. Vivian glanced back at Mary, who looked as stunned and worried as she was.

"Now, I don't want to be an alarmist—I'm sure everything will turn out just fine," Mrs. Zilch continued. "However, the presentations that were scheduled for today will be on hold until she returns."

"But how do you know she will?" asked Molly Shamrock. It was, Vivian thought, the question that everyone was thinking but no one else had wanted to say out loud.

"Of course she will!" Mrs. Zilch snapped, before taking a deep breath and recomposing herself. "I'm sorry. I know this must be upsetting for all of you. What I meant to say is that I'm sure it's just some sort of . . . mix-up. You may read or play board games today as we get things sorted out."

Vivian felt an intense pit in her stomach. What if Ms. Greenleaf didn't return? What happened to her? Was she okay? Vivian grew dizzy as her mind raced with possibilities, none of them good.

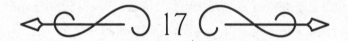

Trick-or-Treat

THE LUNCH BELL rang. Vivian navigated against a sea of goblins, ghouls, and ghosts en route to her usual lunchtime haunt, the stairwell. Today was Thursday, October thirty-first—Halloween, but it sure didn't feel like it.

Three days had passed since the shocking announcement about the disappearance of Ms. Greenleaf, and the trail to find her was cold. The town was on high alert and a strict sundown curfew had been instituted for people under eighteen. At Murkwood, though, students and teachers alike seemed to be in denial and were pushing forward with Halloween festivities as if nothing had happened. Vivian was in no mood to celebrate, and she certainly wasn't dressing up.

Vivian shook her head disappointedly at the excited students bustling about the hallway as she entered the stairwell.

"'appy 'alloween!" bellowed Arturo, holding up a plastic battle-axe. He was wearing a thick, braided beard and football shoulder pads spray-painted silver to look like pauldrons. He had dressed as his Beasts & Battlements character, Durin.

Vivian opened her mouth to reply but then noticed Mary putting the usual electric candles in place beneath the stairs, wearing a long, purple wizard robe—the outfit of her character, Venna. Violet shuffled papers next to her wearing large, pointed ears and brown and green sweats, dressed as Snarfette, Vivian assumed.

It seemed only William, wearing jeans and a T-shirt, was sharing Vivian's cause of boycotting Halloween.

"Hey Viv!" exclaimed Mary as she rose and dusted off her hands. "Are you coming out with us tonight?"

"Oh yeah, you have to," added Violet excitedly. "We're going to hit up mansions on the east side of the lake. They do all kinds of huge decorations, graveyards and stuff, and give out full-size candy bars!"

"It's going to be spoooooktacular!" cut in Arturo in a Dracula voice.

Vivian hadn't been surprised to see the other kids at Murkwood dressed up, but she thought the misfits felt the same way she did and hadn't expected to see them in costumes.

"Um, I'm not trying to be a downer, but do I need to remind you that our history teacher is missing?"

Silence overtook the stairwell. The misfits looked at each other guiltily.

"Did everyone dress up but me and William?" continued Vivian.

"Actually . . . ," William began. "I dressed up too." He pulled a pen out of his pocket, holding it like a sword. "Percy Jackson."

Vivian almost laughed but stopped herself.

She was really disappointed.

"I just . . . I kind of thought you'd feel the same way I did."

"We do, Viv," said Mary. "Honestly. We're just trying to get our minds off it, you know?"

"And I really think things are going to turn out okay," added Violet. "I really believe that—you'll see."

Vivian nodded, but didn't share Violet's optimism. She knew from experience that things didn't always turn out okay.

"Oh, c'mon, Vivian," broke in Arturo. "You'll feel better if you—"

"Sorry, guys," interrupted Vivian. "You can count me out for today, but have fun, though," she continued coldly as she left the stairwell.

They just don't get it, she thought.

"I'm sorry, Vivy," said Mr. Van Tassel as he rested his elbows on the massive desk in the study, squishing his cheeks with his palms. "That's all I know. I've dug up everything I could at the paper; asked the other reporters, but no one's got anything on the disappearance. I even asked to be assigned to the story so I could help, but Troy Grausam insisted on taking it and he's got seniority."

"I thought he was on the animal attack story?" Vivian

mumbled sourly, breaking apart a leftover pizza crust on her plate.

"He was," sighed Mr. Van Tassel. "He jumped to this because it's the 'bigger story,'" her dad said, making air quotes with his fingers. "The animal attack story is now mine, but I don't know how I'm supposed to find a lot of energy around that when Gwen, I mean Ms. Greenleaf, is missing."

Vivian grunted in agreement as she thought about what Amber said about her dad during dodgeball. It was so unfair. There was no doubt in her mind that he was the best reporter at the *Bugle*, but that didn't seem to matter. If they actually wanted a story solved, he was the one to put on it.

"Look, I know how important this is to you," he continued gently. "I promise I'll keep an ear to the ground, okay?"

Vivian nodded.

What a crummy Halloween, she thought.

"So, are you going out with those new friends of yours tonight?" asked her dad. "What do you call them, the rascals?"

"The misfits, and no, I'm staying in," she replied sharply. "And I'm not sure I would call them my friends exactly."

"Well, you've been hanging out with them a lot lately. Those sound like friends to me. . . ." His voice trailed off and he smiled hopefully.

"It's for a school project," Vivian shot back. "I don't have any friends here . . . really. Anyway, I think I'd rather stay here with you and hand out candy."

Mr. Van Tassel's eyes widened as he bit his lip.

"Candy, right!" he said, snapping his fingers.

"You forgot." Vivian crossed her arms and narrowed her eyes.

"No . . . of course not!" her dad replied. "I've got it right here!"

Mr. Van Tassel opened one of the desk's side drawers and pulled out bags of Smarties and Peppermint Patties—both open—and plopped them triumphantly on the desktop.

"All set," he said, looking very pleased with himself.

This was obviously his personal stash.

Suddenly the phone rang, startling both of them.

As it rang a second time, Mr. Van Tassel hurriedly dug through his briefcase to extract his cell phone.

"Who is it?" asked Vivian.

"I don't know," said her dad as he frowned at his phone, studying an unfamiliar local number. "Let me grab this. Hello? . . . Yes, this is Michael Van Tassel . . . Um-hmmm . . . um-hmmmm."

He mouthed the word "sorry" at Vivian as he gestured to his phone and rolled his eyes.

"Darkham? Okay. I can come by first thing in the morning. . . ." As he continued, his frown returned and deepened. "Now? But it's Halloween . . . I'm sure it can wait . . . it can't? But I'm . . . okay then . . . I'm on my way," he finished defeatedly as he touched the end button.

"I'm so sorry, Vivy," he said as he pulled on a cardigan. "That was someone named Dr. Boris Barkov, the caretaker at Darkham Observatory, who insists he knows how to get the animal attacks to stop and had to speak to me in person and immediately. These are usually dead ends, but one thing I've learned as a reporter is the value of showing up. I should be back in an hour or so—can you hold down the fort and do the candy until I'm back?"

"Sure, Dad," Vivian said. It was depressing enough to spend Halloween at home, but even more so to spend it alone. Vivian sighed disappointedly. She had been looking forward to finally spending some time with him, and now he had to leave. She all at once realized that he had probably been feeling the same way about her lately.

"Thanks, Vivy," he said softly as he kissed her on top of the head. "I'll be back soon."

He hurriedly threw his satchel around his shoulder and began to leave but seemed to have forgotten something and returned to the desk. He leaned over it and quickly scanned his eyes about an area map of Midnight Lake while rubbing his chin. Vivian noticed that he had labeled the map "Animal Attacks" in black marker and placed a large red "X" over each spot where there had been an incident. Sure enough, there had been one up near Darkham Observatory at Harmon Bay, but the vast majority were located in a cluster right near the edge of the town of Midnight Lake.

He nodded and seemed satisfied that he had refreshed his memory.

"Okay, back soon!" he said as he rushed out the door.

The minute he left the room, Vivian fetched her copy of the first *Harry Potter* and sat back down to make a new row on her inside-cover comparison chart. For this one she wrote "Halloween," and gave another check to the "Harry" side. By now the page was more than half full of assorted line items, from school and teachers to food and hobbies, and still not a single check for Vivian.

She replaced the book and rested her chin on the desk, listening to the howling wind and rustling leaves outside. Her eyes rested lazily on her father's animal attack map. She found the "X" at Arturo's farm. There was another immediately to its northwest, and another to its southwest. Then there was an attack at the Midnight Lake Resort territory next to the farm; one to its southeast, a couple to its northeast.

Vivian lifted her head up as her eyes focused more closely on the map. She began to notice a pattern that she hadn't before. The cluster of attacks seemed to all circle around a particular site—one that bore no marking on the map. Oddly enough, it was a location she was familiar with, although she had never been there. It had shown up in her study of B&B creator Garrison Arnold—that plot of land his family had once owned and called the Outskirts. Could there be more to the story than she had already discovered? An excited chill ran down Vivian's spine—she was determined to find out.

Her mother's blue eyes looked down on her disapprovingly from the Snape portrait on the wall as Vivian rushed over to a desk drawer, dug out a notepad, and hurriedly scribbled:

Trick-or-treating. Back soon.

Vivian

Without losing a step, she grabbed the bags of candy sitting on the desk, haphazardly threw them into a bowl, and plopped it out on the front porch with a sign she taped above it that read, TAKE ONE (SERIOUSLY, DON'T BE GREEDY!). It took a few tries to get it to stick properly to the oily, uneven paint her father had recently applied to the door. Signs like this never worked, and Vivian was pretty sure the candy would be gone after the first trick-or-treaters came and went, but such was the price of adventure.

She bounded up the steps to her room, where she looked around for anything she might need. Certainly, the flashlight was a must, which she threw into her backpack. She figured the electric lantern might be helpful if she needed hands-free light, so she went into her closet nook and grabbed it along with the map that had the location of the Outskirts she copied from one of the Garrison Arnold biographies. On the way out she noticed something propped in the corner—one of the few things she had kept through the move: the antique combat saber her mom had given her for her tenth birthday. The saber was special not only because it had been given to her by her mother, but also because it had actually belonged to her mother, having been gifted to her on her tenth birthday as well.

The sword was heavier and thicker than a competition saber—almost the heft of a rapier—and featured a beautifully filigreed hilt, a sharpened blade, and a removeable safety tip. With the disappearance of Ms. Greenleaf and all the animal attacks looming over the town, taking it didn't seem like a bad idea. But how would she transport it without drawing attention to herself? She had gotten rid of her fencing bag and the rest of her gear after the "fencing incident." Then she remembered: it was Halloween—a night for costumes and trickery.

The Outskirts

VIVIAN PEDALED AS fast as her creaky, undersized bike could carry her; her three-point hat nearly blew off her head as she rounded the corner onto Main Street. It was awkward riding with puffy pants and a scabbard around her waist, but the pirate costume offered her the perfect excuse to carry her saber in the open without having to worry about drawing unwanted attention.

"Steady as she blows!" she joked to herself as she winked an eye and twisted her face.

As she flew down the street, her mind rapidly came back to Beasts & Battlements monsters as she passed group after group of little Halloween goblins, trolls, devils, and ghosts, most accompanied by nervous-looking parents who were eager to get these Halloween activities out of the way. What was still to be discovered about Garrison Arnold? Could there be some connection between him and the animal attacks that kept happening around town? She had no idea what she expected to find at the plot of land known as the Outskirts, but the circumstances seemed too coincidental to pass up.

Finally she arrived at the entrance to the Midnight Lake Resort, and she began the long ride into the campus. According to the Outskirts map, there were no roads that led directly to the site, but it looked like it could be accessed through the Midnight Lake Resort trail system—it was just beyond its boundary. Her legs began to burn beneath a dimming, orange Halloween sky—she knew she must hurry as she was quickly losing daylight.

After about a half mile into campus, Vivian found the trailhead she was looking for and sped off into the dense woods. It wasn't long before it turned sharply to avoid a rotting, split rail fence with a faded and rusted sign nailed upon it: PRIVATE PROPERTY—KEEP OUT.

"This must be it," she whispered to herself.

She dismounted her bike and, realizing that it would be of no use from here, left it on the side of the trail and descended to the fenced property line. It appeared that the property beyond was mostly open fields with pockets of woodlands and streams cutting jaggedly across it.

In all of her research on Garrison Arnold, there was very little information on this particular property; only that he would occasionally paint here and there was something about him blowing up boulders for fun near a stream and waterfall. With nothing else to go on, Vivian figured that following the stream was probably as good a bet as any.

As she high-stepped through the wet, tall grass, the reality of her situation began to set in. *What am I doing here?* Vivian wondered to herself. *What exactly do I think I'm going to find?*

As the last orange rays of daylight disappeared behind the trees and gave way to a twilight purple sky, Vivian became keenly aware of the situation she had placed herself in: she was walking through woods and fields . . . at nightfall, alone and in an area that was rife with animal massacres.

Vivian drew her saber and began using it to cut through the tall grass as she doubled her pace to a jog toward the meandering stream. Because the area was so overgrown, it was hard to see the stream clearly until she was upon it, and she almost ran right into it.

Wouldn't that be great, she thought. *Getting drenched and then turning into an icicle.*

She followed the stream in the direction of the water as fast as she could manage, but she had to lift her feet high to not get caught in the muddy banks, all while cutting away the dense foliage.

A large, yellow moon had begun to rise high in the sky, illuminating the stream and windswept field. It was all at once beautiful and eerie. The ominous sound of wind howling through reeds kept Vivian focused—the sooner she finished her investigation, the sooner she could leave.

After a few hundred feet, the stream split, one smaller

branch wandering toward a small wooded hollow and the other, larger branch continuing through the field. Vivian paused at the fork, debating which way to go. One way was as good as the other, but then she remembered Arturo's dwarven wisdom: "Right is wrong and lef' is right."

"Left it is," she whispered to herself, and then took a deep breath and bounded on.

The smaller branch was far more manageable to walk next to, and some areas seemed so shallow that she thought she could've walked right across them. Meanwhile, the tall grass dwindled as she approached and entered the hollow. Once she passed the threshold of towering evergreens, there was a sudden drop-off, which created a waterfall and a bubbling pool ten feet below. Vivian carefully hiked around the ridge and finally arrived next to the pool, which frothed white beneath the falling waters, before smoothing out and continuing deeper into the woods.

By now, Vivian's energy was waning and she needed rest. She sat down on a large boulder beside the pool, hugging her arms around herself and shivering, partly due to the cold, but mostly due to her nerves.

She closed her eyes and whispered to herself, "C'mon, Vivy, breathe."

The wind howled with increased force, but after a few moments, Vivian's shivering began to subside. She opened her eyes again and studied her surroundings—as her eyes adjusted, she realized it really wasn't so dark after all. She pressed her hands to the rock surface at her sides and tried to concentrate. *What does this have to do with the mysterious animal attacks?* she asked herself over and over. Her gut told her there was a connection . . . but what was it?

Suddenly she noticed the top of the boulder she sat upon was not smooth; rather there was a large, rough indentation, as if the top had been blasted off. Then it hit her—this must be where Garrison Arnold and his friends would blow up boulders with dynamite! When she began examining the remaining boulders, they all seemed to have undergone similar trauma, as did the walls of the rocky outcropping, including a hollowed-out area around and behind the waterfall itself.

Flashlight in hand, Vivian moved along the edges of the shallow pool to get a better look behind the stream of falling water. At closer inspection, this was far more than an indentation in the wall; it was a cave! Vivian shuddered with excitement. Remembering that getting drenched would be very unpleasant on this chilly fall evening, she pressed her body close to the mossy rock wall and carefully shimmied behind the waterfall, taking on just a bit of misting water.

The cave stunk of sulfur, and darkness enveloped the beam of her flashlight after just a few feet, but even without it she could still faintly make things out. She put her flashlight into her pack and drew out her electric lantern, which would better light all areas of the space. On the ground, rusted cans of cream soda gleamed dully in the lantern light, indicating to Vivian that the cave had once seen some use. Carved prominently on the rock wall was the phrase "GPA 1.0."

"GPA," she whispered to herself, cocking her head.

What did that mean—some sort of inside joke or code? A 1.0 was certainly a terrible grade point average. She waved her lantern around the space for further clues—a small circle of stones enclosed what appeared to be a long-since-abandoned fire pit. Something momentarily sparkled between two of the stones as the light passed by.

Vivian knelt and dislodged the stones from their place. Her eyes caught the glint of brilliant jewels—huge rubies, sapphires, and emeralds cut in jagged geometric shapes like pyramids and octahedrons. Exciting news headlines began spinning in Vivian's mind. *Recent Midnight Lake Transplant Finds Jewels, Retires, and Moves Back to Chicago!*

She beamed as she gathered up the precious gems, but when she scraped them up, she realized they didn't feel quite right—not heavy or cold enough. She opened her hand right in front of her face beneath the intense light of her lantern. Each side on every shimmering jewel was numbered.

"Dice," she whispered to herself disappointedly as she squeezed her hand around what she had thought were treasures.

Vivian's momentary dreams of wealth and prosperity had been shattered, but she couldn't help but chuckle to herself— there'd be no treasure for this pirate tonight! And while she might not have found riches, she did find something else.

"Of course," she said, nodding to herself with a smile. "These are Beasts and Battlements dice."

She looked again at the strange "GPA" inscription on the wall.

And then it dawned on her: Garrison Arnold's middle name was Perry; Garrison Perry Arnold—GPA were his initials; this must be his space; these must be his dice!

Vivian's heart continued to race, but her breathing steadied. She lifted her lantern and padded around an outcropping in the back of the cavern, quickly discovering that there was more to this cave than she had realized. In what appeared to be another result of Arnold's demolition, there was a large opening in the wall that whistled with cool, sulfur-filled air. The tunnel floor sloped downward and continued deep into the blackness.

Vivian's head told her that it was now time to stop, but something else deep inside her—something far more powerful than her reason—made her continue. She had already come this far; what was another tunnel?

Vivian stepped nervously beyond the threshold. It was a narrow shaft, maybe seven feet round, but a comfortable enough amount of space for her. She walked for what seemed like hours deeper and deeper along this solitary path, always sloping down. The compass on her phone told her that she was walking toward the lake, which was confirmed as the passage became dank and rimmed with moisture. But it wasn't the occasional drips of water and the increasingly slippery terrain that bothered Vivian the most; it was the smell. As she descended, the distinct, rotten-egg smell of sulfur and other unhealthy-smelling gases became more and more prominent.

The smell became so intense that she fished the eyepatch out of her pocket and placed it over her nose as a makeshift face mask; she began to grow lightheaded and dizzy, almost slap-happy. These effects further impaired her judgment, making the notion of pushing forward seem like a better and better idea. All the while, her thoughts wandered rapidly—a jumble of different voices swirling in her head, some almost visible to her twitching eyes:

". . . *I know it will be hard at first, but I think you'll love Midnight Lake. I grew up there and it's time that I returned . . .*"

". . . *When I arrived, I found it was a less than warm reception—small towns, ya know . . .*"

". . . *They keep saying animal attack, but how could one animal take out an entire stable like that . . .*"

". . . *Well . . . based on what I've read, this wasn't always a school . . .*"

". . . *Beasts and Battlements . . . Invented and published right here in Midnight Lake . . .*"

"*There she is. The first-edition* Book of Beasts—*a classic.*"

". . . *funny folk around here in Midnight Lake, don't you*

think? Lots of hallucinations, lots of asylums. Or maybe it's somethin' . . . in the water?"

Finally the ground leveled off and her thoughts were interrupted by something new: the tunnel opened into a large cavern, where the odor was at maximum intensity. This cavern wasn't entirely dark, though—there was a faint, multicolored light source far off in the distance. However, it was obscured not only by intense blackness but thick fumes that waved and bent the dim source, while mineral-rich stalactites and stalagmites shimmered against her lantern. The ground here was soft with moisture; the walls were wet, and the ceiling dripped into shallow pools.

This area felt completely exposed compared to the relative safety of the narrow passageway where she could at least see the walls and ceiling around her. She glanced at her phone and realized she had come so far that there was no signal down here. She was truly on her own. Her chest tightened and her breath grew more rapid as she quietly padded through the cavern toward the light source, endeavoring to not make a sound.

Suddenly the cavern echoed with a loud whooshing sound and the light flashed bright, while the dense gas grew nearly as thick as smoke, making Vivian cough and gag as her eyes stung. She knelt behind a pillar trying to regain her senses and keep quiet. The noxious cloud and whooshing echo began to dissipate, giving way to light footsteps and hushed growling that could be heard in the cavern coming her way—Vivian realized that she was no longer alone.

Vivian switched off her lantern and froze behind the pillar—she seemed to stop breathing entirely. The footsteps grew closer—it sounded like several entities were approaching. Meanwhile, the growling continued; it bore frequent changes in pitch and began to sound more sentient than just random animal sounds—it was more like a strange animal conversation. Then the growls stopped abruptly, as if in alarm, followed by the sounds of targeted and deliberate sniffing. It was a terrible sound, something between the harmless snuffing of a dog and the snorting of a pig—they were close now. Vivian quietly drew her saber, one inch per second.

The sound continued slowly around the pillar—it was practically upon her now. More on instinct than thought, Vivian flicked on the lantern and jumped away from the pillar to get distance from her potential assailant. She screamed and it howled back. What she saw before her wasn't a badger or coyote, though, but something far more terrible. It was a scaly, three-foot-high man with the face and tail of a wolf! It wore a rusty chain mail shirt and held a cleaver in one hand and a dagger in the other; its fanged maw dripped and frothed. Vivian froze. Even in her terror, she was able to recognize this creature from the book that she had spent so much time poring over: the *B&B: Book of Beasts*!

Her shock passed as adrenaline surged through her body. She stumbled backward and fell, her eyes and mouth opened wide.

What! The! Heck!

The hideous creature growled and hissed at her as it shielded its eyes from the bright lantern light that dangled from her hand. It barked out something, as if speaking an unknown language, and other footsteps rapidly approached— there were others, many others. Vivian jumped back to her feet and raised her sword, which trembled in her hand. The beast charged her in a growl-filled fury, swinging steel.

Instinct took over. Much to her own surprise, Vivian had little trouble parrying the cleaver strikes with her saber, the creature's strength seeming not greater than her own. What she hadn't trained for, however, was a second thrust from the dagger it held, which she tried to evade, but which slashed her across the forearm, making her shriek and drop the lantern. Even worse, his reinforcements had now arrived—a hissing, snarling gaggle of perhaps a dozen feisty little wolf men.

Vivian's heart pounded. Panic was now the only instinct left, and it told her to run.

She bolted for the tunnel from which she had come as her attacker took another failed swipe with his cleaver. The chase was now on, and she could tell by the excited panting and barking that these creatures shared a wolf's instinct for pursuit. Fortunately, they were awkward and bipedal and what they shared with canines in instinct, they did not share in speed.

Vivian flew through the slippery cavern, somehow armed with a sense of where things were despite the low light that got worse as she got farther away from her abandoned lantern. She gained distance on the pack, but out of the corner of her eye, she noticed others moving in from the perimeter along the walls.

Running frantically, she reached into her backpack and withdrew the flashlight. As the tiny men closed in from the sides of the tunnel entrance, she unleashed a beam upon them, which left them shrieking and averting their eyes for just long enough for her to get inside.

She bounded up the corridor like a gazelle but stopped dead in her tracks as she realized that this tunnel was no longer vacant. Running just as fast toward her was an ominous, dark figure—the gray man from town! His hood and sunglasses were off, revealing his sharp features and long, unnaturally pale hair. He held a katana sword in one hand and some kind of cannister in the other—he must have followed her here. And now she was trapped.

Bleeding, dizzy, and exhausted, Vivian crumpled to the ground as the dangerous man approached with frightening speed and grace. She was finished and she knew it—all she could hope now was that it would end quickly.

Vivian covered her head with her arms as he wound up his sword for a killing blow, and just as she expected it to arrive, she heard the clang of steel ringing through the tunnel. She peeked up through her shivering arms to see the gray man's katana right above her head under the cleaver of one of her wolf men pursuers—he had saved her!

"Run!" he yelled in a gruff voice as he bounded over her in a single stride and engaged the two creatures immediately behind her in the tunnel. His maneuvers were otherworldly fast, his style elegant and deadly. She never saw him make large swings or thrusts with his silver katana, but his attackers fell limp and silent as he passed by, never breaking stride, first the two in the tunnel and then three more at the mouth of the cavern.

Vivian, too mesmerized and terrified to move, just sat and stared. Who was this man?

"Run, you fool!" bellowed the gray man again, as he disappeared in the blackness of the cavern, which now blazed with silver.

Vivian, still paralyzed, finally snapped out of her trance as a loud bang and smoky flash filled the cavern below. She shot to her feet, but her head spun with dizziness and then the tunnel began to tunnel; her legs wobbled, and blackness overtook her.

Dangerous Games

VIVIAN WOKE WITH a jolt, buried under the covers of her bed. The fall sun had just begun to peek through her window, making her squint. She rubbed her eyes and sat up—her head throbbed. Had last night's adventure been a dream?

She looked down and noticed that she was still wearing the puffy pirate clothes from the night before. Her left forearm ached beneath a neatly wrapped bandage. It hadn't been a dream; last night's events were real.

Vivian's neck tingled; the hairs on her arms stood on end.

She scanned her room in search of her bag, her eyes landing on it where it sat on the dresser next to the lantern that she had abandoned in the cavern. Her saber rested safely against the bedpost. How had these things gotten back here? How had *she* gotten back here?

Vivian sprang out of her bed and began pacing the floor frantically, only to realize how tired and achy she was. The sheer distance she had covered last night, paired with combat scars, noxious gases, and a roller coaster of emotions had clearly been too much for her body to handle. It became harder to breathe with every new question that passed through her head.

Who is the gray man? How did he know I was in the cavern—am I being followed? How did I survive the attack of those . . . those . . . ?

Her eyes fell again on her backpack.

She pulled out her *Beasts & Battlements: Book of Beasts* and began hurriedly flipping through it. She knew she had recognized her attackers from the night before in its pages, and it didn't take her long to find what she was looking for—a black-and-white illustration of a wolkflike man holding a cleaver and dagger: a caniman! Even the chain mail shirt this illustrated caniman wore seemed to match the armor that the creature Vivian encountered had been wearing. Her eyes narrowed and then widened with understanding as she read the accompanying description:

. . . Canimen dwell in dark, dank places such as swamps and underground caverns. They have excellent night vision and can see in the dark up to one hundred feet, but they abhor bright light and cannot see well in it. If they are in bright light, they fight at a penalty (-1 from all attack rolls).

That's why the light had worked so well, Vivian thought.

At least according to this game book, these little wolfish men called canimen hated light. She realized right then that she needed to take this "game" book more seriously than she thought.

But how had she gotten home with no memory of it? Was it the gray man? If so, how had he not been seen?

By now, she couldn't stop shaking; her breath was shallow. She needed to do something—to move—so she rushed across the room to her dresser to change into clothes more suitable for school. She picked a long-sleeve shirt that would hide her bandaged arm. Just as she finished getting dressed, she noticed the clatter of kitchen activity downstairs. Her dad! What had become of him last night? Did he know she'd been out?

Convinced that she was slated for the grounding of a lifetime, she tiptoed out of her room and carefully edged down the back stairs to the kitchen. There, she found a pair of legs dangling out from below the sink, the sound of wrench work, and the hummed tune of "This Is Halloween" in her father's baritone voice.

"Good mornin'—Ouch!" he said as his head popped up and banged against the drainpipe.

For whatever her dad was "fixing" on the sink, the last impact seemed to undo his work and then some as the side sprayer began to shower the counter and cabinets. Mr. Van Tassel quickly retreated back below, fiercely twisting the water valve. The pipes whined and the water finally stopped.

"Huh . . . must've been a bad seal," he remarked, rubbing his head as he emerged from the cabinet. "Anyway, I made your favorite, stuffed French toast!" he continued, gesturing to the stove.

He doesn't seem mad, she thought, astounded. *He doesn't seem to know . . .*

"Dad! About last night—"

"I know, I know. I am so sorry, Vivy! I really am—I didn't mean to leave you on your own for Halloween! The interview really got out of hand—"

"But Dad! I've got to tell you somethi—"

"First, he made me wait for almost an hour until he felt satisfied that 'they weren't listening,' then he brings me to this cluttered director's office and starts ranting and raving about some kind of portal beneath the lake—a gateway to another world! It was nuts. He then goes on to explain that these animal attacks are actually creatures that have emerged from this other world and that Darkham Observatory itself was built by the government to not look up but look down—to study the portal and find a way to 'harness its energy.' That's why people like Einstein visited. Ridiculous, right? This guy was a total loon! Too bad those sanitariums are closed these days 'cause I've got them a great candidate!"

"Dad?!" Vivian tried again.

He was so caught up in his telling, that Mr. Van Tassel didn't seem to hear her.

"The only reason I stayed was how incredibly elaborate his fiction was. He had diagrams, schematics, the works. It was crazy!"

He finally stopped for a moment, realizing that he had been ranting, or rambling, or maybe both. "Sorry, girly— what is it you wanted to tell me?"

Vivian suddenly realized that she had a whole lot of explaining to do. Her story was as far-fetched, if not more so, as that of the Darkham caretaker. She had been dying to share her recent discoveries—the Murkwood Sanitarium, the case files, Garrison Arnold, everything. Add that to last night's encounter with the canimen and the gray man and who in their right mind would believe her? Who would understand? Not someone who couldn't believe this "crazy" Darkham story. Vivian was bursting and terrified all at once.

"Vivian, what is it?" her dad asked, concern growing on his face.

Could he believe her? And what if he did? Wouldn't he put her on lockdown? There were still so many questions— so many mysteries—to solve here. In the blink of an eye, she decided that she couldn't risk it.

"Oh, nothing . . . I just, uh, went trick-or-treating with the misfits—it was fun," she said finally.

He let out a relieved sigh.

"Great! I'm so glad you had fun with your friends!"

"They're not my friends," Vivian snapped back, so fast even

she was surprised. "I told you, I don't have any friends here."

Mr. Van Tassel adjusted his collar and cleared his throat.

"Well, thanks for leaving the note anyway—I would've been worried sick," he replied as he produced the message off the table and handed it to her.

Vivian did a double-take when she realized that the note she'd left had been changed. The top was her original message, but a postscript had been added at the bottom: *P.S. I've gone to bed—see you tomorrow*. It was in her handwriting, but she hadn't written it.

Vivian's eyes froze on the note.

"Vivy . . . you okay?" asked her dad, his forehead creasing in concern. "You seem . . ."

"Huh? Oh, me? Yeah, fine . . . great, really," she squeaked, trying to get her eyelids working again. "Uh, so, did the caretaker say anything else?" she continued as casually as she could. "Like any other crazy facts about the 'portal' or how he thought he could get the attacks to stop?"

"Not really. Just a bunch of rantings, really. Oh, darn! I've got to go. I have an interview this morning at Stone Manor with this mystery millionaire who keeps buying up properties around the lake!"

Mr. Van Tassel wiped his mouth and hastily snatched up his briefcase.

"See you tonight," he said quickly as he pecked Vivian on the top of the head. "Are you good to get yourself to school?"

A feeling of dread crept over Vivian as she realized how frightening it would be to go outside right now, let alone all the way to school. What if "they" were still out there?

"I'm good," Vivian managed in a dry whisper, amazed that she and her dad couldn't seem to get on a schedule when one was there when the other needed them.

"All right, girly. Love you," her dad replied as he flew out of the room and moments later out the front door.

Vivian stiffly rubbed her palms over her eyes and cheeks. She needed to think. What should she do; what could she do? There were monsters in Midnight Lake that came out of a portal located in caverns deep beneath the water. Who else knew about this? Evidently, the caretaker at Darkham . . . and the gray man. Who else? Who were these people . . . what did this all mean?

The pounding of Vivian's head increased as she pondered these hard-to-believe realities. She wanted nothing more than to stay home today, but she knew she couldn't. She needed to push on, and the answers were not in here but out there.

She ate the French toast and downed a glass of milk, then fixed herself up as best she could, given the circumstances. It took everything she had to find the courage to exit the house, and when she did, she rapidly scanned the landscape. She immediately noticed that her bike had been returned to the lawn, just as if she had come home under her own power last night. This made her even more anxious.

She was running late, as usual, but she didn't have the benefit of her normal energy to compensate. Vivian cut through backyards and corners of lawns en route to Main Street. She knew she could've ridden her bike and saved a lot of time and energy, but all she needed was the judgments and jeering that would come along with that at school. It was safe to say that she had enough problems already.

As she pushed down Main Street, nervously dodging morning walkers and sweeping shopkeepers, she noticed out of the corner of her eye a graceful, black-clothed figure on the opposite side of the street: the gray man! He was limping swiftly down the sidewalk with his hooded head down and his hands buried in his pockets. Not only did it seem that he had survived last night's combat, but he seemed reasonably intact!

At this sight, Vivian found the spring she was looking for. She slipped along the storefronts, taking cover in each canopied doorway until the shadowy figure had reached the next intersection, where he turned out of sight. Vivian darted across the street and rounded the corner in stealthy pursuit. He had gotten halfway down the block when he disappeared into one of the retail shop doorways. Vivian had kept enough distance that she was confident she had gone undetected. She closed the ground rapidly and, when she got there, discovered that the doorway was actually a steep stairway that went down to perhaps a cellar or basement of one of the shop buildings.

Vivian's curiosity and thirst for answers had taken the place of any fear that had lingered from earlier this morning. She took a deep breath and silently padded down the stairs. At the bottom, there was a narrow brick corridor lit by a single pull-string lightbulb. After just a few feet, the corridor opened into a large storage space full of bicycles and various lawn-care equipment, but the gray man was nowhere to be found.

She had little trouble seeing in the dim environment and she scanned every inch—there was no movement, no nothing. Vivian shook her head and sighed—she was becoming more than a little annoyed with all the mysteries.

She turned around to head back up and almost fainted when she did. There, right in front of her, blocking her path, stood the gray man!

Vivian gasped and stumbled backward, tripping on a nearby bicycle and falling on her behind.

"I bet you're looking for some answers," he said in a rough, low voice.

"Mmm-hmmm" was all Vivian could muster. Her mouth was paralyzed; her heart bursting.

"Meet me at midnight at the old Real Games Limited headquarters on Silver Springs Road and you will find the answers you seek."

Vivian was tense as a drum, but she didn't feel like she was in danger. Maybe it was instinct. Or maybe it was reason.

After all, if this man had wanted to harm her, he certainly had the chance last night. Instead, he had saved her. She dusted off her hands and shifted to stand up. She had only looked away for a moment, but by the time she was back on her feet, he was gone.

Misfit Trouble

"I MEAN IT'S ridiculous," William complained as he dodged students rushing through the hallways of Murkwood. "I mean, what's the point of having chasers, beaters, and keepers, if the golden snitch is the only thing that matters?"

"It's not *all* that matters," shot back Mary, keeping in step with William and evading students as effectively as he was. "You do get points for scoring the quaffle."

"Yeah, a whole ten points," countered William. "Your team's working hard doing that for like an hour and you're up like seventy nothing and then the opposite seeker catches the snitch, gets a hundred fifty points and the game ends. Why not just have like teams full of seekers?"

"Because that's how Quidditch works!" snapped Vivian from behind them, surprising even herself that she had entered the conversation.

Normally, Vivian would've been thrilled to be talking anything *Harry Potter*, but not today. In fact, she had hardly said a word all day in class or otherwise, heavily distracted by the disturbing events of the past twenty-four hours.

Mary and William stopped talking and exchanged a surprised look.

Vivian felt her cheeks grow warm.

"Sorry," she said quickly. "It's sorta been a long morning."

"No problem," replied Arturo with a grin. "If I had Putrim first period, I'd be moody too."

"Thanks," Vivian mumbled as the group pushed on against a flood of students heading for the gym cafeteria.

It was lunchtime at Murkwood, and Vivian and the stairwell misfits were en route to their usual stairwell hangout, where they ate and gamed.

"Okay, enough Potter or William will get going again on his critique of the House Cup point system," announced Mary as they crouched into their seats and activated the electric candles. "Where were we?"

"I think we had just killed that minotaur and returned to the fortress where we were summoned by the king," answered Violet.

"Technically, *they* killed the minotaur, Violet," teased William. "I don't recall your gnome ever landing a hit—she was bait, at best," he continued, breaking into a chuckle.

"Ha-ha, smart guy!" Violet rolled her eyes at him. "Just wait till I get you alone in Scrabble, Traumer."

"You may be the Scrabble whiz around here, Violet, but

today its Beasts and Battlements, and that's my domain. . . ."

"Would you two knock it off so we can get going?" Arturo impatiently tapped his fingers on his binder. "I've got Drabner next period and I still haven't done my homework."

"Good luck with that," Mary said under her breath, her eyebrows raised.

"Okay, okay, okay," rushed William. "So, you're escorted by a dozen guards with spears into the inner sanctum, where the lord of the fortress lives and holds court. You enter a lavish throne room with a high, beamed ceiling with all kinds of crimson and purple banners hanging down, each with a different coat of arms. You approach the throne where the lord sits, flanked by the captain of the guard on his left and an old, bearded man on his right, holding a staff and wearing a long gray robe.

"Greetings, heroes! The fortress continues to be in your debt for your bravery and heroism."

"Ah, it was nothing," squeaked Violet as her gnome Snarfette.

"But a new task is at hand, one that will require your immediate departure back to the Tunnels of Torment,'" the lord intoned, as voiced by William. "'Seer Allred?'"

William continued looking down behind his gamemaster screen and said, "The old, robed man steps forward and you realize that his eyes are all foggy and white—he's blind. Then, in a crackling, dry voice he begins. 'Brave travelers, have you heard the tale of Arborem?'"

"Nothin' comes to min'," answered Arturo as Durin.

William went on in his best Dumbledore impression. "There were three brothers, triplets, born to a powerful elven king—a demigod. One brother was named Urbanem, a great warrior, who was given dominion over cities and towns—the civilized world of humankind, elves, and dwarves. The second was named Aquanem, a wizard, who was given power over water, oceans, seas, and all that lived in them. Last, there was Arborem, a righteous and powerful druid, who was given dominion over nature, forests, and beasts. For over a thousand years, the brothers worked in harmony, fostering peace and prosperity throughout the Great Realm. But over time, the cities of men spread and grew, exploiting the natural resources that Arborem had sworn to protect. Arborem watched as his domain became plagued by deforestation, mining, and pollution. The brothers bickered over a solution."

William quickly took a swig of water. Mary, Violet, and Arturo waited for him to continue, seemingly with bated breath; Vivian followed along distractedly.

"One day, a group of loggers came to Arborem's sacred high forest, cutting and burning with reckless abandon. Arborem snapped, unleashing the beasts of the forest upon them and massacring the whole camp. When Urbanem found out, he confronted his brother, but Arborem's soul had been corrupted by violence and cursed by blood. He had come to the belief that the only way to purify the Great Realm was to . . ."

William grabbed the electric candle and held it beneath his chin, casting twisted shadows upon his face. ". . . to end the scourge of humanity altogether. The brothers went to war, which continues on in many parts of the Great Realm to this day."

William turned his shadowed face to Vivian. "Alissa, I'm sorry to say the war has reached your homeland of Raven Haven. Your mother has been captured by the forces of Arborem and brought to the Tunnels of Torment, which are under the control of one of his high priests."

Vivian's heart sank.

"My moth——" Vivian started and cleared her throat. "Um, William, can it be someone else?"

"I wish it were," William said, still in the voice of Seer Allred, "but the captive is the one they call Marissa Sunstorm, your mother."

"No . . . I'm talking outside of the game, William," Vivian said. "Can it be someone else who has been captured?"

Her breathing became rapid and shallow.

"I don't understand—are you okay?" William switched back to his own voice, a confused look on his face. "Why can't it be your mom?"

All eyes were on Vivian now.

She closed her eyes and spoke, "Because my mom is dead."

There was silence. No one moved and only the flicker of the fake candles broke the stillness.

"Like, your real mom?" asked Violet gently.

"Yes," Vivian replied, fighting back her emotions with clenched teeth and fists. "And I don't want anyone saying 'sorry' or feeling bad for me, all right? I'm fine. I've dealt with it."

She kept her eyes fixed on an artificial candle, daring not to look at any of them.

"Maybe we should pause there today," Mary said after a moment. "Besides, we don't want Arturo to fail science."

Everyone stood up and began gathering their things. Vivian could feel their eyes on her, as if they were all shooting her secret looks of pity. Vivian knew these looks and absolutely hated them. She already regretted having said anything at all.

Without meeting anyone's gaze, she mumbled goodbye to the misfits and rushed up the stairs, finding a quiet corner in the almost empty hallway. She could feel that each had wanted to say something, but none of them did.

She went to open her bag and pull out her Harry Potter chart, but it was the *Book of Beasts* that caught her attention, reminding her of what had happened last night and what was to come. Her emotions shifted from regret to nervous excitement.

"Just a few more hours," she whispered to herself. "Tonight, I'll get some answers."

21

SPECTOR

VIVIAN TWIRLED HER fork over and over again as she sat across the dining room table from her father. The portrait of the woman with her mom's cheekbones peered down from above the fireplace.

"So you could imagine my shock when I walk up to Stone Manor and who but Mr. Braemor comes out to greet me—turns out he's the mystery buyer who bought Stone Manor—that huge mansion on the shore near downtown—and most recently Darkham Observatory!" Mr. Van Tassel said with a mouthful of spaghetti. He paused to take a swig of his root beer. "Guess he even tried to buy up buildings downtown like that game store on the corner, but the owner, Mr. Lynn, wouldn't sell."

"Umm-hmmm," Vivian replied. She realized that she had actually witnessed the beginning of the meeting her dad was talking about.

"You know, Mr. Braemor, that quirky old guy who came

by when we moved in?" continued Mr. Van Tassel. "Well, it turns out he's a gazillionaire and he has all kinds of development plans around the lake."

"Small world I guess," said Vivian softly with a shrug.

"Yeah. Who would've thought. Evidently, he's the heir to the estate of some old East Coast family, and he came to town a few months ago because of all the development opportunities."

"Mmmm." Vivian nodded.

"Hey Vivy, everything okay? You seem distracted tonight—you've barely touched your dinner. You usually love spaghetti!"

"Huh? Oh, yeah, I'm just tired, that's all," she lied. She took a big bite of spaghetti and tried to smile reassuringly.

The truth was, Vivian was horribly distracted. She couldn't stop thinking about her midnight plans—not exactly something she could tell him.

"Okay . . . well, let me clean this up and then we can watch a movie or something," he said as he walked over, rustled her hair, and grabbed the carton of pasta from the middle of the table. "Meet me in the living room when you're done?"

She nodded.

After finishing her dinner, Vivian sat down in the living room, but couldn't stop herself from fidgeting. Her dad joined her armed with a huge bowl of popcorn. Vivian smiled. Crunching on popcorn seemed like a perfect activity to help quell her jangled nerves.

Tonight's movie was one of her absolute favorites, *Indiana Jones and the Raiders of the Lost Ark*, but she was restless and could hardly concentrate on a single scene. Like Indy, Vivian had been a skeptic too about the supernatural . . . until last night. Now she really didn't know what to believe.

At the halfway mark, the popcorn was gone and she couldn't pretend to focus on the movie any longer. She gave her best fake yawn and stretched her arms as she rose from the couch.

"Hey Dad, I'm really tired. I'm turning in."

"Already?" he asked in surprise. "But you'll miss the bad guys getting their faces melted off."

"Yeah, sorry," she answered honestly. "It's been a long week."

He paused the movie.

"Vivy, is everything okay?" He moved the popcorn bowl to the table and shifted to face her. "I feel like I've hardly seen you lately."

"Well, you haven't exactly been around a lot either," she said, a bit more aggressively than she meant to.

He opened his mouth to reply, but stopped and all of a sudden looked guilty and at a loss for words.

Vivian realized that she was opening a can of worms—one she didn't have the time or focus for tonight.

"Sorry," she said quickly. "I just mean we both have a lot going on, but everything's fine. I'm just tired tonight—see you tomorrow, okay?"

He looked at her thoughtfully.

"Okay . . . well, sleep tight, girly. Love you."

"Umm-hmm." Vivian nodded and walked out.

A pit of guilt swirled in her stomach as she ascended the stairs. She hated to disappoint him; she hated lying to him even more. She'd have to make it up to him later. But tonight's meeting was too important, and something inside her told her that she had to see this through.

She closed the door to her room and looked at her desk clock: only nine thirty. She had a few hours to go before her midnight journey and could only hope that her father would be fast asleep by the time she left.

She entered her reading nook and cracked open *Harry Potter*—she was now rereading the third book, *The Prisoner of Azkaban*—to get her mind off things, but it really didn't. She now had a new and deeper understanding of the boy who lived. Like Harry, a dangerous new world had been revealed to her and life would never be the same. Unlike Harry, her life hadn't improved. It felt like it had gone from bad to worse.

Around eleven o'clock, she heard her father's footsteps on the back stairs and the sounds of him entering his bedroom. The bustle of bedtime readiness continued for another half hour, but by about eleven forty-five, everything seemed to be still—a rustle here and there, but still enough, Vivian decided. It was time to move.

Vivian put down her book and tiptoed to get her backpack. As she exited her room, the door creaked extra loudly, as she knew it only did against the backdrop of a silent house. She waited a moment in the hallway to confirm that there was no new activity from her father's room—there wasn't. The floorboards whined with every step as she slipped over to the front stairs, which were carpeted at least, and she padded down keeping her eyes peeled toward the upstairs in case a light turned on.

When she reached the bottom of the staircase, she turned back toward the shadowy front hall and gasped: the front portrait had startled her, and seemed to frown at her disapprovingly with her mother's eyebrows.

Vivian stood in place and panted for several moments.

"Sorry, Mom," she whispered almost silently. "I have to."

She tiptoed through the entry hall and edged out the front door.

It was a crisp and dark night, the moon mostly obscured by thick clouds. Vivian's bike was waiting where she had left it on the front lawn. She hopped on and zipped into the blackness. The ride to Silver Springs Road was only about a mile, but because of the citywide curfew, Vivian traveled via unlit neighborhood back streets to stay out of sight. The only place there was really nowhere to hide was Silver Springs Road itself, which was well lit and isolated on a hill that held a barren business park. This complex included the old Real Games Ltd.—"RGL"—headquarters, Garrison Arnold's company and the publisher of Beasts & Battlements. But RGL moved out of town years ago after Arnold's death and, according to a road sign, the building now housed an organization called SPECTOR.

To minimize her time in the open, Vivian tore up the hill as fast as she could. Her legs burned as she rounded the bend of Silver Springs Road, where her worst fears were realized. Sitting right in front of the former RGL headquarters was a Midnight Lake police cruiser!

She quickly veered off to the side of the road and hid in a shallow drainage ditch, mostly out of sight from the street. She crouched next to her bicycle and waited in the cool mud while her heart pounded in her ears. There wasn't much cover here, but it was better than nothing. She just hoped that the officer had been looking away when she came up.

She tried to slow her breath, which was making dragon steam in the ice-cold air and further giving away her position. Nothing happened. She slowly crept along the muddy ditch, walking her bike the rest of the way until she was directly across from the police car. She cautiously popped her head up for a look—the car was empty!

Vivian freed her bike and Gryffindor sneakers from the muck, and darted across the street and into the shadows of the light-industrial office building. A modest sign out front read SPECTOR INTERNATIONAL. Vivian figured that whatever

SPECTOR International was, it must be a twenty-four-hour operation as the front office lights appeared to be on and the parking lot was half full.

"You're late," called a rough voice from the shadows, making Vivian nearly leap out of her muddy shoes.

The gray man slipped out of the shadows practically right next to Vivian.

"S-s-sorry," Vivian stammered. "I ran into some . . . complications."

"Follow me," he said briskly as he brushed by her toward the front entrance where he knocked three times, waited a beat, knocked a fourth, and then a fifth a few moments later.

Vivian could hear the lock on the heavy wood door click, and the gray man pushed it open.

"Wait just a second," Vivian cried out of instinct. She planted her hands on her hips. "I'm not going in there until you tell me who you are."

"Name's Drusen," replied the mysterious man as he disappeared into the entrance of the building.

Vivian waited and shivered in the cold for a moment. Could she trust him? He did save her life and there was a police car out front, so that was something. Also, something else, something deep inside, told her that he could be trusted.

She took a deep breath and followed.

The front portion of the building had small offices around the perimeter and an open space in the middle with a large reception desk. It was unremarkable except for the décor—she had never seen anything quite like it in an office. Elaborate medieval-style tapestries and unusual crests adorned forest-green walls; carved natural-wood desks and beautiful, nature-inspired artifacts filled the space. And plants. Tons of plants and planted trees of every imaginable species took up every corner.

"Hurry," Drusen urged as he moved with purpose toward the back corridor, his limp having improved dramatically since this morning. "We're already late."

Vivian scampered to catch up with the mysterious man, who led her around a corner where they were met with a perfectly round, mirrored corridor.

"What's this?" Vivian blurted out.

"Shhh!" shot back Drusen as he handed Vivian a gleaming silver talisman engraved with an eye, arrow, leaf, and sword. "Put this on."

Vivian could tell she was already pushing her luck with her questions, so she complied.

"Now c'mon," whispered Drusen as he zipped through the strange tunnel.

Vivian followed, but the moment she stepped in, she felt as though she was inside some sort of magnetic field. Her hair stood on end and something like electricity seemed to flow through her body. She paused in shock.

"What's happening?"

"It's magically protected," Drusen explained. "The talisman is granting you access. Now hurry up!"

Vivian's body hummed as she made her way through the tunnel. As soon as she exited, she felt normal again, but her senses were now assaulted by yelling as they entered a large council chamber of some sort. There were a dozen pews on the floor and an elaborate multitiered judge's bench carved with trees and forest imagery anchoring the room. It was a lavish and elegant space—much more like a temple than the windowless warehouse portion of an office building. The walls were adorned with colorful green, brown, silver, and gold banners, each featuring mysterious symbols of arrows, swords, eyes, and dragons—it reminded her of the Great Hall at Hogwarts.

The floor seats were chock-full, but a few of the seats on the raised council bench were noticeably empty, including the highest seat—almost a throne—placed right in the center. As Vivian scanned the room, she froze when her eyes found the front. She recognized these people! The man speaking was Mr. Arrowsmith from the museum; seated upon the bench was Mr. Thornwood, her school principal; and to his left was Mr. Greenbriar, a thin, bald man with piercing blue eyes who was Midnight Lake's mayor. Deputy Brookfield from the sheriff's department filled another one of the seats of honor.

Her eyes finally found Drusen, who was standing, arms

crossed, behind the back pew looking at her. Vivian scurried over to stand next to him.

"He has returned!" bellowed Mr. Arrowsmith. "How else can you explain the animal attacks; the disappearances?"

"Nonsense!" Mr. Thornwood's voice was just as loud but quite a bit colder. "We've always had attacks and disappearances. This is a sad a reality of guarding the gate. These recent incidents are no different."

"No different?" gasped Mr. Arrowsmith. "The attacks are happening every few days! We've recently lost some of our best sentinels! This is no coincidence! *He has returned!*"

A roar of agreement came from the members seated in the audience, many of whom stood and shook their fists in support.

The mention of animal attacks instantly got Vivian's attention. She had rarely ever seen grown-ups yell at each other this way, and she knew whatever they were debating must be serious.

"Order!" yelled Mr. Thornwood as he smacked a gavel upon the bench. "Order! I will have order!"

Mr. Thornwood froze with his gavel lifted as his eyes caught those of Vivian standing in the back of the auditorium. His eyes widened and then narrowed to join the rest of his face in a sneer. In a split second, the chamber was silent as all heads turned toward her.

"What is *she* doing here?" asked Mr. Thornwood through curled lips.

Drusen stepped forward and cleared his throat.

"She found the entrance at the Outskirts last night; she entered the portal chamber and was attacked by a group of canimen that had emerged. I believe she has a right to know what is going on."

Heads turned to each other as muffled whispers and gasps bounced off the walls of the chambers for several moments.

"She has no rights here!" said Mr. Thornwood sharply. "Sentinel Verrick, you should not have brought her here! You will remove her at once and tell her nothing. Then you shall return to face disciplinary action of the council!"

"But this is—"

"I know who she is!" shouted Mr. Thornwood. "And she is not welcome here. Now escort her home and return. And Drusen . . . you're not to tell her anything."

He knows who I am? Vivian thought. *That's what I get for all those detentions.*

Drusen glared at Mr. Thornwood and glanced around the room at the shocked faces of the attendees.

"C'mon, Vivian," he snapped as he turned and stormed back to the entrance tunnel.

Vivian wasted no time in following right on his heels, straining to hear what was being said in the chamber as they left.

"My apologies for that unpleasant interruption," she could hear Mr. Thornwood saying. "Now for the next order of business. It seems that Darkham Observatory has been purchased by a developer, which could adversely affect our access to the northern entrance. . . ."

Vivian took a deep breath and followed Drusen back into the tunnel. The sound cut out immediately and she felt the same sensations she had noticed when coming through the first time, as if her body was buzzing with some sort of otherworldly energy. Drusen's face was stiff, his jaw was clenched tight, as he pushed ahead in silence. He was walking so fast that Vivian needed to jog to keep up with him as he flew out the front door of the building.

"Wait," Vivian pleaded as it became clear to her that he was intent on following Mr. Thornwood's orders to not tell her anything. "Can we talk for a second!"

"No!" Drusen growled as he threw Vivian's bike onto his shoulder and began walking down Silver Springs Road. "Evidently, I am forbidden."

No, not when I'm so close to finding out the truth, she thought, shaking with frustration.

She chewed her lip as the pair walked in silence for several blocks into the still and frigid night. Unlike her roundabout journey to Silver Springs to avoid curfew attention, with Drusen here this time they stayed on the main roads.

As they passed an upscale antique shop, Vivian could no longer contain herself.

"This is ridiculous!" she blurted out. "I'm the one who was attacked! I've been on this wild goose chase now for weeks and I deserve some answers!" She stopped in the middle of the sidewalk and sighed. "Drusen, please. Please tell me what the heck is going on around here."

Drusen stopped and looked at Vivian for several moments.

"I agree," he said finally. "Follow me."

The Truth

DRUSEN AND VIVIAN walked in silence, each making misty breath in the black night air. At this hour, Broad Street was deserted, lit only by gas streetlamps, which created shadowy pools of light every so often. Finally, they reached a half-timbered storefront building that resembled an English cottage. A painted wooden sign depicting the head of a falcon and eagle facing each other hung over the door. It read PHOENIX & GRIFFON TAVERN.

"Phoenix and Griffon?" Vivian asked.

"I know the owner," said Drusen as he plopped Vivian's bike down next to a parking meter and disappeared through the door.

Vivian was getting used to Drusen's pattern of curt responses followed by hasty retreats and by now she understood the need to keep up. By the time she stepped into the cozy, firelit tavern, Drusen was already near the back of the room. As she rushed after him, he settled into the back corner table, nestled in shadow and shielded from the light of the great stone hearth.

When she finally sat down on the wooden bench across from him, she noticed that he had put his sunglasses back on, which seemed odd to her, given the dim candlelight of the restaurant. He sat stiffly with his hands folded on the table.

"Where to begin," he said to himself softly.

They sat quietly for several moments.

"How about at the beginning," Vivian replied lightly, doing what she could to break the awkward silence.

"Okay," he sighed deeply while cocking his head, as if to say *you asked for it.*

"Imagine that just about every bedtime-story fantasy creature you ever heard about— dragons, unicorns, trolls, and goblins—was real. That they weren't just made up and drawn from our mythology, but rather real creatures from our own history."

Vivian's arms began to tingle with goose bumps.

"But these creatures are not originally from our world; they are from another and have emerged over time through portals from this other world. Throughout history, when humans encountered these creatures, they would draw them or write about them, providing the basis for some of earth's most famous mythology."

"Oooh, like phoenixes and griffons, too," Vivian said, nodding and making the connection to the name of the tavern.

"Yes, Vivian, phoenixes and griffons, too," he replied. "But these portals have a much darker history. According to the scriptures, about five thousand years ago there were three brothers, triplets, born to a powerful elven king and demigod of this other world."

"Wait, I know this one," interrupted Vivian. "It's about the druid—Arbor-something—who wants to end humanity! We just encountered this in our Beasts and Battlements game!"

"Very good," said Drusen. "That's the story of Arborem and that was a real war in our world that went on for one hundred years—a long and bloody conflict—that pitted humans, dwarves, and elves against Arborem's unholy alliance of hobgoblins, canimen, vulturebears, and other monsters of the forest. Do you know how it ended?"

"No, we haven't gotten to that yet," said Vivian sheepishly, just now remembering why today's game had ended so abruptly.

"Over time, the armies of Urbanem, the city lord, began to overtake the scattered creatures, but it was then that Arborem discovered a great power in the High Forest of Greenmoor: the secret of the Founder's Tree. It gave him the ability to access and create portals to other worlds. And he set his sights on a young and fertile world with a large population of able human warriors, beasts, and abundant resources."

"Earth?" asked Vivian excitedly.

"Indeed," continued Drusen. "He sought to exploit the resources of this world in an effort to conquer his own. Soon, he was controlling massive armies made up of humans from this world and monsters from his own, leading to a level of bloodshed his world had never seen. The third brother, Aquanem, who had remained neutral up until this point, witnessed this abuse of power and joined Urbanem's side, using his control over the water and its creatures to aid the efforts of humanity. Now, with the very power of water on his side, the forces of Urbanem were able to defeat those of Arborem. And as for Arborem himself, the two brothers banished him to the lower planes—an, uh, unpleasant different dimension, one might say—never to return. But the portals—or gates as they are usually called—remained, all set at different locations around this world—in Europe, in Asia, in Africa, in South and Central America . . . and one in a cavern beneath a freshwater lake in North America."

"Midnight Lake!" Vivian blurted out.

Drusen nodded, seemingly pleased that Vivian was following along.

"After the war, Urbanem conscripted the finest wizards in the realms to try to destroy the gates but to no avail. Concerned for the welfare of this fledgling planet, and because the portals move on the other side, Urbanem recruited a force of some of his finest elven soldiers, rangers, clerics, and mages to take residence on earth as sentinels to protect it from the horrors that might emerge from the gates until the secret to their destruction could be found."

"The group that was meeting tonight at Silver Springs, these are the sentinels sent by the Urban guy?" Vivian asked.

Drusen laughed.

"Yes and no. That was five thousand years ago and even elves don't live that long. No, what you see today—what you saw at the former Real Gaming Limited headquarters—is the ancestral remnant of those sentinels that protect the Midnight Gate. They are now more than ten generations removed from the originals, having lived here all this time and kept the traditions, scriptures, and mission, but intermarried with humans over the years, making most of them today far more human than elf. These 'trace elves,' as they are called, have only a fraction of the skills of their ancestors—a bit of night vision here; enhanced coordination there; a strong connection to nature and magic—and usually live no more than a couple hundred years."

"You keep saying 'they'—aren't you one of these trace elves?" Vivian asked with a confused frown.

Drusen shifted uncomfortably in his seat, while a subtle, but unmistakably pained expression shone across his face. Even beneath his sunglasses, Vivian could tell he had turned his gaze elsewhere.

"I . . . I'm a bit different," he said sadly. "I have elven blood to be sure, but my ancestors were a different type of elf.

A subterranean-dwelling elf called the Drelve. In our home-world, Drelve are believed to be . . ." His voice drifted off and Vivian had the impression he wasn't sure how to continue.

"Yes?" Vivian's voice was encouraging.

Drusen took a deep and bothered breath.

"Believed to be ruthless killers," he said finally. "These people—my people—supposedly worship evil gods in their vast underground cities. In the surface world, Drelve are outcasts, just as my ancestor was. But Urbanem, for what-ever reason, trusted her and sent her with the sentinels to the Midnight Gate. She was never accepted among them and I suppose some things never change. Even today among the trace elves, I'm something of an outcast, but I have a very particular—a very useful—set of skills. A 'necessary evil' I've heard them say. . . ."

"I'm sorry," said Vivian, also averting her eyes. "I didn't mean to . . . I'm sorry."

"Don't be," he replied gruffly. "Whether they accept me or not, I take some satisfaction in knowing that SPECTOR needs me."

"SPECTOR?" Vivian asked.

"Ah yes. That's what we call ourselves. The Society for the Protection of Earth from Creatures Transplanar, Other-worldly, or Realm-born."

"Boy, that's a mouthful," Vivian replied, earning a sharp look from Drusen.

She cleared her throat and sunk low in her seat. "I mean, I like 'SPECTOR' better . . . it's a good name."

"The sentinels of SPECTOR will be here until we can solve the secret to closing the gate; then we can all return to our homeworld—the Great Realm."

There was silence at the table for a few moments as Vivian digested everything Drusen had just told her.

"Do you meet with the sentinels from the other gates?" she asked.

"We are the last. The other gates have since been closed. One by one, each society discovered the secret to their gate and closed it and then returned home. The Midnight Gate is the last."

Vivian felt as though she was pushing her luck, but if she was going to get to the bottom of this, she needed to dig for information like a reporter would. Like her father would if he was going after a great story.

"So, what's it like through the portal . . . in your world? In the 'Great Realm'?"

"I wouldn't know," Drusen said wistfully. "It is forbidden for sentinels to go through until our task is complete. I was born here as were the other sentinels—we've never seen our homeland and only know what's in our ancient texts. We are refugees of a sort and we all long to return. We're out of place here. That's probably why we all live up at the Sanctuary. It's mostly known as a resort today but was originally built by the society in the old ways of the elves to help us feel at home."

"I know what you mean," Vivian said quietly. "I mean about feeling out of place. Ever since my moth—Ever since we moved here, I've felt like I really don't belong."

Drusen met her eyes and opened his mouth to say something, but he stopped when a ding rang from his coat pocket. He pulled out his phone, eyed it for a moment, and slipped it back in his pocket.

"I need to go," he said sharply. "Let's get you home."

"Wait!" Vivian cried. "Just one more question—promise. How does this all connect to Beasts and Battlements? I mean, it's obviously not all a big coincidence."

"Aha. I almost forgot. That's how you tripped upon the portal in the first place. Garrison Arnold and B and B . . . ," he said, his voice trailing off as he looked around. "Let's talk more on the way."

Vivian followed Drusen out of the tavern and back out into the chilly, dark night. Drusen picked up her bicycle and heaved it over his shoulder, never glancing back to make sure Vivian was following, yet seeming to know she was there. He walked in silence for a block, Vivian practically jogging to keep up with him, before he spoke again.

"So, Garrison Perry Arnold was a local boy and an adventurous sort—a troublemaker really—he spent lots of time at the Outskirts—"

"You knew him?" Vivian asked.

"I did, a bit. As a young man, he used to visit the Outskirts and play games in the cave beneath the waterfall. He'd blow up boulders with dynamite—that's the kind of things bored people do in small towns."

"Boy, he must've been *really* bored to do that," cracked Vivian.

"One day while reading in the cave, he set the dynamite bag too close to the open flame. He got out of there just in time to avoid blowing himself up, but the blast still knocked him unconscious. When the dust settled, he realized that he had opened up a fissure in the back wall that connected to a vast system of underground tunnels."

"That's where I entered!" Vivian exclaimed.

"Yes. In those days we didn't know about that entrance. Garrison wandered into the tunnels all the way to the Midnight Gate and he went through. We don't know exactly what happened on the other side, but we know he almost died and would have if not for the help of a powerful wizard from that world—my world—named Merlyn the True, who took pity on him."

"Merlyn?" repeated Vivian. "That sounds familiar."

"Yes, I'll get to that. . . ." Drusen paused, hitching Vivian's bike up higher on his shoulder, and then continued. "When he returned, and upon several subsequent visits, he began cataloguing the monsters he had found and recording their characteristics and weaknesses as a practical reference book for defending the earth from these creatures, should its residents ever need to."

"The *Book of Beasts*," Vivian whispered as they rounded the corner onto her sleepy, neighborhood block.

"Sort of," replied Drusen. "When SPECTOR found out about what Arnold was up to, they threatened to . . . discipline him if he didn't stop his work. Garrison, who was already a passionate gamer, came up with a compromise."

"B and B!" Vivian blurted out excitedly.

"B and B," repeated Drusen. "We agreed to let him continue his work as long as it was always under the guise of the game. And his work went well beyond monsters. He developed maps, detailed descriptions of the places you'd find on the other side, and lore from our world like that of Arborem. He even made his own character for games he'd play in—the famous Merlyn the True, based on his friend from the other side. And as the game took off, he became a critical ally and friend of SPECTOR. He built his Real Gaming Limited Silver Springs headquarters next to one of the entrances and allowed the society to operate from there."

"Wow," Vivian said in amazement as they arrived at her driveway. Her head spun from all of this information. Everything she had ever learned told her this was impossible . . . but everything inside her told her it was true. It was all true.

"Now, Vivian, you must listen to me very carefully," Drusen said, pausing in her driveway. He turned to face her, his voice quiet and serious. "I've told you far more than I should have. These are dangerous times and you need to keep your head down. You are not to return to the caves; you are not to go snooping around the society; and you're not to tell *anyone* about this."

"But, what about—"

"Vivian," he interrupted sternly. "No one. Do you understand?"

"Okay, Drusen."

"Dru," he said more gently, with something resembling a smile. "You can call me Dru."

He turned and began to walk away.

"Dru!" she called after him.

He stopped but didn't turn around.

Vivian still had a million questions, but there was one she really needed the answer to.

"Why are you helping me?"

He went rigid.

"I . . . I knew your mother," he said somberly over his shoulder.

Vivian's breath caught in her throat.

"She was always kind to me," he added.

Before Vivian could say anything, he disappeared into the night with what she swore was a subtle green flash.

Vivian stood in her driveway in silence. This had been a lot to take in, but she felt an odd sense of relief mixed with uneasy excitement. She knew. She now knew what was going on—that was freeing to be sure, but the realities of the situation were not at all comforting. Monsters—real monsters— threatened their town and their livelihood. Even worse, there was nothing she could do and no one she could tell. In a strange way, she was more alone than ever.

In the dim light of the porch, she drew out of her backpack her copy of *Harry Potter and the Sorcerer's Stone* and added a new line to her comparison chart: "Safety." She thought for a moment. It's true she had SPECTOR, and Drusen, but Harry had magic. She'd have to give Harry the advantage here also, as she had done for everything else.

Her thoughts weighed heavily on her as she crept back into her lightless house, up the stairs, and into her room. When she entered and flipped the light, she gasped.

Sitting on her bed was her father, who looked both frazzled and fuming.

"Vivian," he said sternly. "We need to talk."

Study Monster

WILLIAM'S EYES GLEAMED excitedly as they always did when he ran a game of Beasts & Battlements.

"You walk down the narrow tunnel, which appears to be an old mythril mine—a rare and magical silver metal much prized in the Great Realm. Finally, the passage opens up on your left into what appears to be a mess hall with a bunch of venomors, which are like muscular humans with snake heads, sitting around tables eating and slurping rancid-looking food. They haven't noticed you yet. What do you do?"

It was the Wednesday before Thanksgiving and tonight was game night at William's house, just two streets over from Vivian's. They played in his wood-paneled basement around an old pool table. It was the first time she'd seen the misfits outside of school in nearly a month, as she had been grounded since her midnight journey to the old RGL headquarters— now SPECTOR International. Today her father had finally agreed to end her after-school and weekend imprisonment.

"Aw, 'ell," cursed Arturo in his best cockney. "I'll get me ol' axe ready."

"Snarfette hides in the shadows near the entrance with her dagger drawn, ready to poke ankles," declared Violet.

"Minions of evils, prepare to feel the wrath of Venna," proclaimed Mary before pretending to blow dust out of her hand. "I cast slumber."

"Okay, I'll resolve that in a second," replied William as he readied some dice. "Vivian, what are you going to do?"

After a month of being grounded, choice was not something Vivian had been very used to lately. Of course, she knew her punishment could've been way worse. When she had arrived home that night after her visit to SPECTOR, she felt certain that her father knew everything. It turned out that he thought she had been out secretly looking for Ms. Greenleaf—nothing more. She went along with that. Like the last time she was grounded, the time had been filled with lots of eighties movies at home, but her father seemed more concerned this time. With all that she had learned that fateful night, she had been absolutely bursting to get out again, to discover, to solve. Instead, she had been stuck at home, spending most nights in her reading nook continuing her study of the *Book of Beasts* alongside her reading of the third and fourth books of *Harry Potter*. It was good to be out again—and, it was good to see *them*.

"Vivian," repeated William. "What does Alissa do?"

"Time-out," declared Vivian while flipping open her notebook and preparing her pencil to take notes. "So, about these venomors. What do we know about them? I mean, do they have known weaknesses? What combat tactics do they usually employ?"

"What are you, some sort of Beasts and Battlements biologist all of a sudden?" cried Arturo. "You kill 'em!"

"Vivian, what is this all about?" Mary demanded. "All night, and even in our school games, you've been pausing the game and digging in the weeds on every monster we encounter. No offense, but it's kind of annoying."

"Is this more research for your Murkwood Garrison Arnold paper?" William asked.

Vivian hadn't realized she had been so obvious. For them this was a game, but for her this was important research that might someday prove to be the difference between life and death.

"Sorry, guys—you got me," Vivian lied as she closed her notebook. "Yep, I'm still digging into that Murkwood Sanitarium–Beasts and Battlements project—I'm really trying to get into Arnold's head. . . ."

"But Vivian, the project is postponed until Ms. Greenleaf—" Violet began, but then she stopped herself.

Silence overtook the room, as if the air had been sucked out of it. Everyone was well aware of the reality of their missing teacher, but no one liked to speak about it. The possibilities—probabilities really—were too disturbing.

"I should go," Vivian said, breaking the silence. "I'm still on probation at home and I don't want to push my luck."

"Oh, come on, Vivian!" exclaimed Mary. "It's your first time out and it's only been a couple of hours."

"Probation for what exactly?" asked Violet innocently. "You know, you never did tell us why you were grounded."

"Yeah, Vivian, time to spill," Mary added.

"Oh . . . uh, you know. School stuff," Vivian mumbled. "All those detentions."

She lowered her gaze to her backpack as she shoved in her B&B books and papers, but checked nervously out of the corner of her eye to see whether they would keep digging. Violet and Mary exchanged a look, and Mary subtly shrugged.

"Well, do come again," said William in his best spooky narrator voice. "The Tunnels of Torment will be waiting for you."

"Will do. Sorry, everyone," said Vivian as she threaded her arms through the backpack straps, which caught on her sleeve and pulled it back, revealing the still fresh scar on her forearm.

"Whoa, what happened to your arm?" blurted out Mary.

Vivian quickly pulled her sleeve back down.

"Oh, that?" squeaked Vivian. "It's nothing. Just fell off my bike a while back. See you later," she continued as she zipped out the door, certain that Mary and Violet were sharing another skeptical look.

It was nearing dusk and a frigid winter wind was whistling through the bright brown and yellow trees that were quickly losing their leaves. Even though the town had since lifted its curfew, Vivian moved at double time. Her father had set a curfew of his own for her tonight: "sundown."

As she dashed, her father's disappointed words from the night she was caught passed through her head: *"I can't believe you did that . . . this isn't a game. It's dangerous out there, Vivian."* Of course, he had no idea how right he was about the danger. But weirdly enough though, this *was* a bit of a game, or at least it had been turned into one by Garrison Arnold. In fact, one reason she was in such a rush now was that she wasn't going straight home. Instead, she was making a detour to the Catacombs Game Shop. All that time spent at home while grounded studying her existing books had brought her to the conclusion that she needed more information. She needed more B&B books.

As she reached the door, the cotton candy sunset over Midnight Lake told her she had just a few minutes left.

"Hello again, young one!" exclaimed Merle as she entered the shop. "Back for more, are you?"

"Yeah," Vivian said, giving him a quick smile. "I'm in a bit of a rush, but I was hoping to pick up some more B and B stuff."

"Aha!" bellowed Merle triumphantly as he patted the head of his droopy bloodhound, who was awake this time, but panting heavily. "You've caught the bug! New or old?"

"Some more Arnold stuff, if you have it," Vivian replied, trying to sound casual.

"Can do!" answered Merle as he headed into the back aisles of the shop.

"But I don't have a lot of money," she called after him, realizing she would need him to help her find the best materials within her very limited budget. "So I was hoping you could help me choose an inexpensive but really complete book. . . ."

"No worries!" Merle answered from somewhere deep in the store. "Your credit is fine."

Did he mean Mr. Braemor? Vivian thought. She couldn't keep taking advantage of his generosity.

Merle emerged from the back aisle with a stack of old and tattered B&B books.

"About my credit," said Vivian awkwardly. "These won't be from Mr. Braemor—"

"They're not," interrupted Merle. "They're from me. Just pay me what you can when you can."

"Wow!" blurted out Vivian. "I definitely will . . . and thank you so much!"

Vivian quickly shuffled through the old B&B books from the seventies and eighties, and noticed there seemed to be two different types. There were rulebooks, which included things like character options, combat rules, equipment lists, and spell descriptions—everything anyone would ever need to know to run or play in a game. Then there were the adventure module booklets, which were for gamemasters only and contained a general storyline along with maps, treasures, and villains that could be plugged into anyone's home game.

She stopped and stared for a moment when she came near the end of the module stack and landed on the *Fortress on the Frontier* adventure, which William had been using to guide the story and action for their game. Under normal circumstances, Vivian would have never even considered reading ahead and spoiling the adventure, but this potentially being a matter of life and death, she wanted to keep her options open, so she hastily shoved that and the other books into her bag.

Half doubled over, weighed down by the bag full of heavy books, Vivian lumbered home as fast as she was able. Even with the frosty air, she was sweating by the time she arrived on her porch, but she had made it!

She watched as the western sky abandoned its last traces of pink, giving way to the deep purples and turquoises of dusk. She exhaled deeply and entered the house for the night.

24

Thanksgiving

"WELL, WHAT DO you think?" asked Mr. Van Tassel as Vivian sipped her root beer.

"About what?" Vivian asked absently.

"About the food!" her dad sighed playfully. "Not bad, right? Certainly better than any Thanksgiving dinner I could've cooked at home."

Compensating for his lack of cooking skills and their less-than-functional kitchen, Mr. Van Tassel had taken Vivian to Meisterburger's, a Bavarian-themed Midnight Lake establishment known for its burgers, cheese curds, and homemade root beer.

"Oh, yeah. It was good, I guess," Vivian replied, trying not to glare at the ridiculous (and embarrassing) cardboard alpine hat her dad was wearing—Meisterburger's answer to the Burger King paper crown. Vivian felt lucky they didn't carry lederhosen shorts, socks, and suspenders or her dad would be wearing those, too.

"You guess?" repeated Mr. Van Tassel. "Vivian, you hardly talked all through dinner. What's going on with you?"

"Sorry," Vivian said. And she was. She knew her dad was trying. "Lots on my mind I guess."

"It's okay," her father replied. "I know there's a lot going on right now. Lots of worries around town. I'm sure they'll find . . . I'm sure everything will turn out okay . . . Vivy, you know you can talk to me about anything, right?"

"Yeah, I know. . . ." Vivian nodded, but then realized her dad was going to keep digging—he *was* a reporter after all. She decided a change of subject was needed fast. "So, what's going on at the paper?"

Mr. Van Tassel raised his eyebrows and chuckled softly to himself.

"Lots," he said. "I thought joining a small-town paper would be pretty low-key, but the pressure has been crazy high. Mr. Bellowman seems to think it's our job to solve all the mysteries of this town, and there happens to be a lot of those right now."

"The disappearance?" Vivian asked, not wanting to make it more real by using Ms. Greenleaf's name.

Mr. Van Tassel nodded as he took a swig of his root beer. "*And* the animal attacks. We've stopped running many of the stories as we don't want to cause a panic, but there are reports of attacks around the lake every couple days now—they seem like they're all around us. Meanwhile, the fish keep turning up dead along the shore in droves. It'll actually be nice when the lake freezes. . . ." Mr. Van Tassel's voice wandered off as he drummed his fingers on the table. "C'mon, let's get out of here. Unless you want dessert?"

"Nope, I'm stuffed," Vivian responded, springing up from her seat and grabbing her coat. "The food really was pretty good, though," she added, earning a satisfied grin from her father.

It was early afternoon when they began the walk home, crossing over the Williams Wetland Preserve bridge that sat adjacent to the outflowing Green River. The wetland wasn't flooded this time of year, but what was there today was far more worrisome. The woodsy park was chock-full of soldiers—real, medieval-type soldiers—donning armor, swords, battle-axes, flails, and dozens of other pieces of weaponry and equipment that Vivian had learned to identify since playing Beasts & Battlements. There were two distinct legions on opposite sides of the preserve, one in red and one in blue, facing each other nervously.

Vivian froze in place. Someone blew a horn from inside the park.

She watched in horror just as the two sides began charging at each other. It had begun!

One or both armies must have bubbled up from the portal and they were now out in the open! She only hoped that one of them was allied with earth and the sentinels of SPECTOR.

Vivian instinctively positioned herself in front of her father.

"Run," she shouted to her father as the first clank of steel reverberated through the greenway.

Mr. Van Tassel just stood there dumbly.

"Run!" she screamed. "Don't you see them! I don't have time to explain right now, but we're in great danger!"

The clink of swords and cries of battle were now in full force amid the sea of heavily armored soldiers. What was most distressing though is that she couldn't seem to make out the good from the bad within the fray. Regardless, this wasn't a place to be without a weapon in your hand.

"Vivian," said Mr. Van Tassel comfortingly as he grabbed her shoulders. "It's okay."

"Okay?" she asked hysterically as she shrugged off his hands. "Okay?! At least one of those armies wants to kill us and you're saying it's okay? Run! I'll explain at home!"

"Vivian!" Her dad's voice sounded both concerned and confused. "I don't know what kind of game you're playing or if Beasts and Battlements has gotten to your head, but everything is fine—look!"

Mr. Van Tassel pointed to a sandwich board sign someone had erected near the park entrance.

10TH ANNUAL TURKEY DAY LARP

"It's a LARP, Vivy, please settle down!"

"A LARP?" she repeated slowly.

"Live action role-playing—a LARP," her dad explained, his tone gentle. "They're just pretending—it's like a Civil War reenactment, or more like a live-action game of B and B. See?"

Vivian squeezed her eyes shut and opened them again, willing herself to calm down. Now that she looked more closely, and not through panicked eyes, she could see that the weapons did appear to have padding on them; some of the battle cries were actually arguments between opponents over who hit who and where.

"You can't cast mana missile unless you're holding up the scroll!" yelled a fully armored knight to a wizardy-looking opponent.

"I was holding up the scroll, dufus," shot back the wizard. "And I got the spell off before you hit me, which got my armor anyway!"

"You're a mage—you can't wear armor," countered the knight.

"Ref!" they both yelled in unison.

This was make-believe combat. Vivian felt her cheeks flush, mortified by how she had reacted.

"It's okay, girly," her dad said. "It does look real. And I think we're all struggling with a lot right now. Let's go home and we'll have some tea and settle down."

The pair walked home in silence amid cartoonish turkey decorations that adorned the downtown. It was awkward for both of them. Vivian was embarrassed and Mr. Van Tassel didn't seem to know what to say.

If only I could tell him why I reacted the way I did, Vivian thought.

When they arrived home, they slowly made their way into the kitchen where Mr. Van Tassel put a teakettle on the stove—one of the few implements that did work in the ancient kitchen.

"Let me just run into my office and check my messages," he said as he slipped out of the room.

Vivian just sat on a stool rubbing her still-icy hands to her face.

"Get a grip, Vivy," she whispered to herself.

Was she losing it? Had all of the events of the past couple of months been too much for her?

No, she thought as she rolled up her sleeve and looked down at the scar on her arm from the caniman attack. She wasn't overreacting. She wasn't sure one even could overreact to the kinds of things she had learned and seen.

A few minutes passed before Mr. Van Tassel rushed back into the room, visibly agitated.

"What is it, Dad?" asked Vivian.

"I'm so sorry, Vivy," said Mr. Van Tassel as the teakettle began to whistle. "I've got to go. I just got a message from my editor—Mayor Greenbriar has gone missing."

25

Darkham Observatory

VIVIAN WATCHED OUT the bus window as thick trees gave way to stubbled, brown cornfields and then back again along meandering lakefront roads. A light snow had begun to fall from the pale November sky.

"Next stop, Lakewood College at Harmon Bay," blared the voice of the bus driver over the PA system.

Vivian looked at the map on her phone. She was close.

The bus turned down a winding wooded road that opened up to a rustic complex of small dormitories and lecture halls set into the steep hillside.

"This stop, Lakewood College, Harmon Bay," called the voice again as a half dozen college-aged students stood to exit the bus. "Next stop, the Sanctuary Resort."

"Well, this is it," whispered Vivian to herself as she slung her father's guitar bag over her shoulder and followed the stream of older students toward the exit.

She noticed the bus driver do a double take at her as

he pulled shut the door handle, probably wondering if this young girl with the guitar case could possibly be a college student. Vivian smiled to herself at the thought as the bus pulled away. She was left in a cloud of dust in front of a lodge-style student union.

It was the Friday after Thanksgiving and Vivian had the day off from school. Less than twenty-four hours had passed since they had gotten word that Midnight Lake's mayor had mysteriously disappeared. Her father had been out most of the waking hours since then, but he did check in briefly (and apologetically) late on Thursday night to get a quick bite and a short sleep before returning to the paper first thing this morning. Of course, Vivian knew that the disappearance was far more serious than anyone at the paper understood. Mr. Greenbriar was not only the mayor, but also one of the highest-ranking members of the secret trace-elf society known as SPECTOR. Vivian knew that this couldn't be a coincidence and it meant that something was up.

Vivian pulled out her phone to check her map, but the loading icon was spinning continuously, and no bars were showing in the corner. She had no service here.

She looked up and scanned the area trying to get her bearings. She found something better—a campus map sign right next to the union.

Even though she had just emerged from being grounded and was still on "probation"—and even though her father had explicitly told her to not leave the house today—Vivian had decided she couldn't wait any longer to see the caretaker at Darkham Observatory, who had claimed that he knew how to get the attacks to stop. Whether this was true or not, he clearly knew something, and Vivian knew that there was no time to waste. That was why she had used the pizza money her father had left her and taken the local bus to Lakewood College.

As she studied the color-coded campus map, she set the bag down for a few moments to give her shoulder a break. Inside it was her sheathed fencing saber, a ski mask, and a flashlight . . . nothing that heavy, but the single cross strap was awkward and irritated her neck and shoulder.

According to the map, there was a trail that led from the small college campus right to the observatory, which was on the next lakefront parcel over. Realizing that being out by herself wandering around was bound to draw questions, she got off the main drive and jogged to the wooded trail where she was not as likely to be spotted by passersby.

Before long, she arrived at a chained-off road that led to a huge clearing. Located at the end of the long, tree-lined driveway was Darkham Observatory, which looked much more like a castle than a science facility. Each end of the hulking structure hosted a retractable observatory dome, the largest of which was so big it looked like it could hold a full-size basketball court inside.

As she neared the front entrance, she couldn't help but

marvel at the building's ornamentation. Large stone grif-fons sat atop ornately carved pillars, while now crumbling arched cornices and pediments featured stars, globes, and strange creatures of mythology. The place had the aura of a once great medieval castle that had since fallen into dis-repair. Out front, a sign read CLOSED. NO TRESPASSING, while another promised a ONE-OF-A-KIND DEVELOPMENT OPPORTUNITY with a SOLD sticker slapped crookedly across the bottom.

As Vivian scanned the impressive-looking building, her heart leaped. Among the dragons, griffons, and phoenixes, she noticed some more peculiar creatures hidden in the stone-carved foliage: the bear seemed to have a hooked beak; the wolf had subtle tentacles emerging from its back; a large, horned sphere with a mouth and many eyes peered out through carved stone vines and branches. These were vulturebears, worm wolves, and leer spheres—which was more than enough to prove to Vivian that whoever built this structure knew about the portal and the creatures that came out of it. There was no way *this* was a coincidence.

The entrance plaza of the building lacked any of the cover that she'd had on her way there, so when the trees ran out, she darted across the large circular drive and to the covered entranceway, limiting her exposure to any potential onlookers as best she could. With all that had happened, she knew she needed to keep a low profile. When she reached the door and turned the handle, she was shocked to find that it was unlocked.

The interior of the building was as elegant, if not more so, than its exterior. In the grand entrance rotunda, a mosaic tile floor gleamed from the light coming through the vibrant stained glass dome overhead. Both the floor and dome depicted the same glowing doorway—it was the portal, the Midnight Gate. Long, dark passages led off in three directions, lit only by occasional rays of exterior light that seeped out from beneath office doors. A directory sign suggested that the administrative offices and large observation dome were one direction, and the smaller domes were the other.

Vivian remembered that her father had met the caretaker in the director's office, so she figured the administrative offices were the right path. She padded lightly down the hallway, each step seeming to squeak and echo through the vast, empty building. Framed black-and-white photographs hung on both sides of the lavishly trimmed walls. One showed a huge group of serious-looking scientists standing on the building's front steps with a ribbon across the door on what must have been the facility's opening; another featured a face that Vivian knew the moment she saw it. Albert Einstein proudly posing in front of the facility with a group of annoyed-looking scientists, who perhaps didn't have the time or patience for grandstanding.

It wasn't long before she reached a prominent office in the middle of the hallway that read OFFICE OF THE DIRECTOR on the door. She could see a light was on inside through the cracked, frosted-glass window on the door's upper panel. She knocked lightly and waited. Nothing.

"Hello?" she called through the door, trying to keep her voice directed toward the office so to not create an echo in the hallway. "Is anyone there? I'm looking for the caretaker."

There was no sound or movement inside. Vivian tried the handle—this door was also unlocked. Vivian slowly inched the creaking door open. Inside, the office was so cluttered it looked like there had been some type of ruckus here; maybe it was hasty packing and retreat, or maybe it was a scuffle or something worse. Even the banker's light that sat on the desk had been left on. Books covered the floors while papers and schematics were strewn about the desk, surrounded by globes, planetary models, strange rocks, and model spaceships.

The hair on Vivian's arms and neck prickled. It was like being the first to arrive at the scene of a crime. She spent several minutes silently inspecting the dilapidated space without touching a thing. Nothing stood out.

Finally, she moved to the desk and nudged the mouse, causing the hulking computer to flare to life. As the screen began to glow beneath a poorly affixed webcam, she recognized the familiar homepage of YouTube. Unfortunately, the user, bbarkov@darkhamobservatory.com, was signed out. No other windows were open. There were, of course, a million reasons why one might come to YouTube, but Vivian figured that if she could see what he had been watching or posting, it might prove a worthwhile clue.

She typed "Darkham" into the password field and hit enter. The computer spat back "Incorrect Password." Then she tried "Password," having heard that it was one of the most popular passwords in the world, used largely by people who had no business being on the web in the first place. Unfortunately, this was also a no-go—she knew she probably had only one more chance before she'd get locked out. She plopped down on the leather swivel chair and rubbed her chin as she thought. Her eyes scanned the chaotic desk scene, but the schematic of a glowing portal was the thing that caught her eye most. It was labeled "Midnight Gate."

Vivian's eyes narrowed; her heart fluttered as it came to her. She didn't quite know how she knew this was the password, but she was suddenly quite sure that it was.

Vivian excitedly returned to the keyboard and entered "midnightgate." Voila!

A video window appeared in the asset library, which featured the frozen image of an old, pasty-looking man with frazzled white hair and saucerlike eyes, magnified through thick, Coke-bottle glasses. He wore a suit and paisley tie that looked like it came from the 1970s. The video, according to the dashboard, was unpublished. Vivian clicked play.

"My name is Dr. Boris Barkov and if you're watching this,

then I am probably dead," he said dramatically in a thick, Eastern European accent.

Whoa, Vivian thought. *Jackpot.*

The man cleared his throat and continued, "I was once a scientist at Darkham Observatory on Midnight Lake in Wisconsin, the last in a team assigned by the US government to observe, study, and ultimately harness the power of a mysterious portal that rests in caves deep below the lake. However, the project was disbanded nearly fifty years ago, its records burned, and all of its personnel have died, usually under mysterious circumstances. I left and went into hiding for many years, but returned under a false name and took the position of caretaker of this facility since that time. My goal was to finish the important work that we started all of those years ago. After all my study, I have concluded that the portal beneath the lake is in fact an interdimensional gate, powered by an unknown source not of this world. It cannot be controlled, and its power cannot be harnessed, at least using our known technologies. The portal is also very dangerous, for what emerges is . . . is the stuff of nightmares. Monsters that do not belong here and pose a great danger to those they encounter."

Vivian gripped the chair's armrests.

"Fortunately, for many years, only an occasional creature would emerge, with small spikes of activity every now and again—like that in the summer of 1891 when, we suspect, there was substantial portal activity, unleashing a large group of lizard men who infested the lake and sunk the *Lucius Sunberry*. But these incidents were mostly small and isolated, usually taken care of by a secretive, local hunting group. But over the last few months, there has been more portal activity than in the last century combined and the rate has accelerated every week. And it is not just the monsters that are the problem. With every entrance, the portal releases an energy byproduct, something similar to what we know as radiation. This byproduct surges into the water above and represents a great danger to the lake, its fish and wildlife. In the past, the activity was so low that it rarely ever made a discernible impact, but I suspect the current levels of activity are causing the mass fish deaths—like they did in 1891. If the rate of activity continues to increase, not just the town, but perhaps even the world will be overrun by these creatures, while the town is turned into a biohazard."

The wild-eyed man looked up from the webcam as the sound of heavy footsteps could be faintly heard storming down the hallway in the background. He shuddered and pressed in close to the camera, now talking in a whisper, "There isn't much time! The only option is to destroy the portal and I believe I know how."

Vivian involuntarily leaned toward the screen, now hanging on the man's every word.

"A targeted nuclear blast would provide the appropriate energy to collapse the portal's powerful electromagnetic field.

You must contact the US government, have them evacuate the town and arrange for a nuclear explosive to be built and set near the portal to my exact specifications," he ranted as he held up a schematic—one that was still on the desk.

The background footsteps in the video grew louder and the sound of yelling and perhaps even growling could now be heard.

The man's eyes rose again and then back to the webcam, his face now quivering and closer than ever.

"Good luck, whoever you are. You're our only hope," he said with quiet intensity as his eyes shot up at the sound of an opening door and the video ended.

The Caverns

VIVIAN SAT WIDE-EYED and speechless for several moments after watching the video. Her stomach twisted in knots as she slowly processed everything the man had said. A targeted nuclear blast? If this was Dr. Barkov's solution to making the attacks stop, then thanks for nothing, Vivian thought. How in the world could she arrange for a nuclear blast to go off deep in an underground cave in little Midnight Lake, Wisconsin? Was she to write the US government, "Dear Mr. President, Please send armed forces immediately to Midnight Lake to help us stop an invasion of interdimensional monsters."?

Just then, Vivian heard voices and faint footsteps down the hall. She quickly rolled up as many graphs and schematics as she could and shoved them into her guitar bag, then tiptoed to the door and peered around the corner. She could now hear the voices more clearly and she caught a glimpse of movement at the end of the hallway. As she gazed down the corridor, she noticed a pair of broken glasses on the floor—the Coke-bottle glasses of Dr. Barkov, Vivian was certain. He had been taken that way.

Taking a deep breath, Vivian crept out of the office and down the hallway toward the large dome. By the time she reached the stairway, the shadowy figures had just disappeared around the corner. She padded up the stairs, two at a time until she reached the top. Here, there was virtually no light except small amounts that crept in through cracks and seams in the massive retractable-dome ceiling. Nonetheless, Vivian could make out a giant cylindrical instrument in the room's center— the telescope—as well as bench seats that circled the perimeter, broken up by occasional exits to the exterior balcony.

There was no sign of the mysterious figures, but the noisy clang of boots upon iron steps reverberated throughout the cold, dark space. Vivian quickly realized that she was standing right near a wrought-iron spiral stairwell that led straight down through the wooden platform floor and into the depths of the dome building.

Vivian shuddered as she looked down into the blackness. She knew she was going to have to be as quiet as a mouse going down these stairs. She waited until the racket of boots descending the stairs finally ceased. She tightened the guitar bag strap across her torso and grabbed the narrow railings on both sides, using her arms to lower herself down on each step to reduce the noise. It worked pretty well—even she could barely hear her own steps above the sound of her breath and the blood pumping in her ears. She descended down, and down, and down, into a cool, lightless void. She went slowly and after some time felt certain that she had descended far deeper than the building's ground floor. By the time she reached solid ground at the bottom, her arms ached from using them so much to lower herself, and the figures she had pursued seemed to be long gone. Only a dimly lit entryway was visible across the otherwise pitch-black room.

She crept toward the doorway, noticing the floor here felt like rough stone and gravel. When she arrived, she again could hear noise, but this time it was something far more terrifying than deep voices and clanging boots. What she heard was a mixture of growls, roars, slithers, and snorts coming from all directions. They were coming from inside cells that lined the walls of the tunnel, Vivian realized.

What monsters were inside? And could they get out?

Now nearly frozen with fear, Vivian knew she had come too far but that quitting was not an option. She had never been this terrified, and she knew she couldn't afford to make any mistakes.

"C'mon, Vivy, breathe," she whispered to herself.

She exhaled and pulled her saber out of her bag. Something about having the familiar feel of steel in her hand calmed her nerves just a bit. Then she secured the scabbard around her waist and withdrew the ski mask and pulled it down over her face. Midnight Lake was a small town and she couldn't afford to be recognized by would-be enemies. She placed the bag next to the door, planning to retrieve it on the way out, and slipped into the hallway.

Vivian dared not look into any of the cells as she silently crept along the opposite wall, and before long, the smell of sulfur met her nostrils—the same terrible odor she had experienced during her visit to the caves at the Outskirts. This must be another entrance to the portal beneath the lake, she reasoned.

She darted from shadow to shadow, crevice to crevice, trying to ignore the hideous sounds emerging from each cell. Some cell doors were battered and bowed from impact from the inside; the locks and handles on some rattled forcefully. Then, out of her periphery, she saw a green tentacle wrapped around one cell's window bars. She returned her eyes to the ground, kept crouched and moving.

What are you doing, Vivian? she thought to herself. *Even Harry never did anything this reckless . . . and he had magic!*

After passing what seemed like dozens of cells, she made out a large opening with a brighter light at the end of the hallway, which ended at an intersection. Considering that it was probably only a matter of time before someone patrolled the corridor, Vivian quickened her pace until she heard those deep voices again, coming from what appeared to be a guard station that was situated in a carved-out area of the stone hallway. Inside, she could make out two people playing darts (or using a dartboard for a game of daggers, actually), speaking in some dialect of choppy English. To hear what they were saying she'd need to get closer, and fortunately there was a deep wall crevice right outside the station, but she'd need to make a dash for it in the open to get there.

She waited tensely for her moment, and it came when a stray dagger went clanking to the ground. She darted for the crevice and made it safely, but not before her scabbard scraped against the wall, making one guard turn toward the hall. When he did, Vivian gasped. His face was that of a grimacing pig, with a distorted snoutlike nose and great fangs that protruded from his top and bottom lips. The hair on his head and face was patchy; his ears pointed and uneven. These were not men at all, she realized. They were hobgoblins!

Vivian pressed herself into the tight, dark corner. She held her breath, waiting for the hobgoblins to descend upon her.

"Hey Orik, did you 'ear sumpfin'?" asked the larger, thicker, and more brutish-looking guard.

"Yeah," replied Orik, the smaller of the two. "The same fing I 'ear every moment in dis place, Grif—beasts!"

"No, this was sumpfin' different," continued Grif, the first hobgoblin.

"Nah!" exclaimed Orik. "Jus' your mind playin' tricks on ya. It 'appens down 'ere in 'dis cursed dungeon. I jus' can't wait for the master to give us the ol' go-ahead."

Vivian let out the breath she'd been holding. They didn't seem to know she was there. Even still, she stayed pressed deep into the crevice.

"Th' go-ahead?" asked Grif with a confused scowl.

"Yeah, to release the monsters. He can control 'em, ya know, and he's usin' the gate to build an army of 'em to take over the town. These are our soldiers—don't you ever listen? From there, we drain the lake, dig up the portal, then we'll have a free flow o' reinforcements and nuffin' will be able to stop us!"

"Great! I can't wait to see the look on those hoity-toity human faces as we roll in with a horde a' monsters. When do we start?" replied Grif.

"Soon, I think," said Orik impatiently. "No one knows for sure."

"Well, the sooner the better. I'm getting' tired of bein' holed up here eatin' rations—I need sum fresh meat," said Grif bitterly.

"Speakin' of, did you give the professor his slop for the day?" asked Orik.

Professor? Vivian's ears perked up at that. She dared to lift her head up out of the shadows ever so slightly, straining to make sure she didn't miss a word or a gesture.

"Nah. He was moved this mornin'," said Grif, and he tossed a bull's-eye with his rusty dagger.

"Where?" asked Orik.

"An' you say I never listen!" jabbed Grif with a chuckle.

"To the cells at Master's fortress—One Roman Street. They took 'im through the caves—the map's there," he continued as he gestured to the table.

Vivian could just make out the curled edges of a piece of parchment that rested on the table. If that was a map of the tunnels, then she needed it.

Suddenly a huge roar reverberated throughout the hall.

"Aw 'ell," groaned Orik. "It's the Taloned Terror again . . . Grif, go check on 'im. . . ."

The brawny Grif grabbed a rusty battle-axe off the table and the key ring hanging on the wall and lumbered down the curving hallway and soon out of sight. Orik, the remaining guard, looked around the corner to make sure his companion had left and then returned to the guard station and began riffling through one of the bags.

"I know he's got sumpfin' in 'ere," he muttered as he hastily dug through. "Aha!"

He pulled out what appeared to be a dead rodent and bit into it greedily.

Vivian almost gagged at the sight, but she also knew that it was now or never. As Orik was distracted, she slipped out of the dark crevice and silently crept to the table, staying low and obscured by its chairs. Vivian slowly looped her arm above the tabletop and felt the crinkle of parchment beneath her hand. She grabbed the edge and slowly pulled the paper off the table toward her.

Clank!

Orik turned and stood, catching Vivian cleanly in his sight, her hand still holding the edge of the parchment on the table. A small dagger had been left on the paper, which had fallen to the floor.

"What's this?" he said as he pulled out a rusty, curved dagger and began to slink over. "Looks like dinner."

Vivian's eyes widened, reflecting the glint of the dagger.

"No, thanks," she squeaked as she grabbed the map and ran.

"Hey Grif, we've got a live one 'ere!" he yelled as he rang a wall-mounted bell and galloped after Vivian.

The bell seemed to agitate whatever was in the cells, as the growling, gurgling, and hissing grew to a fever pitch. Vivian darted full speed down the hall from which she had come, not at all worrying this time about stealth, but Orik was surprisingly fast for such a misshapen creature and kept pace with her, only a few steps behind.

Heavy, iron-clad footsteps reverberated throughout the hallways seemingly in all directions, but still only Orik was in view. Vivian reached the stairwell door in virtually no time and beelined through the unlit room below the dome to the spiral staircase, abandoning her guitar bag that she had left by the entrance.

Vivian thought she had gained a step over the last stretch and made the mistake of pocketing the map and looking behind her. She tripped on the opening steps of the narrow staircase, almost fumbling away her saber. Orik was upon her instantly, followed by three new shadows that appeared in the doorway.

As Vivian scrambled to regain her footing, Orik made a heavy swipe with his dagger, just missing Vivian's face and clanking into the wrought-iron filigree, where it stuck. Vivian gave Orik a mule kick to the chest, which knocked the wind out of him, but her foot caught on his rusty, engraved breastplate, pulling her down a step as he fell.

As she sprung up, new stubby hobgoblin hands emerged from the dark openings in the staircase and grabbed Vivian around her left ankle, while a bald, portly hobgoblin began lurching up after her.

"Give up, little 'un," he said in a low, gravelly tone. "It's over."

Vivian thrusted her saber down into the hand around her ankle. She felt the hand let go just as the creature attached to it let out a blood-curdling howl. The hobgoblin on the stairs tried to cleave the very same ankle, now at his eye level, with his sickle, but Vivian's sword was low and in a perfect position to parry.

She deflected the swipe and used an upward circular movement to flare out his arm and expose his torso, where she then skewered him through the shoulder. The hobgoblin hissed loudly as he tumbled backward on the stairs, knocking over Orik, who had reemerged and was right behind.

Even she was surprised as to what she had just accomplished, but this was no time to look back and admire her work. She flew up the stairs, taking two at a time with precision and speed. She could tell by the clanging ruckus below that she was quickly gaining ground on the hobgoblins, who were too large to take these stairs quickly.

By the time she reached the top and emerged back onto the wooden platform of the telescope dome, her legs and lungs burned with exhaustion. But her attackers were still coming, so she sheathed her sword and pushed on down the marble stairs that led up to the large dome and back to the hallway where Dr. Barkov's office was. Much to her dismay, she could hear loud voices and footsteps emerging from the other end of the hall toward the entrance, marching in her direction. She frantically slipped into the nearest office and waited right inside the door, trying to control the volume of her heaving breath. The footsteps got closer and closer until they passed by the room she was in and charged up the stairs.

Vivian sighed in relief, but her exhalation wasn't the only breathing she could hear. Deep rattling breaths filled the space. She turned and shrieked.

She was face-to-face with a spiked, floating sphere the size of a beach ball, covered in eyes, which were, for the moment, closed tightly. But what really caught Vivian's attention was its mouth full of razor-sharp teeth. She knew immediately what it was: a real-life leer sphere . . . and her shriek had just woken it up!

The largest eye shot open, followed by the smaller ones. With its lids open, the hideous creature was somehow even more terrible.

Vivian backed out of the door, tripping over the threshold as the leer sphere snapped its massive jaws, just missing her head. Its eyes stared at her hungrily as it advanced. Vivian froze, not sure how she was going to get out of this, but then she heard a squeaking sound from the doorframe—it was too wide to fit through! As the creature struggled to wriggle out, Vivian didn't wait around to see what would happen. She pulled herself to her feet and shot down the hallway.

She paused for a moment near the entrance. All was quiet, but she didn't make the mistake of looking back this time. She ran, and ran, and ran, through the entranceway, out the building, across the fields, and back on the wooded path to Lakewood College. The entire time she was half convinced that her enemies were right behind her, but that only made her run faster. She ran so fast and frantic she didn't even notice how heavily it was now snowing. When she finally did turn around, there was nothing behind her and only her footsteps could be seen in the heavy snow cover. She doubled over, panting and practically numb with exhaustion. Even with her eyes closed, all she could see was the terrible eyes of the leer sphere as she shivered.

As her breath slowed, she realized she was wearing her saber in broad daylight. Her eyes hurriedly searched the area for a hiding spot, but she found something better: a trash can. She rushed over to the receptacle and quickly extracted the heavy-duty plastic bag inside, which contained only a few empty cans. She stuck the sword inside and wrapped it taut in the bag. She sighed in relief as her blood again slowed, and shuffled back to the Lakewood College bus stop.

It was only a few minutes before the bus arrived.

I've never been so happy to get on a bus, she thought as she boarded. She settled into the first open seat and told herself she was safe.

"Next stop, the Sanctuary Resort," blared the bus driver's voice over the PA system.

The Sanctuary, Vivian thought. *I can find help there . . . I hope.*

27

The Sanctuary

AS THE BUS pulled up to the Sanctuary Resort, Vivian began to understand what Drusen had said about it. The lodge did not seem to be something of this world and rather looked like a dwelling right out of an elven city from *Lord of the Rings*. Huge fountain-filled gardens surrounded pointy, high-roofed structures that looked like crosses between Swiss chalets and Polynesian long houses. It was certainly one of a kind.

"This stop, the Sanctuary Resort," the bus driver announced.

Vivian bundled up the awkwardly large garbage bag she had lifted from the Lakewood College receptacle that now concealed her saber and mask. For the second time today, the bus driver threw curious, if not suspicious, eyes at her as she exited. This time, Vivian didn't care. She had much more urgent matters to worry about.

The snow had picked up as the temperature dropped, so Vivian wasted no time in entering the lobby.

"Excuse me," asked Vivian to a young, kind-faced woman behind the reception desk. "I'm looking for a resident here. Drusen."

"Drusen?" the woman repeated. She looked confused.

"Uh, or maybe Dru. I don't remember his last name, but he's a resident here," Vivian continued.

"Vivian?" called a familiar, gravelly voice. "What are you doing here?"

Vivian turned and found the sentinel standing menacingly behind her. Vivian thought he looked even more haggard than usual.

"Dru, we need to talk," said Vivian quietly as she led him to an unoccupied corner of the lobby.

"I thought I told you to stay out of this and keep your head down," Drusen replied. "I thought we had an understanding." He looked upset, but also genuinely concerned. Vivian suppressed a pang of regret and forged ahead.

"I'm sorry, Dru," she said, hoping her apology would be enough to make him listen. "I had to. I have information you must know . . . It's an emergency."

Drusen gave her a sharp look and then sighed.

"Follow me," he said curtly as he walked to a stairway in the back of the lobby.

He threw on his sunglasses and led her outside along a frozen marina-front walkway and then up to a path that meandered through a series of cottages that dotted the hilly back edge of the wooded campus. Each elegant A-frame villa had large windows and colorful crests centered above each door, similar to those she saw on the walls at SPECTOR headquarters.

Just as he had the last time she saw him, Drusen walked quickly, never looking back to make sure Vivian was following, but he somehow knew she was. They passed house after house and didn't stop until they came to a nondescript concrete stairway that led straight down into the hill itself. A sign next to its windowless steel door read UTILITY HOUSE.

Drusen zipped down the stairs and whispered something Vivian didn't catch, but whatever it was, it didn't sound like a word she recognized. She could hear multiple heavy-sounding locking mechanisms click and clank, and then the door opened. Drusen finally turned briefly and gestured for Vivian to follow. Then he slipped into the darkness while removing his sunglasses. Vivian rushed to keep up with him.

The space was dimly lit by unseen green light sources, which illuminated cold stone walls and two stalactite pillars that anchored the center of the large, open room. A small kitchenette with a table and single chair occupied one corner, and a simple bed and wardrobe occupied the other, next to a door that she guessed was the bathroom. Next to the bed hung a collection of swords, daggers, and small cannisters each labeled "Flash Bang Stun Grenade." In another small nook hewn into the rock was a simple wooden desk that held a laptop computer in front of a tall bookcase overflowing with antique, leather-bound books.

"Um, where are we?" Vivian asked.

"I'm sorry," Drusen muttered. "I'm not used to guests."

"It's okay," Vivian said awkwardly as she realized this was his home. "It's . . . homey."

"More like 'home-like.' This is what Drelve dwellings are like in my homeworld," he replied wistfully. "The underground is comfortable . . . at least for me."

"I like the green lighting," she remarked. "Where does it come from?"

"It's called fey fire," he said. "A Drelve enchantment from the world of my ancestors."

"Hmm. And that's quite a collection of weapons," she said nervously, unable to tear her eyes away from the wall full of blades and modern weaponry. "But I would've expected bows and arrows instead of any new stuff."

"When it comes to combat, the other trace elves follow the old ways—they use only weapons and technologies from our homeworld: swords, shields, bows and such. I follow my way. That means being prepared and practical . . . But anyway, I'm sure this is not what you came to talk about."

"Oh, right," Vivian said, nodding as she pulled the map from her pocket and unfolded it. "I just came from Darkham Observatory, and I think we're in trouble."

Drusen frowned and opened his mouth to respond, but then stopped himself and gestured for her to sit at the table.

"Would you like something to drink?" he said awkwardly as he walked to the mini refrigerator and opened it, which, Vivian noticed, was full of bright-green cans of Mountain Dew soda. Vivian wondered whether he had ever had guests here before.

"Sure," said Vivian. "Looks like you like Mountain Dew—I'll have one of those."

"Oh, those," said Drusen, embarrassed. "Yeah, it's quite similar to what people in the Great Realm call—never mind. Yes, I like them."

He plopped the can in front of Vivian on the table and rested against the kitchenette counter, his arms crossed.

"Well?"

Vivian cracked open the can of soda and took a long drink, which she found especially refreshing after all that she had been through. She took a deep breath and told Drusen everything: Dr. Barkov's YouTube video; the monster holding cells beneath the observatory; the hobgoblin guards, and, most important, the plan they had mentioned.

Drusen didn't say a word during Vivian's entire retelling. When she was finished, he stood for many more moments in silence rubbing his chin and studying the elaborate, hand-drawn map, which showed the entire cavern and tunnel system with labels next to each entrance. Finally, he spoke, his voice almost a whisper.

"The 'master' they mentioned. Did they say anything else about him? Try to remember, it's important."

"No," replied Vivian. "Only what I told you. He evidently has a fortress at 'One Roman Street' but it's hard to figure out where that is because it's a tunnel map and not one of the surface."

"Roman Street?" Drusen repeated.

"Yes, it says it right here," she continued as she pointed to the entrance labeled "One Roman St." on the map. "Do you know it?"

"There is no Roman Street in Midnight Lake," he replied pensively. "What else?"

"It's like I said, he supposedly can control monsters and has some master plan to take over the world."

Drusen walked over to the bookcase and pulled an ancient-looking tome off the shelf and set it on the table.

"Did the guards wear any crest or insignia on their armor?" he asked.

Vivian hadn't really thought to mention it before, but when her foot had gotten caught in Orik's breastplate, it was embossed with a tree with an elaborate root system made of snakes. She described it the best she could.

Drusen quickly flipped through the musty, rune-filled book and stopped.

"Was it this?" he asked as he splayed the book in front of her.

A drawing on the page depicted exactly the symbol Vivian had seen on the armor. Below the drawing was an inscription in an unfamiliar language.

"Yes, that's it," Vivian said quickly.

"Are you sure?" Drusen asked.

Vivian nodded. "Positive."

Drusen took a long swig of his Mountain Dew and then placed the can on the table. He had a haunted look on his face.

Vivian knew something was very wrong.

"So, it's true," Drusen whispered finally, more to himself than to Vivian. "He has returned."

"Who?" asked Vivian. "Who has returned?"

"Arborem. Arborem has returned," he said solemnly. "Do you remember the story I told you about the war between the three powerful brothers? Well, that was the story of Arborem, the Tree Lord. It seems that he has finally escaped his imprisonment and has come here to finish his work."

"What's his work?" Vivian asked nervously.

"Hard to say at this point," Drusen muttered as he flipped through the tome and landed on an illustration of what appeared to be a once-great city now overgrown in thick foliage with human skeletons riddled about the ground. "But I suspect his masterplan hasn't changed. To purify the multiverse by ending the scourge of humanity."

"Huh?" Vivian's head was spinning.

"He wants to eliminate all people, leaving only beasts and

nature behind," Drusen said. "Probably to first conquer earth and then back to his homeworld, the Great Realm, for a second act."

"Oh . . ." Vivian nodded, completely unsure of what to say to that. This was somehow even worse than she had ever imagined. Her mind went to the gate, and to what Dr. Barkov had said.

"Can the gate be destroyed?" she asked softly.

When Drusen didn't respond, Vivian repeated herself. "The gate, Dru! Destroying the gate—that's the answer, isn't it?"

Drusen shrugged. "While I'd be fine using a nuclear bomb, as Dr. Barkov suggested, the council would never approve it, and how would we get one anyway? I've read that there may be magic of such power in my homeworld, but we have nothing like that here."

"Like Beasts and Battlements spells?" she asked. "I knew it! So we do have magic—just like in *Harry Potter*!"

"Well, maybe not quite like *Harry Potter*, but yes," he replied matter-of-factly. "As I've told you before, pretty much everything from your bedtime fairy tales—and from your B and B books—it's all real."

Vivian's eyes lit up as she was struck by a realization.

"And you used the magic hand spell to forge my bedtime note after bringing me home from the Outskirts, didn't you?" she asked, her voice quivering with excitement. "That's a level two spell from B and B, so that must mean that you're at least—"

"Vivian," he interrupted sharply. "Stay focused."

"Sorry," mumbled Vivian. "So, what do we do?"

"*We* don't do anything," replied Drusen pointedly. "*I* will take this information to the council and insist they act. There's a seven p.m. meeting tomorrow at SPECTOR headquarters."

"Oh, c'mon, Dru!" pleaded Vivian. She felt the familiar flame of anger rising up inside her. She wasn't going to be pushed aside just because she was a kid. She was a part of this, whether the council liked it or not. "I'm the one who discovered the plan; I'm the one who got the map; I'm the one who was almost torn to shreds by the guards! I'm coming! I want to—I deserve to!"

"Vivian!" snapped Drusen, with an edge that she had not heard from him. "You don't know what you are asking! It's not safe! Your mother would never forgive me if—"

"My mother's dead!" Vivian screamed. "She's dead and she's not coming back! What do you know about her anyway! This is all I have now—I want to do something important. I can help!"

The fire left Drusen's eyes in an instant and he looked at her with such empathy that Vivian had to look away.

"Vivian," he said calmly. "You have to trust me. We'll develop a plan and I'll let you know."

261

Vivian could tell that there was no use arguing any further. She knew she could trust him, because she sensed that he actually cared.

"I'll ask Mr. Arrowsmith to take you home."

Close Calls

VIVIAN WATCHED OUT the back-seat window of Mr. Arrowsmith's car as the final rays of dusk illuminated a backdrop of leafless, snow-covered trees. Not a word had been spoken on the ride home.

"Pull over there," said Vivian as she pointed to an area about a half block from her home. "I don't want my dad to see me getting dropped off and start asking questions. I'll be in for it as it is."

Mr. Arrowsmith nodded and quickly pulled the car over.

"Drusen told me what you discovered," he said as his steely blue eyes reflected in the rearview mirror. "That was great and brave work, little one, and it's just as I suspected. Rest assured that I will support Drusen with the council and we'll end this threat, once and for all."

"But shouldn't I be there if they have questions?" Vivian asked hopefully.

"I'm sorry, Vivian, but Drusen's right." He shook his

head. "Our duty is first and foremost to keep you and this town safe, and the further you are away from this, the safer you'll be."

"Okay, well, thanks for the ride," Vivian sighed as she opened the car door and gathered her garbage bag full of things.

"It was no trouble at all," he said. "I have to drop by the museum anyway to clear some space for our upcoming mining exhibit. Mr. Thornwood has made it clear that I need to get that collection of equipment out of the attic of Murkwood School by the end of the year—it's like a miner's camp up there. Good night, Vivian, and be safe."

Vivian nodded and exited the car. She gave a final wave to Mr. Arrowsmith and disappeared down the dark, snow-covered sidewalk thinking about what she might say to her father when she returned.

As she approached her house, Vivian saw something that made her stop in her tracks: her father! He was just a few feet ahead of her, slowly trudging up the front steps and pulling out his keys. He hadn't come home yet . . . he didn't know she'd left!

Vivian instinctively leaped behind a shrub. She thought for second, which was all the time she had, then darted around the side of the house to the overgrown garden in back.

There, she threw down her garbage bag and began scaling up the trellis attached to the back of the house. A lattice snapped under her foot when she was near the top, but she caught herself, her hands barely able to hold on to the icy wooden structure. She gritted her teeth and steadied herself, then hurriedly continued to the top where she shimmied onto a second-floor air conditioner, which protruded from the wall of one of the back bedrooms. She stood on her tippy-toes to reach the rear window, which, like most windows in the house, was not capable of locking. Brushing off the snowy ledge, she edged it open and with her last remaining strength, pulled herself up and in, thumping onto the floor just inside.

"Vivian!" called her father as he shut the front door. "Are you upstairs?"

Vivian pulled herself up off the floor, tore off her coat, kicked off her boots, and scurried to her room. She could hear the creak of her father's footsteps as he made his way up the stairs. Breathing heavily, Vivian slipped into her desk chair and crossed her legs casually as she grabbed the fifth install-ment of *Harry Potter*, which she noticed was upside down as the bedroom door swung open.

"Oh, here you are!" exclaimed her father. "It looked for a second like no one was home."

"Where else would I be?" Vivian asked as sweat began to bead on her forehead. She did everything she could to stop herself from panting.

"Vivian, I know you're upset and I'm so sorry," he said as

he walked over to her bed and sat down on its edge. Vivian felt a wave of relief as she realized her dad thought she was acting oddly because she was mad at him for working late.

I can work with this, she thought.

Then her dad sighed deeply. He kept his head down, his eyes fixed on the floor as he spoke. "I thought this job was going to be a refreshing change of small-town news like local birthdays, county fairs, and the opening of new stores, but it's been . . . it's been nothing like what I thought it was going to be. And I just . . ."

He didn't finish, but only slumped his shoulders and shook his head slowly.

He looks so sad, she thought. So sad and so tired. And for a brief moment, she understood him better. She knew this feeling—it was guilt.

"You couldn't have known, Dad," said Vivian gently. "It's not your fault. . . ."

Her dad looked up and his face broke into a sad smile.

"And it's not yours, either," he replied softly.

A pit opened wide in her stomach. She knew what he meant, but she couldn't convince herself to agree. Things fell apart when Mom died, and Mom died because of *her.* Whether she agreed or not, he deserved to know what was going on. She opened her mouth to speak, but then bit her lip. A part of her desperately wanted to open up; to tell him what was happening—everything—but something again stopped her.

"Anyway, I love you, girly," her dad said as he stood, struggling slightly to get up from the saggy mattress. "Boy, that bed is soft—I'm going to have to fix that."

"Please don't," replied Vivian with a smile.

The Blowup

"THE SOUNDS OF angry, guttural voices and armor-clad footsteps echo throughout the tunnel and seem to be getting closer as you continue to clear boulders from the blocked passage," narrated William.

"Blimey, 'ow long is this gonna take!" exclaimed Arturo in the voice of the ornery dwarf Durin.

"We wouldn't be in this situation if you hadn't decided to snoop around the high priest's chamber," quipped Mary, speaking as her character, Venna.

"What, are we supposed let 'em keep doin' his evil without consequences?" shot back Arturo as the feisty dwarf. "I jus' took a few souvenirs."

"Oh, would you two quit it!" cut in Violet in her Snarfette voice. "We need to work together to get out of here!"

"I don't see you doin' much other than lifting pebbles, gnome!" snarled Arturo.

"William, how many rounds do we think it will take to

clear the tunnel?" asked Mary earnestly in her own voice.

William smiled and rolled some dice behind his gamemaster screen.

"Ten more rounds," he said with a wicked grin.

"And how long till our enemies show up?" asked Violet.

William's smile stretched from mischievous to downright grinchlike.

"As you're bickering, you see the high priest step around the bend and into the wide, three-way intersection behind you, in front of the storage barrels stacked along the walls. He's surrounded by two black-robed cultists with maroon cowls, two grotesque-looking zombies, four skeleton warriors, and a half dozen armored hobgoblins. The chief priest looks like Ming the Merciless from *Flash Gordon*, with thick, pointed black eyebrows and a thin goatee. He is adorned in all black robes and wears an evil-looking goat-horned headdress and a talisman around his neck with a healthy tree above with roots made of snakes."

William pulled the cowl of his hoodie over his head to make like the high priest and went on.

"He points his twisted, snake-headed staff at you and yells, 'Infidels! You dare to defile the Temple of Arborem! Prepare to die and then you will serve me for all of eternity in my army of the dead!'

"Okay," William continued as he began rolling a die behind the screen. "Everyone roll for initiative—just gimme your final totals—your roll plus your dexterity modifier."

"Fifteen!" exclaimed Arturo.

"Seventeen," declared Mary, shooting a wry smile at Arturo.

"Aw, shucks," said Violet in the small voice of Snarfette. "Seven."

"Vivian?" asked William.

"Huh?" replied Vivian dumbly, and she broke from a pre-occupied trance.

"What did you roll?" he continued excitedly.

Vivian hadn't been able to keep her mind on the game all evening. Instead, her mind was fixed on the meeting that she knew was happening at SPECTOR headquarters even as they gamed tonight in Mary's dining room. Mary lived just on the edge of Midnight Lake's central business district on Center Street, just a couple blocks away from Murkwood. Outside, they could hear the mechanical hum of bucket lifts operated by public works crews who had begun decorating the downtown for Christmas and the upcoming Winter Solstice Festival.

"Oh," said Vivian as she rolled unenthusiastically. "Ten."

"Okay, it's Mary first, then Arturo, then the high priest, the skeletons, the cultists, Vivian, the hobgoblins, Violet, and zombies last," continued William, all in a single breath.

"You mentioned barrels stacked along the walls of the intersection," said Mary. "Do we know what's in them?"

"You don't," replied William. "Could be ale, could be oil or foodstuffs—you don't know."

"Hmmm," Mary muttered to herself.

"This is no time for inventory, Venna," blared Arturo as Durin. "We've got some fightin' to do!"

"Shut it, Durin!" exclaimed an unusually bold Violet speaking as Snarfette. "Let her think!"

"Okay," continued Mary resolutely. "I . . . I cast mana missile, directing one missile at three different barrels."

William obviously liked the move and couldn't help beaming.

"Okay," started William excitedly. "You see three bolts of fiery energy shoot from Venna's fingers and whiz through the air like fighter jets in slow motion, doing loop-the-loops, dodging right past the stupefied bodies of your enemies. The three bolts land simultaneously at the barrels, at which point you are blinded by an extraordinary flash; the sound of the explosion practically splits your eardrums!"

William smirked as he gave a few quick rolls of the dice behind his screen.

"Then, you hear the heavy rattle of stone giving way as the ceiling above the intersection begins to cave in," continued William before making a hollow crackling sound effect from the back of his throat. "The sound is deafening and the dust all-consuming. As the smoke slowly clears, you can see that the cave-in has completely blocked off the intersection and other tunnels. You can hear yelling from behind the blocked passages and there appears to be some efforts in getting through—so at least some of your enemies were blown into the other passages or managed to escape during the cave-in."

"Ha-ha!" exclaimed Arturo. "Just what I was thinkin'—and just the time we need! Durin goes back to removing the boulders from their original tunnel—light speed."

The in-game explosion had gotten Vivian's attention and an idea began to bounce around her head.

A cave-in, Vivian thought. *Maybe the gate doesn't need to be destroyed, maybe it just needs to be obstructed! A cave-in below the lake could flood the tunnels and make it really hard to move creatures into our world!*

"So, you finally remove enough boulders from the obstructed passage you had been working on to crawl through. It opens up quickly and flows freely for several hundred meters until it emerges at a cave opening behind a waterfall deep in the forest somewhere southwest of the caves. Where do you go?"

"Great game, guys," said Vivian abruptly. "But, I've got to go."

"Oh, c'mon, Vivian," protested Mary. "You can't leave now—we're so close! We can go back to the fortress, get rein-forcements, and finally finish off the high priest."

"Yeah, what's the deal, Vivian?" demanded Arturo. "You're always running off when things are getting good."

Vivian couldn't help feeling irritated. Mary and Arturo

couldn't even imagine the kinds of things that she was wrestling with. The burden was immense, and here they were complaining about her gaming schedule!

"Mind your own business," said Vivian sharply. "I said I need to go and I'm going."

"Is this about that thing with your mom?" asked William carefully. "I'm really sorry about that, but I changed who the hostage was so—"

"No, it's not about my mom," Vivian snapped. "I just need to leave."

"Okay, it just seems like you always need to go much earlier than everyone else," William mumbled.

"Buzz off, William," snarled Vivian, as her temper began to flare. "It's my decision. You have no idea what I'm dealing with."

"What are you dealing with?" Violet asked, the concern obvious in her voice. "Is everything okay at home?"

Vivian realized she had said too much.

"Yes, everything's fine!" she insisted. "I just need to go."

"Vivian, we're your friends and we just want to help," Mary said softly.

Mary was trying to help—they all were—and deep down, Vivian knew that. But as she felt her temper boil over, it didn't matter. They were clueless! Clueless about her mother. Clueless about the challenges of being a new kid. Clueless about the very monsters that threatened to take over their town.

Whether it was their fault or not, they were clueless and that made her furious.

"You're not my friends and you can't help!" shouted Vivian. "You can't. No one can!" She snatched up her backpack and stormed out of the room and out the front door.

Vivian's face flushed red as she exited into the cold evening. A crescent moon glowed bright against the dark winter sky.

What the heck do they know, she thought. Vivian puffed hot vapor into the frozen air for several moments. Just as quickly as her temper had flared, she calmed. She began to feel bad—guilty even. How could the misfits know what she was up against? She never told them. . . .

Vivian had a momentary urge to go back in and apologize, until she remembered why she had left in the first place: a cave-in! She had a solution to SPECTOR's problem and, even though Drusen had warned her to stay far away from the meeting tonight, she felt she had to tell him now.

Vivian picked her bike up off Mary's lawn and pedaled as fast as she could down the icy street, past twinkling streetlamps and quiet storefronts now decorated with wreaths, bows, and candy canes, en route to SPECTOR headquarters.

When she arrived, she could tell the meeting had just let out as dozens of folks were exiting the building, solemnly heading for their cars and bicycles. As the congregation departed one by one, Vivian noticed a dark shadow leaning against the wall near the entrance, arms crossed. It was Drusen and he was fuming.

"What are you doing here?" he growled without looking up.

"I . . . I'm sorry, Dru," Vivian said quickly. "But I had to. I have an idea. I know how to get the attacks to stop! A cave-in! We need to collapse the—"

"Do you ever stop!" snarled Drusen. "It doesn't matter now—none of it does! That blasted Sentinel Thornwood still does not believe Arborem has returned, calling your claims 'the delusions of a confused young girl.' He has convinced the council that there is no need for immediate action—the blind fools! The matter will be reevaluated at an all-council meeting he has called to be held during the Winter Solstice Festival."

"The solstice?!" repeated Vivian. "But that's three weeks away! By then—"

"I know that, Vivian," he shot back angrily. He closed his eyes and took a deep breath. He continued in a softer tone. "But there's little I can do. I'm only one person and I can't completely defy the will of the council, even if I am . . . different."

"But Dru, what if Arborem strikes sooner? We need to be prepared!"

"The sentinels will be watching—me especially. Now, I'm going to tell you one last time—stay in and keep your head down. SPECTOR will handle this."

"SPECTOR can't handle this unless they are prepared!"

Vivian shouted, her face reddening in anger for the second time that evening.

"I'm sorry, Vivian, I really am," mumbled Drusen. "There's nothing more to say."

"Okay, well, thanks for nothing," Vivian fumed as she began to stomp away.

"Vivian," Drusen called after her. "Please be safe."

Vivian didn't turn or reply, but only brushed her hand toward him and stormed off toward her bike in a huff.

30

The Waiting Game

"IN SUMMARY, IF you vote for me for student council, I'll make sure that Murkwood is a place of safety, respect, and acceptance," blared Amber's whiny voice over the gym's PA system. "Get an 'A' this year at Murkwood—vote 'A' for Amber Grausam!"

Polite applause churned through the smelly gym turned lunchroom. Vivian rolled her eyes, sitting in the safety of the bench nook nearest the entrance. Most of those clapping obviously didn't know Amber, and those who did, knew full well she hadn't written her speech and she certainly didn't mean it.

"Thank you, Amber," boomed Principal Thornwood. "You've now heard from all the candidates. Please make your selections and drop them in the basket on your way out and proceed directly to your third-period classes."

It was Friday, December twentieth, the day before winter break. Vivian couldn't wait to get some time off because the last few weeks had been atrocious. Since her blowup with the misfits and then Drusen, the school days had felt especially cold and gray, filled with boring lectures given by mean teachers. Meanwhile, tense encounters with now student council nominee Amber Grausam and her cronies were an almost daily occurrence, Vivian often coming out on the wrong side and ending up in detention.

Vivian looked down at her ballot—she didn't know a single person on it other than Amber, which wasn't good because Murkwood wasn't that big a school. Of course, she knew the misfits, but none of them were running and she hadn't spoken to any of them since she had stormed out on their game. The more she thought about that night at Mary's house—the way she had acted and the things she had said—the worse she felt. There was no way they could understand, though . . . unless she told them the truth.

But the worst part of these bleak December days was the waiting—waiting for what could only be impending doom. It was like the feeling of a doctor approaching with a needle for a shot, but the apprehension never ends. It was a jittery and hopeless sensation. How could SPECTOR not see what was happening? Weren't they supposed to be the Society for the Protection of Earth from Creatures Transplanar, Otherworldly, or Realm-born? She felt pretty certain Arborem and his minions fell into at least one of those categories.

In spite of all of this, Vivian's spirits were a touch higher today because starting tonight the misery of school would be delayed by two weeks. More important, it was only one day till the solstice and there would be another meeting at SPECTOR—she could only hope they would make the right decision this time.

As students began to turn in their ballots and file out, Vivian quickly scratched something out with her pencil, folded the paper, and dropped it in the basket near the door, where she received a suspicious glare from Mrs. Wickams.

If Mrs. Wickams had audited her vote, she would've come to realize that Vivian had followed the rules. She had exercised her right to write in a candidate in the appropriate place on the ballot. It read, *ANYONE BUT AMBER GRAUSAM!*

As she exited, she heard amid the jumble of conversations behind her the unmistakable sound of William's voice when harping on a point.

"I just don't get it," William exclaimed as he dropped in his vote. "In *Harry Potter*, do you need a wand to do magic or not? Are wands like the all-purpose tools of the wizarding world?"

"Well, of course you need a wand," Mary responded.

Vivian froze at the voices of the stairwell misfits—they were close behind her and exiting the gym. She panicked and zipped to the wall next to entrance, kneeling down and pretending to get something from her bag.

"Okay, but then how does Harry make the glass go away with the snake?" William countered as the group passed by.

"How does his hair grow back to the same length right after it's cut?"

"The wand is what allows a wizard to harness their innate magical power and control it to make specific spells," chimed in Violet.

"But what's the point of being a wizard if you need a wand to do anything?" shot back William as they began up the hall.

"That's like saying what's the point of being a pilot if you need a plane to fly?" replied Mary.

"Yup," Violet agreed.

"It's fantasy, William," added Arturo. "The rules don't need to make perfect sense."

"Oh, yeah," huffed William. "Remind me that rules don't matter the next time we play B and B! It's the rules that keep you alive. If it were up to me . . . ," he said, his voice fading as the misfits disappeared down the hallway.

Thankfully, they didn't see her, but her heart ached all the same. She would've loved to help Mary and Violet fight off William's attacks on *Harry Potter*; even more, she would've loved to go play Beasts & Battlements with them in the stairwell. The fact was, she *missed* them.

The walk home that day was especially slow and cold. It was nearing sundown when she arrived. The house was dark and quiet.

"Dad? You here?" she hollered out of habit as she entered. She didn't try a second time—she already knew the answer.

Her father had been working around the clock at the newspaper. He was under constant pressure from his boss, Mr. Bellowman, to keep up with the increasingly active animal attack story or start looking for a new job. The attacks now occurred every day, but the story was still back seat to the disappearances of Ms. Greenleaf and Mayor Greenbriar. Before, Vivian thought she knew what it felt like to be alone; now she knew what it was to be truly alone.

Vivian sighed and softly padded up the stairs to her room, heading straight for her nook. While her days may have been miserable, her evenings were filled with meaningful study. By now, she had read every word in the stack of antique *B&B* books she had picked up at the Catacombs Game Shop. She didn't know if all of this research would ever make a difference, but at least it was doing something rather than nothing. Somehow, poring over these books made her feel less helpless.

As Vivian settled in amid the glow of her electric lantern, she picked up *Fortress on the Frontier*, the module she had been playing with the misfits until their fight. She had now read it, figuring she wouldn't be invited back to play anyway, but as she looked it over this time, she stopped at the mention of making a successful "charisma check" to convince some adventurers controlled by the gamemaster to join your party.

"That's what I need to do," she whispered as she looked up from the dusty booklet.

If they won't take Drusen's word for it, I need to convince them myself—I need to make my charisma check, she thought.

An idea began to form in Vivian's mind. She would attend tomorrow's council meeting at SPECTOR headquarters— she wasn't going to let another chance go by. And, for the first time in weeks, her heart filled with hope as her mind raced with the possibilities.

With a renewed sense of optimism, Vivian knew sleep would come slowly tonight. So, again she read, and read, and read. It was sometime very late in the night, or perhaps the early morning, during her umpteenth study of the furley, a B&B monster that looked like a jagged cave rock, that her eyes finally grew too heavy to keep open.

"When you're older you'll get to make decisions like this, but right now the decision is ours," said Mrs. Van Tassel firmly.

"Shut up!" screamed Vivian. "Stop trying to control me—to wreck my life! I hate you! I hate you both! I'll . . . I'll run away!" she added frantically as she grabbed her backpack and darted out the door, slamming it behind her.

She ran down the long, dimly lit hallway toward the lobby, which glowed with daylight. She could hear their door open behind her, no doubt her mother in pursuit. She stepped into the lobby and zipped by the mail slots and a finely dressed older man she had never seen before, who sat in the pleather lobby chair. He looked up from the newspaper he was reading—the Midnight Lake Bugle— *and smiled at her as she darted out the building's entrance doors.*

Vivian awoke in a cold sweat. Light poured in from beneath her closet door telling her that it was morning. She had spent the whole night in her nook and she had the neck stiffness to prove it. That face from her dream—who was it? It seemed so familiar, but she couldn't remember it. What she could remember was that today was the solstice—the meeting at SPECTOR headquarters was tonight!

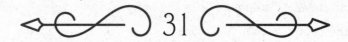

31

The Solstice

VIVIAN WAS A pink-and-purple blur as she sped on her bike toward SPECTOR's headquarters, dodging townsfolk who crowded the streets. The winter solstice was finally here, and half the town had gathered near a stage they had built for the Midnight Lake Winter Solstice Festival. Tonight, the sky had an eerie green glow and there was electricity in the air. The nearly full moon hung low in the sky above the bell tower of Murkwood Middle School, which was nothing but an ominous silhouette that loomed over the town.

SPECTOR's all-council meeting was currently in session and Vivian wasn't going to miss it. Her father would be covering the festival for the paper for the next hour, so she'd have just enough time to get out and back without detection.

The nervous voice of the assistant mayor blared over the PA system:

"Now, it is my district . . . I mean *distinct* honor to present the key to the city of Midnight Lake to Mr. Carlisle

Barmoor . . . excuse me, *Braemor* rather, a recent transplant to this area who has big plans for us!" The assistant mayor looked up from his notes, took off his glasses, and dabbed his brow. His struggles with public speaking served as a stark reminder of who should've been there presiding over this evening's activities—the missing Mayor Greenbriar. "Mr. Braemor's recent accusations . . . *acquisitions* rather and development plans, which now include the old quarry across the lake, will revitamin . . . sorry, *revitalize* this town! Congratulations, Mr. Braemor!"

The spectators broke into polite applause as Mr. Braemor stood awkwardly on the stage next to the assistant mayor, holding his fancy lapels and blushing tulip pink beneath his gray beard.

Good for him, Vivian thought as she zigzagged through the crowd on her bike, keeping her eyes peeled for her father, who she knew was working from the second stage a few blocks away. Her encounters with Mr. Braemor at her home and the bookstore had been some of her few bright spots since she landed in town almost four months ago. Once she cleared the main stage area, she found traffic-free streets due to closures from the festival. Holiday decorations flew by as she passed the understated sign of the Phoenix & Griffon Tavern en route to SPECTOR headquarters. Her legs burning and blood pumping fast, she had to stand on her pedals to conquer the final stretch—the hill of Silver Springs Road.

Pressing hard against the pedals, Vivian kept her gaze fixed on the pavement until she was practically there. When she finally lifted her eyes, she couldn't believe what she saw. A thick wall of tangled brush sheathed in razor-sharp thorns surrounded the building, hugging tightly to its perimeter.

She dropped her bike on the front lawn without ever taking her eyes off the building.

"How in the heck—" she muttered to herself as she approached.

She had never seen anything like it. The thorn wall was probably ten feet high and several feet thick—it was absolutely impenetrable!

She ran to where the front door should've been and shuddered.

The entrance was completely obstructed and tightly vined shut, while the building itself appeared to be completely enveloped in the deadly shrubbery.

A chill ran down Vivian's spine as she glanced at the parking lot full of cars and then back into the tangles.

The sentinels of SPECTOR are trapped inside . . . Arborem must be making his move tonight!

And if the sentinels were sealed in, who was going to protect the town—who was going to stop Arborem now?

Vivian's breath caught in her throat as the reality of the situation hit her. Her mind swirled with questions: Who could help her? Who could she trust?

Vivian grabbed a thorny vine and pulled it as hard as she could to try to make an opening in the hedge wall, but it was so heavy and thick she couldn't get it to budge an inch. She couldn't do this on her own.

Behind her, a brilliant flash and loud pop exploded high in the sky. Vivian knew that fireworks marked the end of the Solstice Festival—it must have ended early!

Dad! Vivian thought. His coverage of the festival would be ending and he would be home any minute. For a brief moment, her panic intensified as she realized she'd be in big trouble if her dad came home and she wasn't there. She hopped on her bike as a realization hit her: *Maybe Dad can help.* She wouldn't be able to beat him home from here, but it didn't matter now. It was finally time to tell him everything.

Vivian pedaled as fast as she could and made it home in record time. Even still, it appeared her dad had beaten her home as the lights were on. She left her bike in its usual spot on the snow-covered front lawn and bounded up the creaky front steps.

She huffed and puffed by the time she reached the front porch and took a moment to catch her breath.

"C'mon, Vivy, breathe," she half whispered to herself, shivering from nerves.

Would her dad believe her? It was time to find out.

Just as she was about to open the front door, she

realized it was splintered and slightly ajar. The door had been forced open!

She shuddered and quietly slipped inside.

"Dad?" she called tentatively. "Dad, are you here?"

There was no response. The floors creaked as she padded toward his office door, which was closed. She pushed the door open and gasped.

The place had been ransacked, with books and office effects strewn everywhere about the room.

Her father was nowhere to be found.

Vivian frantically searched through the wreckage and began to suspect that this had been less a burglary and more a struggle.

"Dad?" yelled Vivian, beginning to panic. "Dad, where are you!"

As she went around the desk, her blood went cold. There, resting on the floor, was her dad's phone, which had been smashed and lay next to the guitar case she had used to conceal her saber during her journey to Darkham Observatory. The bag she had left near the entrance to the catacombs . . . the bag that had a fully completed name and address tag right on top! How could she have been so foolish!

"No!" moaned Vivian as she picked up the bag and stared at the tag in disbelief.

They had captured her father, and it was all her fault. Vivian staggered backward, slowly hitting the wall behind her and sliding down to the floor as she tried to calm her racing thoughts.

"Dad," she whispered, her voice shaking. "Dad, I'm so sorry. . . ."

How could she have been so stubborn, so stupid! As usual, she had wanted to help, but she had made things worse—much worse.

She squeezed her eyes shut and took a deep a breath. When she opened them again, she caught the eyes of her mom peering down at her from the Snape portrait. As she stared at the painting, Vivian could somehow feel her mom telling her not to give up. She looked down at the guitar bag still in her hands. Gritting her teeth, she rose and headed up the stairs.

She knew what she needed to do.

Vivian shivered anxiously on the porch of Mary's house, the guitar bag over her shoulder. She could tell by the bikes scattered on the snow-covered lawn that all of the misfits were there. Vivian knocked again. A few moments passed and finally the door opened. It was Mary, who didn't react to the surprise of seeing Vivian.

"Hello Vivian," Mary said, her voice lacking its usual warmth.

"Hi Mary . . . Can I come in?"

Vivian knew she had a lot of explaining to do, and she was ready to do it. She had to.

Mary shrugged and gestured for Vivian to enter. Inside, the group was very much as she had left them three weeks ago, sitting around Mary's dining room table.

Mary came back around the table and stood behind her chair, crossing her arms.

"Well?" she said impatiently. "What are you doing back here with us losers, your nonfriends?"

Vivian winced as she remembered the terrible things she had said.

"I'm here because . . . you *are* my friends," she said, her voice shaking. "And I'm sorry. I'm sorry for everything. Since . . . since my mom died, I didn't think I needed anybody, but tonight I realized that I do. I need help and I need you."

The misfits all exchanged a look. Vivian held her breath, waiting for anyone to speak.

"Go on," William said finally.

"Last time we were together, you asked me if everything was all right. . . . Well, it's not and I have something to tell you," Vivian blurted out. The misfits exchanged a look of concern but Vivian kept talking. "So, you remember the thing I discovered about Garrison Arnold seeing the Murkwood Sanitarium case files and using those delusional descriptions in his game as Beasts and Battlements monsters?"

"Sure," said Violet slowly. "It's an amazing discovery."

"Well . . . I was wrong," Vivian said. "He didn't find those monsters in case files; he saw them with his own eyes. . . ."

The room went still. Mary and Violet shared a stunned look. Vivian went on.

It got easier as she continued. But the eyes of the misfits got wider and wider as she walked them through her adventure at the Outskirts; her encounters with Drusen and SPECTOR; Darkham Observatory; and ending with what she had found at home tonight with her dad missing and his office ransacked.

She had put it all out there. She took a deep breath as she waited for someone to say something, but the misfits seemed to be stunned into silence. Did they believe her or did they think this was some type of twisted joke, Vivian wondered. Then, she got her answer.

"You expect us to believe that?" William snapped.

Vivian's eyes dropped. Even *she* could hardly believe all that had happened. How would anyone else?

Then Violet stood up.

"I believe you, Vivian," she said with absolute calm and sincerity.

"We *all* do," chimed in Mary, directing her eyes sternly at William.

"Speak for yourself," William muttered, and he hugged his knees to his chest and turned away.

The room again fell silent.

"I don't blame you, William," said Vivian softly as she walked over to him. "I sometimes don't believe it either, but it's true and it's been happening to me. It's happening to *us* and we're the town's last chance—maybe even the world's last chance."

Vivian put her hand on William's shoulder.

"Please believe me, William."

William glanced up at her—he looked terrified.

"It's impossible," he whispered desperately.

"I know," answered Vivian. "But it's true."

Violet scooted her chair right next to William's. She spoke softly. "It's okay to be scared, William. We all are."

William stayed very still for a moment and then buried his face in his hands, breathing heavily.

"I'm not just scared . . . ," he said finally, his voice muffled by his hands. He lifted his head. "I'm sad. Fantasy is supposed to be fun. If this stuff is actually real . . ."

His voice trailed off and the room fell silent. No one needed to finish the sentence for him because they all seemed to understand how he felt.

"Don't worry, William, we'll still play B and B," said Mary lightly. "Heck, we'll need more sessions now for our own survival!"

William chuckled as the tension in the room broke.

"Now, how can we help, Vivian?" asked Violet.

Vivian smiled at Violet and then at the others—her *friends*—as they all began to beam back at her, each standing one by one.

"It'll be dangerous," Vivian warned.

"You have my axe," declared Arturo.

". . . and my spells," said Mary confidently.

". . . and my stealth," added Violet.

". . . and my . . . uh . . . quick wit, I guess," William said awkwardly.

Vivian's heart swelled with emotion, overwhelmed with gratitude for her friends. Tears rose up behind her eyes, but she quickly swallowed them back.

She walked over to the front bay window and peered out.

We need to create an explosion strong enough to collapse the caves beneath the lake, she thought to herself as her friends chattered excitedly behind her. The moon continued to glow ominously down on Murkwood Middle School and just like that, Vivian had an idea.

"Okay," said Vivian resolutely. "Follow me."

Friends

"OW!" CRIED MARY. "Arturo, that's my foot!"

"Well excuse me, princess!" Arturo grumbled. "I'd happily stay off your foot if I could see a dang thing down here!"

"Would you two keep it down!" whispered Violet. "If there's any security here, you'll give us away—ouch!" she yelped as she bumped into something.

"C'mon, guys, this way," Vivian whispered as she led the group through the maze of service tunnels. "We're almost there."

"I don't know how you can see anything down here, Vivian, it's pitch-black," replied William. "You know flashlights would've been nice."

"Well, sorry I didn't think of *everything*," teased Vivian. "Now stop whining, it's not that dark, and look, there's an exit to the entry hall."

Breaking into Murkwood Middle School during winter vacation had proved easier than Vivian expected. Maybe the prospect of breaking into what was a former sanitarium was enough to keep most people away as it was. The school seemed to have no security systems, shaky locks, and several ground-level windows where the bars had been pried wide enough apart to slip through. As far as she could tell, this place had been broken into (or out of) quite a lot.

The group had chosen to check the ground-level windows first and, on only their third try, found one where the wood had rotted enough on the sill to create a space where Mary could slip her small hand into and pry it up (she whispered, "Resero," the name of the B&B unlocking spell, when she did it, making Vivian chuckle.). From there, the group snaked their way through the service tunnels and up to the entrance hall, which was lit by dim emergency lights, where they found their bearings.

"We're going to get expelled for this," William fretted as he grabbed a flashlight from the emergency firebox.

"Well, if we're going to be expelled anyway, we might as well do it in style," Arturo replied, and he nudged William out of the way and grabbed the fire axe that was in the case. "Crowbar anyone?"

"Me please!" called Violet.

"C'mon, we need to hurry up!" Vivian couldn't help but smile as she watched the real-world manifestation of her Beasts & Battlements crew.

"Easy for you to say," Arturo said as he gestured to her guitar bag. "You have a sword!"

"Where are we going anyway?" asked Mary nervously.

"The attic," Vivian answered over her shoulder as she bounded up the stairs.

The group hurried up the staircases, grabbing two more flashlights and another crowbar out of fireboxes along the way, until they reached the top floor, where the classrooms of Ms. Greenleaf and Mr. Putrim were. When they arrived, Mary disappeared into Ms. Greenleaf's class and reemerged with an ornately carved walking staff for herself—one that usually rested in the corner behind the teacher's desk. Now fully equipped, the group came to a narrow doorway labeled "Storage."

When Vivian tried the handle, it was locked.

"Dang it, locked," Vivian muttered. "Now what?"

"Let me see it," said Violet as she pulled a hairpin out of her long black hair and pushed to the front.

She inserted the hairpin into the skeleton keyhole and began jostling it as she continued. "My great-grandma has a bunch of old trunks at her house and these old locks usually have a—"

Click.

The group watched in stunned silence. Vivian smiled.

"And we're unlocked," said Violet triumphantly as she gestured for Vivian to continue.

The door creaked open to reveal a narrow, cobwebbed staircase leading up into blackness.

Nothing creepy here, Vivian thought to herself.

The group climbed the creaky stairs until they arrived into the musty, cold attic space. Vivian led the way and arrived first. As she looked around, she saw the room was filled with mining tools and equipment as well as a bunch of antique classroom furnishings such as skeletons, maps, and globes.

The group gave a collective shudder.

"So, what are we looking for?" Arturo asked.

"Well, Mr. Arrowsmith had mentioned that all of this mining stuff was being stored up here . . . ," Vivian began. She looked at the faces of her friends to see if anyone saw where she was going with this. No one did. "We're looking for explosives," she said bluntly.

"Oh dear," exclaimed Violet.

"We're getting expelled for sure," William added nervously.

Vivian tried to figure out where to go from there when Mary jumped in and handled it for her.

"Oh, quit it, you two," Mary said in exasperation. "There won't be anywhere to get expelled from if we don't help Vivian save the town. So, let's all fan out and find some explosives!"

"Dang straight!" called out Arturo with an affirmative nod as he disappeared into the darkness of the attic.

Dusty beams of light showered the space, illuminating all kinds of mining equipment from primitive, ground-penetrating radar machines to metal detectors, gas masks, helmets with headlights, and tons of other rusty tools and machinery. Only a minute or two had passed when Violet rushed to the center of the attic.

"Hey guys, I think I found something!" she exclaimed. "Follow me," she continued as she led them to a back wall.

Sitting against the wall were two identical boxes labeled "TNT."

"Really *dynamite* work, Violet," Mary joked.

"Thanks," replied Violet, a confused frown on her face. "But you know what's odd? I could've sworn that a minute ago there was only one box, not two."

"Well, we're all moving fast," Vivian said distractedly as she knelt before the box on the right and lifted the lid. Inside, it was full of dynamite sticks, connecting wires, and a small push detonator.

"Jackpot," said Vivian, smiling as she turned back to her friends, who were now looking past her with wide eyes and gaping mouths. "What's wro—"

"Vivian, look out!" screamed Violet as she pointed next to Vivian.

Vivian turned back in a flash and to her horror, the second box of dynamite had opened its top to reveal razor-sharp teeth dripping with ooze-like saliva. Small bumps atop the lid housed what appeared to be soulless, reptilian eyes.

Vivian stumbled back as the creature viciously snapped at her head, almost catching the wisps of her bangs in its mouth.

"Run!" screamed Vivian as she backed away, while William, Mary, and Violet scattered in different directions.

The creature slithered toward Vivian, vaguely keeping its box shape, but with its hungry mouth fully open and its grotesque tongue extended toward her. Vivian rolled backward to create more space, but before she was again right side up, she heard a loud, dull thud and then silence. When she looked up, Arturo was standing above the fleshy box, his fire axe buried deep into its top.

"There's no life left in that one," he announced.

The others emerged from their hiding places one by one. Everyone was breathing heavily.

"Wh-what was that thing?" Violet asked.

"An imigator," William responded, his eyes wide with shock. "An imigator is a nonsentient monster that can assume the form of inanimate objects, always in search of its next meal . . . from B and B." William paused and turned to Vivian. "I'm . . . I'm sorry I ever doubted you, Vivian."

Mary stepped forward.

"So, what do we do now?"

"The map seems to suggest that his fortress is here at One Roman Street, but Drusen told me there was no such address in Midnight Lake," explained Vivian, pointing to her stolen tunnel map, which was now unrolled on a desk in Ms. Greenleaf's classroom.

The group was huddled around the map. They were now all outfitted with headlit miner's helmets, breath masks, picks, and of course the box of dynamite that proved *not* to be a monster.

"There isn't," said Violet as she rubbed her chin and furrowed her brow, but suddenly her face lit up. She zipped off to Ms. Greenleaf's game shelf and returned with Scrabble.

"No time for games, Violet," chided Arturo. "We've got work to do."

Violet rolled her eyes and hastily poured the tiles on the desk, quickly arranging the letters exactly how they appeared on the map: "ONE ROMAN ST."

"Look," she continued excitedly while she shuffled the letters. "One Roman Street is an anagram. Move the 'S' and 'T' before the first word and unscramble 'ROMAN' and voila!"

The room went silent.

"Stone Manor?" read Vivian slowly.

"I thought that place was abandoned," said Arturo.

"Nope, it sold recently," Mary replied, raising an eyebrow at Arturo. "Don't you read the newspaper?"

"Well, who lives there now?" asked William.

"Mr. Braemor," Vivian answered, rubbing her chin as she studied the tiles.

"What, the developer and philanthropist who moved here a few months ago?" asked Arturo.

Vivian nodded.

"Braemor. B-R-A-E-M-O-R?" Violet asked as she began assembling a fresh set of tiles.

Vivian nodded again, and Violet went to work, rearranging the tiles on the smooth surface. Moments later, she had something new. Vivian gasped; Mary put her hands over her mouth; William shook his head in disbelief.

The rearranged tiles on the desk read "ARBOREM."

"So, that's it," Vivian murmured in amazement. "Mr. Braemor is Arborem—he's the druid that has come back to conquer our world and end humankind."

"A druid . . . of course!" William exclaimed. "This makes perfect sense."

"Why?" asked Mary. "It makes sense that he's a druid?"

William began to pace the room as he thought out loud. "It's just the control of animals with all of the attacks; the thorn wall and . . ." His voice trailed off, a pained expression on his face as he realized something.

"What is it?" asked Violet anxiously.

"Well, it's just that tonight is the solstice—as a druid, it will sorta be the height of his power. . . ."

A chill ran up Vivian's spine.

"But . . . ," William continued. "We may have one more thing up our sleeve. This map, I've seen it before—sort of . . ."

"What do you mean?" asked Arturo.

"Well, I noticed the placement of the entrances, the different elevations and caves—it's the map of the Tunnels of

Torment from the *Fortress on the Frontier* B and B adventure we've been doing. Garrison Arnold must have used the caves beneath Midnight Lake as its model. Presumably, the bottom of the valley is the cavern with the gate. Maybe Arnold has got some other Easter eggs in there."

Vivian took a deep breath to calm herself and then spoke quietly.

"Guys, I know I've already asked you for a lot, but I need you to do one more thing."

"Of course," Mary said quickly as the others nodded.

"Arturo, do you know that vacant field right near your house where the Green River flows out and splits into two streams?"

"Of course, been through there dozens of times," he said confidently.

"Well, I need you guys to take the dynamite and go there. Follow the left fork of the river until it comes to a small waterfall, which will probably be frozen right now. There's a cave underneath the waterfall with a tunnel entrance in the back. That's here," she said as she pointed to a tunnel entrance on the map labeled "The Outskirts." "I need you to put on your breath masks and follow that all the way until you get to a huge cavern—you can't miss it. Assuming the cavern is uninhabited, I need you to wire dynamite around every column and into every hole and crevice. Then, leave the detonator in the clearing in front of the glowing portal—again, you can't miss it."

"Wait . . . you want us to do what?" asked William worriedly.

"Vivian, we don't know how to wire dynamite," added Violet.

"I do," declared Arturo.

Each head swiveled toward Arturo and stared.

"Well, sort of," he added. "I took a look in the box and it's a really simple circuit, the kind I've worked on tons of times with stuff at the farm."

"Yeah, we can figure this out," chimed in Mary. "Three years of STEM club must be worth something."

Vivian smiled and turned her eyes back to the map.

"Okay, so you'll leave the detonator here, but make sure to save a few sticks of dynamite and then you'll take this tunnel," she continued, pointing to a different one, "out to where it says Silver Springs—it should let out right near the old RGL head-quarters where SPECTOR is now located. Use the remaining dynamite to see if you can blow through the thorn wall at the entrance and free the sentinels."

"Wait, what are you going to do?" asked Violet as she placed a concerned hand on Vivian's shoulder.

"I'm going to Stone Manor," Vivian said quietly. She threw the guitar bag with her saber inside over her shoulder. "I'm going to get my dad."

Stone Manor

VIVIAN ALMOST LOST control of her bike as it slipped, slided, and glided across the frozen Midnight Lake. She knew that travel atop a frozen lake was both foolish and dangerous, except that she had lately watched local ice fisherman set up their seasonal cabins several hundred feet from shore and even watched cars drive atop its slippery surface. So Vivian figured it was safe for the moment, and it was the only way she could think of to get to Stone Manor quickly and undetected.

After parting from her friends at Murkwood School, she had ridden to Stone Manor's front entrance on Lake Shore Drive, only to find the gates closed and suspicious-looking figures looming nearby. It was dark and she didn't get a good look at them, but many of them appeared twisted, bent, and heavily armored—she suspected they were hobgoblins. The otherworldly, green-tinted sky was most brilliant above the mansion, as if somehow the source of the strange phenomenon.

The property was walled off all around down to the lake, so Vivian zipped downtown to the Paradise marina as a departure point. The frozen lake was her last chance, and by the looks of it, the coast was clear.

As she sped toward the mansion's massive shoreline, she could vaguely make out a dock jutting out into the frozen water, which connected to a gravel path that led up the hill to the manor. Vivian thought that this area would be way too visible, so she veered to a more wooded part of the shoreline covered with barren bushes and large weeping willows. She pressed her brakes as she entered the willowy, moonlit shadows, but the bike didn't stop. Instead, the nearly treadless tires slid full speed over the glass-smooth ice and caught the lip of the shoreline, catapulting Vivian into the thorny, leafless brush.

Vivian lay in the scratchy bushes for several moments. She was stunned but mostly unharmed except for a few scratches on her hands and face. More important, she remained undetected.

"That was smooth," she said to herself as she stood up and dusted off.

At this point, she didn't see any need to hide her saber, so she drew the sword from the guitar bag, threw the belted scabbard over her shoulder across her body, and clipped a flashlight she had gotten at school onto one of her belt loops. She peered up at the massive structure—looking at it from here, its shape seemed oddly familiar. Vivian's hair prickled as William's recent observations about the map and the Tunnels of Torment bounced around her head.

If Garrison Arnold put the cave maps into Fortress on the Frontier, *maybe he included some other "Easter eggs" as well.*

She pulled the flimsy adventure module out of her bag and began paging through until she arrived at a map of the fortress. The shape was unmistakable—it was definitely modeled after Stone Manor. Vivian hastily skimmed through the details of each area, which provided the gamemaster the information they needed to properly narrate and referee each room and encounter. Apparently, the top floor hosted the chambers of the lord who was in charge of the fortress in the game—those must be Arborem's quarters. Perhaps most important, according to the booklet, the cellars below hosted a dungeon area with "a dozen stout cells." That was the most likely place where they would be holding her dad.

Vivian could vaguely make out shadowy figures along the perimeter of the property, but the steep, lakefront yard seemed to be otherwise clear. She slowly crept up the snow-covered hill, bouncing from tree to tree for cover.

In only a couple of minutes, she had arrived at the stairs of the mansion's massive stone veranda. She hid in the shadows of the grand staircase, peering through the carved stone spindles to make sure she hadn't been spotted. The guards on the property's perimeter continued their lazy patrol, seemingly most concerned about warming themselves near the makeshift campfires they had set up. Vivian edged up to the top.

Warm light flooded out of the estate's enormous lakefront windows, illuminating the expansive, frozen terrace. Inside, the mansion seemed to be abuzz with guests, but on the cold back terrace only a single guard could be found—a very small soldier wearing chain mail armor, a rusty, full helm, and a crimson-colored cape secured by a large golden brooch forged in the snake-rooted tree symbol of Arborem. He was seated in a chair near the door, snoring loudly with a bottle in his lap.

Vivian took a deep breath and exhaled, which misted all around in the frozen air. There was no turning back—it was now or never.

Realizing she didn't have the luxury of time or indecision, she darted across the terrace into the shadows of the structure and next to where the sleeping guard rested. Without making a sound, she began to carefully lift the helm off the soldier's head. The guard abruptly snorted and flipped his head to the other side, leaving Vivian fear-frozen above him, wondering whether he was waking up. Vivian held her breath and waited, trying to control her shivering. The guard again seemed to relax and go back into his deep slumber. Vivian resumed her delicate work and slowly lifted the helmet off his head. She shuddered and nearly screamed. Beneath the helm was the twisted, gremlinlike face of an old goblin. This was going to take some getting used to.

Vivian silently set the helmet down and tiptoed around to the back of the chair where she made quick work of unfastening and freeing the battle-stained crimson cape. She fastened it around her neck. The garment was filthy but more than large enough to cover her whole body if she held it closed. Then, she placed the heavy helm over her head, but immediately gagged. It stunk of rancid meat and goblin sweat. Vivian fought the urge to remove it, knowing she would need to fight through the awful stench if she was going to make the disguise work.

She grimaced and tried breathing through her mouth. It didn't work; the smell was too overwhelming.

She frantically lifted the helm and vomited all over the snow-covered back porch. The sleeping goblin stirred but appeared to be impaired beyond disturbance. When she placed the helmet back on her head, the smell was still unbearable, but there was nothing left in her stomach to react to it.

Now practicing her best goblin hobble over to the door, Vivian turned the elegant brass nob and slipped inside. The sudden change of temperature almost made her pass out, to say nothing of the continued smell of the helmet she was wearing. Stone Manor's back entrance hall had all of the fine gilded detailing of a Parisian palace, with high, chandeliered ceilings, carved, wood-paneled walls, and grand marble staircases. Unfortunately, the inhabitants weren't the finely dressed, powdered-wig variety one might expect to see at a French landmark. Instead, it was a carnival of horrors inside.

"Happy Solstice, comrade," growled a large, pig-faced hobgoblin, who saluted Vivian while sitting sprawled on the stairs.

Vivian was so startled that she instinctively almost ran away, but she composed herself enough to give an awkward bow and nod back to her pretend brother-in-arms.

"In service to the master!" he continued as he lifted a smoking chalice in a toast and guzzled it, not seeming to mind that the mysterious green liquid dribbled down upon his neck and chest plate, which bore the symbol of Arborem.

"In service to the master," many others in the room and on the stairs joined in a chorus of monstrous voices as they lifted their various glasses and drank.

Vivian's eyes boggled through her helmet as she staggered through the crowd of monsters. Besides the heavily armored hobgoblins, there were dozens of tiny, humanoid servers, which included those wolflike canimen and small green creatures with pointed ears and scowling, fanged faces: traditional goblins like the one she was impersonating. The servers feistily dodged through the crowd with trays of live insects and worms for the larger creatures to snack upon.

At the carving station, huge eight-armed men with grimacing bearlike muzzles were cleaving raw and unidentified meat for the other guests. Vivian recognized these from her Beasts & Battlements books as "spiderbears." Meanwhile, and worst of all, were a handful of tall, blade-thin creatures with slimy, green-colored heads covered in squid-like tentacles who stood motionless in the corners penetrating the other guests with their solid black eyes. One of them was nibbling a fleshy, bulbous gray delicacy with its beak. Vivian realized in horror it was a brain!

"Brainbiters," Vivian whispered to herself in disbelief—yet another notorious monster she knew from her study of B&B. She tried to steady her shaky breath and keep calm.

Vivian put her head down, pulled her cape tightly around her shoulders, and stumbled toward the west wing of the mansion, which, according to Garrison Arnold's *Fortress on the Frontier* adventure module, held both the master's quarters and the dungeons. She decided it would be best to keep her eyes down from now on, and she followed the seams of the polished marble floors, dodging around assorted creatures when their feet (or tentacles) came into view. Fortunately, and curiously, it seemed that most of the creatures did their best to stay out of her way as she passed.

Finally, she reached the end of the lavish, mirrored hallway that ran nearly the length of the building's lakefront side. It ended at another marble staircase, which went up to the second floor, guarded by two tall and fully armored soldiers—hobgoblins, she thought. Vivian halted for a moment. She had rather hoped to find a staircase leading down, not up, as the dungeons were no doubt below ground. But it was too late to turn back or to overthink it now, and she continued on to avoid looking suspicious or out of place. As she slowly hobbled over, her mind raced around what she would say or do if she was questioned. She quietly began to fill her throat with phlegm to mimic the hoarseness of the goblin voice.

The guards stiffened up as she arrived.

"Capm'," said the larger one. "Goin' up to th' master's quarters?"

Captain? thought Vivian frantically as she looked down upon her crimson-colored cape. She had stolen the cape and helm of a goblin captain! That must be why so many creatures had cleared the way for her.

Vivian straightened up and nodded with as much authority as she could muster.

The sentries looked at each other, nodded, and then stood aside.

Vivian's heart nearly stopped, but she managed to amble past them, expecting any moment for a rusty cleaver to come down on her from what she thought must be a failed impersonation attempt, but none came. She wasted no time in shuffling up the long staircase.

When she reached the top, there was an open door to her left that appeared to lead to an apartment and to her right was a long, gilded hallway that ran the length of the mansion—a match to what she had walked on the first floor. She could see the tail end of a nightmare-filled procession that included stoic brainbiters, twisted hobgoblins, leashed vulturebears, and even a hovering leer sphere in the back. They all flanked a brown-robed man in a horned helmet holding a twisted staff. As the last of them disappeared down the grand staircase, located halfway down the hall, Vivian gave a sigh of relief—it appeared "the master" had just left.

"Now let's find those dungeons," she whispered.

The Master's Quarters

VIVIAN TOOK A deep breath, but stopped it short when she remembered how terrible her helmet smelled. She took another glance down the now empty upper hall and quietly slipped into the open apartment door on her left. As she entered, she noticed it matched the lavishness of the rest of the mansion in every way, except its rooms were chock-full of plants. Huge palm plants in the corners, potted trees, large ferns and flowers of every variety filled nearly every inch of the place. It looked more like a Rainforest Cafe than an apartment.

Dominating the common room was a long wooden table with a dozen chairs around it including an especially ornate chair at one end in front of the fireplace. Carved at its top was the familiar tree with twisted snake roots—the symbol of Arborem, Vivian realized.

Resting on the table, held in place by daggers in the corners, was a huge map of Midnight Lake and its surrounding areas with carved red and green miniature soldiers placed on certain locations. There were perhaps a dozen red figures at the Darkham Observatory; four at the old quarry at the far side of the lake, and six more at Stone Manor. Meanwhile, there were green miniatures—over a dozen—all placed at SPECTOR headquarters, which had a red circle around it. It looked like an elaborate game of Risk, but she suspected that this wasn't a game at all, and those miniatures represented real squadrons made up of soldiers, monsters, and SPECTOR sentinels. This was Arborem's war room.

Vivian's hair stood on end when she saw another red circle drawn around a house on Maple Street—hers.

Thoughts of her father snapped her back into the present; her stomach twisted in knots. Where was he? Was she right that they had taken him to the dungeon at Stone Manor as they had Dr. Barkov? If so, how did she get there?

She rushed to a room off to the side, which she thought must be the master's study. This room was also full of plants. Sitting atop a huge, wooden desk were several small bowls and vials of dried flower petals and fine powders next to scrolls, a potion bottle filled with blue liquid, a large jewel, and a hefty skeleton key. Along the back wall, a tall bookcase full of ancient leather tomes was pushed aside, revealing a gloomy stone shaft with a spiral staircase that descended into the darkness.

Vivian removed her helmet to take a closer look at the items on the desk.

"Vivian! What are you doing here?" said a voice from behind her in the doorway.

Vivian's heart almost leaped out of her chest as she turned and instinctively grabbed the hilt of the saber on her back. Standing in the doorway was Principal Thornwood, dressed in his SPECTOR council robes.

"Oh, Mr. Thornwood, thank goodness it's you!" Vivian exclaimed as she released the saber hilt. "It's Mr. Braemor, he's Arborem and I think he's planning on moving tonight! The other sentinels are locked inside SPECTOR headquarters; he's taken my father! And—"

"It's all right, Vivian," said Mr. Thornwood reassuringly. "I've got everything taken care of. You can go home and relax."

"Relax!" Vivian sputtered. "Did you hear what I said? Arborem has kidnapped my father! He is planning his conquest tonight! We must free the sentinels, defeat his army, and collapse the caves!"

"I admire your spirit, Vivian, but I'm afraid I can't let you do that," Mr. Thornwood said as he pulled a jeweled saber from his scabbard and stalked toward her. "The master won't allow it."

Vivian's whole body tingled; her blood rushed hot as she slowly stepped backward, reaching again for her own saber.

"It was you," she said bitterly. "You betrayed SPECTOR! That's how Arborem knew they would be there tonight.

That's how he's been operating so smoothly underneath their noses." She pulled her saber from its sheath.

"Go home, Vivian," Thornwood snarled. "Everything is as it should be. If you leave now, I'll even spare your father's life, if the Tree Lord allows it."

Vivian glared at him, a familiar fire igniting inside her. Her blood beginning to boil, she charged him, unleashing a flurry of furious attacks.

Mr. Thornwood's eyes widened in surprise. He stepped back and almost missed deflecting a thrust to his chest, followed by Vivian's swift combination of swipes to his head and side.

Vivian had the advantage but it only lasted a moment as he quickly regained his footing. He came back with three lightning-fast swipes of his own, which drove Vivian back to the bookcase, forcing her into a last-ditch thrust. Thornwood skillfully repelled the attack, using the momentum to throw Vivian off-balance and careening into the desk.

"Very good, Vivian," mocked Mr. Thornwood. "You have much talent indeed. It's a shame it will never be fully realized," he added as he slowly walked toward her.

"Not if I can help it," said a low, gravelly voice from the doorway.

It appeared to be one of the fully armored hobgoblins that had guarded the stairs up to Arborem's quarters, until the figure removed his helmet—it was Drusen!

"Vivian, grab that key and release the prisoners in the dungeon," ordered Drusen as he gestured to the stone shaft and withdrew his silver katana. "I need to have a word with Mr. Thornwood."

"Drusen, I should've known," spit back Mr. Thornwood as he approached. "You always have a way of mucking things up!" With that, he withdrew a dagger from his belt and unleashed a vicious two-weapon attack.

Drusen's sword flashed with such speed it almost seemed a helicopter propeller, expertly fending off all the deadly strikes, and mounting furious parries that drove Mr. Thornwood on his heels.

Just then, the sound of heavy footsteps and guttural voices flooded the war room next door.

"Go!" yelled Drusen over his shoulder to Vivian as he reengaged in another flurry of lightning-fast clanks.

Vivian threw the heinous helm back on and grabbed the key, the potion, and the jewel off the desk. She took one last worried glance back at Drusen and zipped into the darkness of the secret stairwell. The key felt heavy in her hand, and Vivian squeezed it tightly as she hurried down the steps. She didn't even know why she had taken the rest of the items, but the key . . . the key, she hoped, would allow her to set her dad free.

The Dungeons

VIVIAN WAS DIZZY by the time she finally reached the bottom of the long spiral staircase. The floor was dirt and a cold wind whistled through the dim and narrow stone corridor. This cell block looked eerily similar to those she found beneath the Darkham Observatory, but the sounds that echoed through the halls here were not those of monsters, but the pained moans of people.

With no guards in sight, Vivian removed her helmet and placed it on the ground in front of the first cell door. She stepped on the helmet to gain enough height to peer through its barred viewing window. Inside were two scruffy-looking, unconscious men with long, unkempt locks, one with black hair, the other blond. Vivian felt sorry for these prisoners who looked malnourished and covered in painful-looking scars. She didn't know these men, but she recognized the familiar symbols of SPECTOR on their hunting clothes. These were sentinels.

She unlocked the door with the skeleton key and swiftly

moved to the next door, using her helmet again as a booster. Here, she saw a familiar person huddled in the corner: Dr. Boris Barkov!

Vivian stepped down and opened the door.

"My name is Vivian Van Tassel and I'm here to rescue you!"

The head of the tattered scientist popped up, and he slowly lifted himself off the floor.

"Vivian who?" he replied confusedly in his thick, Eastern European accent.

"Van Tass—never mind. I'm here to help. I watched your video at Darkham and we've got trouble."

"Yes, of course," said Dr. Barkov as he limped toward the door. "That's exactly what I've been trying to tell everyone."

"Dr. Barkov, my father is a reporter named Michael Van Tassel. He interviewed you recently. Have you seen him?"

"The reporter? Yes. Yes!" he replied excitedly. "They brought him in here just a couple of hours ago. He was unconscious and they dragged him that way!"

Vivian bolted down the hall in the direction he pointed, frantically checking cells. The first was empty. The second contained a powerful-looking sleeping hobgoblin that she thought best to leave alone. But in the third cell, she found who she was looking for: her dad.

He was lying on a wooden bench, but he wasn't moving. She frantically unlocked the door and rushed in. She noticed his chest heaving softly—he was breathing! She let out a breath of her own that she hadn't realized she was holding as relief washed over her. She quickly looked him over. He seemed unharmed but fast asleep.

"Dad! Wake up!" Vivian shook him as hard as she dared. "We've got to get out of here!"

Vivian gently slapped his face from side to side to wake him. His clothes, she noticed, were covered in fine sand and he reeked of lavender.

Mr. Van Tassel didn't even stir.

Vivian grabbed him by the shoulders and began shaking him much harder.

"Dad!" she shouted. "Wake up!"

It was no use, she realized. He was out cold.

As Vivian dusted the fine sand off her hands, she suddenly understood that this was no ordinary sleep.

"It's a slumber spell," she murmured to herself, remembering that according to her B&B books, sand and lavender were necessary components for a sleep enchantment.

Relief shifted to anxiety as she realized that she would need to drag him out of here, but he was far too big for her to carry by herself. She looked back and considered Dr. Barkov, but he could barely stand up in his condition. She would need more help.

"Hold tight, Dad," she said as she gently kissed him on the forehead. "I'm coming back for you."

She began to exit the room, but suddenly turned back.

"I love you, Dad," she whispered—words she hadn't muttered since her mom had passed away. Words that were much easier for her to say to the sleeping than the awake.

She nearly ran over Dr. Barkov, who had finally caught up with her, as she darted out of the cell.

"Dr. Barkov, stay with my dad. I'm going to get help."

"Of course," he said, nodding and inching toward her father's cell. "What else would I do?"

Through the window of the next cell, Vivian could make out a slight figure sitting in a tucked position on the ground against the far wall. Long, dirty-looking black hair hung down over the figure's face.

"Hello?" Vivian said. "My name is Vivian and I need your help."

A pair of brilliant green eyes shot up, piercing through the hair and the darkness, followed by an all-too-familiar smile. Vivian's insides nearly burst with excitement and relief. It was Ms. Greenleaf!

"Vivian!" Ms. Greenleaf said weakly. "You've come! I somehow knew you would!"

Vivian unlocked the door and ran inside the cell.

"Miss Greenleaf!" Vivian exclaimed as she threw her arms around the ragged woman. "I can't believe it. I thought for sure you were . . ."

"Dead?" Ms. Greenleaf finished when Vivian paused. "I should be . . ."

"Oh, Ms. Greenleaf, there's so much I want to tell you!" Vivian rambled as she knelt down next to her teacher. "The assignment you gave me led to discovering that the people in the old Midnight Lake asylums weren't mentally ill—they were really seeing monsters! They come out of a portal to another world beneath the lake. Fortunately, there is a secret society in town called SPECTOR and they are sentinels descended from elves who protect us from these monsters. Years later, Garrison Arnold would discover the portal and made B and B based on what he found! Then—"

"Yes, yes, Vivian. I know," Ms. Greenleaf said.

"You know?" Vivian repeated.

"I do." Ms. Greenleaf nodded as she brushed her hair behind her generous ears. Now visible, they had an ever-so-subtle point at the top. "I'm a SPECTOR sentinel myself. I had quite hoped with the assignment that you'd figure all of this out, but I certainly hadn't planned on the return of Arborem in the meantime . . . or getting captured."

"You *wanted* me to discover these things?" Vivian asked, anger bubbling up as the words sunk in. "But why didn't you just tell me? Why lead me down all these rabbit holes to find out the secrets of this town? Was this some sort of joke to you?"

"No, Vivian, you don't understand," Ms. Greenleaf replied. "I didn't put you on this path just so you could know the secret of Midnight Lake . . . I did it so you could know yourself."

Ms. Greenleaf leaned forward and brushed Vivian's hair back to uncover her ears. She gently placed her finger on the tiny, slightly pointed piece of cartilage on top of Vivian's ear.

"Vivian, have you ever wondered why you could do things that no one else could do—feats of speed and reflex; hear things that no one else could hear; maybe see in the dark better than your friends? You are one of us . . . *you* are a trace elf. Your *mother* was a sentinel."

"My . . . my mother?"

"Yes. She was an amazing warrior and an even more amazing friend. As the last offspring of the Silverthorn family, she was slated to be the chief sentinel. If you've been to SPECTOR headquarters, then you would know there's an open chair at the head of the council—that was supposed to be hers. But after she met your father and had you, everything changed. She moved away to protect you. She loved you so much . . . and she'd be so proud of what you've become. . . ."

Vivian tensed as she felt a wave of emotions overcoming her—feelings she had fought so hard to suppress since her mom passed—but she couldn't fight them any longer. Months of pain hit her and tears bubbled up from her eyes and began to stream down her face.

Ms. Greenleaf gently put her arms around Vivian. Vivian's

body went limp as she buried her face in her teacher's shoulder. Rivers of grief, bitterness, and guilt poured out as she sobbed in Ms. Greenleaf's arms.

"You put me on this path," Vivian mumbled finally through her tears. "You made me get the school building assignment—you knew the whole time what I'd find; you made it happen! But I thought you said, 'Fate knows better than we do.'"

"That's true," said Ms. Greenleaf gently as she stroked Vivian's hair. "And yes, I did use a touch of magic to get the ball rolling. Fate, after all, sometimes needs a bit of help."

The word "help" echoed in Vivian's ears; her tears rapidly subsided. Her work wasn't done—there was still much to do and perhaps fate was demanding that she be the one to do it. She wiped her face with the back of her hands.

"Arborem," she blurted out as she stood up. "He's holding my father in the cell next door and has him in some type of sleep trance. Can you help me get him out and free the other prisoners?"

Ms. Greenleaf tried to rise, but her legs immediately gave way as she stumbled back into the wall.

"I'm afraid I'm pretty weak and I suspect you'll find the same with the others."

"Well, what do we do?" Vivian asked desperately.

Ms. Greenleaf's eyes fixed on the blue potion vial that hung from Vivian's belt.

"Where did you get that?"

"Arborem's desk," Vivian replied. "Ms. Greenleaf, what do we—"

"Give it to me," Ms. Greenleaf said eagerly, cutting Vivian off.

Vivian unhooked the potion from her belt and gave it to Ms. Greenleaf, who quickly pulled out the cork and took a sip.

"Wait! I-I don't know what that is!" Vivian exclaimed.

Ms. Greenleaf winced and breathed deeply for several moments.

"Are you okay?" Vivian asked anxiously.

"Yes," she replied as her eyes popped open and she began to rise, slowly but stable on her feet this time. "It's just as I thought—it's a healing potion."

"Awesome!" exclaimed Vivian. "Finish it and let's get going!"

"No." Ms. Greenleaf shook her head. "There are too many for you and me to get out of here by ourselves. I'll need to preserve it—a sip for everyone so they can leave on their own power. There's more we can do for them at SPECTOR headquarters."

"But Arborem is launching his invasion tonight," Vivian argued. "If we don't stop him now—"

"I'm sorry, Vivian," Ms. Greenleaf insisted. "But there's no other way. Only the sentinels of SPECTOR can help us."

Vivian bit her lip nervously.

"Um, about that. SPECTOR is surrounded by a thick, thorn wall. The sentinels are trapped inside."

Ms. Greenleaf's jaw tightened. She closed her eyes and let out a deep sigh.

"Then he's already won," she said softly, more to herself than Vivian.

"No, not yet. Not if my friends, the stairwell misfits, come through."

"Your friends?" asked Ms. Greenleaf in surprise. "I thought you didn't have any friends, just 'acquaintances' helping with your 'research.'"

"I was wrong," Vivian said firmly. "They are my friends— my true friends."

"But Vivian, they're not warriors. How are they going to free the sentinels? I don't see how—"

"Please, Ms. Greenleaf," interrupted Vivian calmly. "Just trust me. Work with Dr. Barkov to revive everyone down here and get them over to SPECTOR—hopefully you'll be able to get in by the time you get there. And for my dad—"

"Don't worry," Ms. Greenleaf jumped in. "I'll take care of him—I promise."

"Thanks," Vivian replied with a relieved smile. As she made her way toward the door of the cell, Ms. Greenleaf called after her.

"Vivian, what are you going to do?"

Vivian hesitated. She was worried Ms. Greenleaf would try to stop her. She turned around and looked at her teacher— her mother's former best friend—and realized that Ms. Greenleaf would understand what she needed to do.

"I'm going to collapse the caves."

The Midnight Gate

THE ENDING OF each *Harry Potter* book played over and over again in Vivian's head as she rushed down the tunnel from the dungeon at Stone Manor to the cavern below the lake. She couldn't decide which of Harry's final trials this was closest to, but she was reminded that they always involved a dangerous encounter. While Harry had usually fared well with his face-offs against He Who Must Not Be Named, she personally hoped that she might be spared a showdown with Arborem.

Unlike her last journey from the Outskirts entrance on the edges of town, this path was far shorter, Stone Manor being right next to the lake.

Her sneakers squished as the ground softened beneath her. As she reached the spot where the tunnel let out into the cavern, she stopped and listened: nothing. Not a sound down here tonight, but Vivian didn't consider that to be good news.

She knew things were quiet because tonight, the creatures were gathering above and getting ready to strike. She took a deep breath and stepped into the cavern. It was dark and polluted, like last time, with the heavy stench of sulfur in the air. In the distance, a faint light source glowed from the cavern's center—it was the gate.

Vivian dashed toward the portal, dodging huge stalagmite pillars as she ran, all the while wondering if her friends had succeeded in their mission. The sulfur burned her lungs, but she kept going.

Finally she reached the pillared area that surrounded the gate and her question was answered. Around the base of each pillar was a bundle of dynamite.

"Well done," whispered Vivian. "I knew you'd come through."

Vivian found the connecting wire and followed it into the spacious opening in front of the portal, which glowed like a pulsing, fiery rainbow. There, sitting in the extreme heat and brightness of the glowing door, was a rotting wooden box with a push handle on top—like something out of *Looney Tunes*. It was the detonator, and she desperately hoped the stairwell misfits had set it up correctly.

She picked it up and headed toward the passage that would lead her to the Silver Springs entrance, letting out the connecting wire from a spool the misfits had left next to it.

She figured she'd depress the lever as soon as she reached the passage, which would give her the time she needed to escape before the caves flooded.

Vivian had barely left the ring of pillars when a strange, gaseous form began to materialize a few yards in front of her. Vivian stopped, frozen in fear.

The green smoke spun and twisted and then formed into an ancient, bearded man. He gripped a gnarled staff and wore a long brown robe. It was Mr. Braemor; it was Arborem.

"Well, well, well," cackled Arborem in his gravelly voice. "If it isn't the great Vivian Van Tassel. The fearless fork fencer and brave savior of Midnight Lake."

Vivian gulped and tried to speak, but terror had seized her voice.

"Oh, yes. I've been watching you closely since you arrived, and I know all."

"B-but, you helped me," Vivian sputtered. "You bought me the *Book of Beasts*."

Arborem grinned. His crooked, yellow teeth looked like fangs in the shadowy light.

"I *wanted* you to learn," he bellowed. "I *wanted* you to understand. A girl of your talents, I was quite hoping you'd see fit to *join* me . . . and it's not too late."

Vivian's head spun; her breath grew short. Was it the fumes or something else?

"And all you have to do is bring me the box," he added as

he held out a bony, clawed hand. "If you join me, I'll be merciful and even spare . . . your *father*."

The mention of her father was like cold water on her face. Her vision sharpened; her thoughts cleared.

"No."

Arborem's grin mutated into a venomous scowl.

"No?" he growled.

"Why are you doing this, Arborem?"

"Because the universe needs to be cleansed!" Arborem shook his fists as he preached. "Humankind is the scourge of all nature and it's time that things return to the ground."

"There's another way," Vivian pleaded. "We should teach people to cherish nature—to protect it. You could show them how!"

"Nonsense!" snarled Arborem. "Don't you see? Humans have had their chance—the earth itself has warned them for years and still they don't change. No, the land requires retribution and tomorrow . . . it will be watered in blood."

"You're mad," Vivian shouted.

"Am I?" replied Arborem, his eyes wild. "I'm merely doing my part to appease fate. Have you never read the prophecy of thorns? Let me enlighten you:

"Yet still a frightful vision remains
of the Tree Lord's return, the world he gains
To finish work he once began
To cleanse all worlds of human's span

He shall succeed except this claim
A girl who bears a special name
a silver thorn right in his side
If she returns, his plan shall die

"You see, that's why your *mother* had to die—she was the 'silver thorn' and the only one who could have stopped me."

Vivian felt the blood drain from her face.

"My mother?" she gasped.

Vivian looked at Arborem's ragged face—that strangely familiar face—and suddenly it all came together. She now knew where else she had seen it outside of her encounters with Mr. Braemor. His was the face from the lobby that morning when she had run away—the day her mother died; the face from her nightmare.

"Yes, it was *I* who killed her—I had to. The last of the Silverthorns, now gone."

Vivian stumbled back in shock. The memory of her mother's funeral surged through her mind, then the countless tear-filled mornings and guilty sleepless nights, all scenes she was seeing through a new lens. She suddenly realized, everything she had been carrying over her mom's death had not been hers to bear—it wasn't her fault!

It had been Arborem . . . It was *his* fault.

"She was a selfish coward," crowed Arborem. "She abandoned her duty and her destiny as Chief Sentinel of SPECTOR to pursue her own fancies—to marry your foolish father and have you. What a waste," he continued. "Her failure is now complete."

"She was not a coward!" Vivian fumed, setting down the detonator and drawing her saber. "She was coming back before you *murdered* her!"

Arborem smiled, his jagged teeth glistening in the dim light. Vivian trembled with rage.

"You should've seen the look on her face when she saw that tree falling toward her car," he taunted. "She knew exactly what was happening. Her last thought was of her own failure."

Vivian's gaze burned through Arborem as she lifted her saber up in salute. In reply, Arborem twisted his grizzled face into a fake grimace. Vivian's anger swelled.

"Come on, Vivian," Arborem spat. "Cut me down and avenge your mother."

Vivian's muscles tensed. She was going to slice him to pieces.

Arborem opened his arms wide and puffed out his chest. His wild eyes momentarily shifted to the detonator box at Vivian's feet and then back to her.

Even through her anger, Vivian had noticed something. *He's afraid of the box . . . He's baiting me to get the box away from me,* she thought. *But my temper's not going to get the best of me today!*

Vivian gritted her teeth, squeezed her toes, and forced herself to swallow her fury. As she sheathed her sword, the words of the prophecy played in her head:

He shall succeed except this claim

A girl who bears a special name
a silver thorn right in his side
If she returns, his plan shall die

"What are you doing, you foolish girl?" Arborem shouted frantically.

"Hey Arborem—not to be a silver thorn in your side, but there is one more Silverthorn . . . Me."

"Nonsense!" Arborem laughed. "The prophecy is clear— it is she 'who bears' the name of Silverthorn . . . the blood running through your veins isn't enough, my dear Vivian Van Tassel. You need the name as well!"

Vivian smirked.

"That's Vivian *S.* Van Tassel, Arborem," she replied as she placed her foot on the detonator's push handle. "The 'S' stands for Silverthorn."

Arborem's bloodshot eyes widened.

Vivian closed her own and took a deep breath—she was ready.

"Noooooo!" shrieked Arborem.

Vivian depressed the handle and a massive explosion shook the cave. Stone crumbled from the ceiling, followed by the violent rush of black water, which instantly filled the cavern.

Vivian smiled peacefully as the raging, dark waters swept over her.

She had done it.

The Catacombs

WHEN VIVIAN OPENED her eyes, all she could see was a bright white blur, but she didn't feel like a weightless, ethereal spirit flying in the heavens. Instead, she was freezing cold, sopping wet, and dizzy. As her eyes slowly adjusted, the white blur began to take the form of white ceiling tiles illuminated by bright, fluorescent shop lights. She seemed to be lying on a couch; a heavy wool blanket had been thrown on top of her.

Vivian rubbed her eyes and slowly sat up to find herself face-to-face with a pair of big, droopy eyes, and a slobbery snout. It was Merle's bloodhound, who had been resting his head on Vivian's lap. He nuzzled her gently and began licking the salt off her hands and face. Vivian realized that she was in the Beasts & Battlements section of the Catacombs Game Shop. Merle was whistling cheerfully while stocking books on the corner shelf. He turned as she rose.

"Oh good, you're up," he said lightly as the hound

lumbered to his side. "I thought you'd be out for a while. You took quite a bump on the head."

"Merle?" Vivian asked in confusion. "What are you doing here? What am I doing here? What happened?"

"All is well, Vivian," replied Merle as he poured her a cup of tea from a nearby teapot and handed it to her. "Things have been returned to balance—for now."

"The gate? My friends! My father!" exclaimed Vivian as she tried to get up but fell back down from dizziness and exhaustion.

"The gate has been flooded—handily obscured, but not destroyed," Merle said before taking a slow sip of his own tea. "That should keep things at bay for a while. Your friends—the misfits, I am told you call them—amazingly made it to SPEC-TOR and managed to free the sentinels. The dynamite they had left over made short work of that thorn wall," he added before chuckling to himself. "And the front door of SPEC-TOR for that matter—not an elegant solution, but it worked well enough. Without the leadership and magic of Arborem, most of the monsters retreated or scattered, and the sentinels, led by Drusen and Ms. Greenleaf, made quick work of captur-ing those that remained. As for your father . . . he is safe. He's resting comfortably at home."

Vivian sighed in relief.

"He won't remember anything of what has happened—such is the way of sleep enchantments," continued Merle.

"And Mr. Braemor, I mean, Arborem?" Vivian asked nervously. "Is he—"

"Dead?" Merle cut in. "Unfortunately, no. He's still out there. As a druid, he's pretty handy at controlling the elements—even breathing under water. I saw him slip through the portal when I . . . retrieved you."

"How did you—" Vivian sputtered. "I mean, are you a sentinel too?"

"Not exactly." Merle paused and looked around his shop as if he was trying to decide what—or how much—to say next. "It looked like you needed help, so I helped. You see, I don't usually like to interfere in matters of this world, but I made a special exception today."

"Matters of this world?" Vivian repeated. "Who are you?"

"Like I told you when we met, the name's Merle. Merle Lynn," he said matter-of-factly, a warm smile on his face. "Of course, I guess I'm better known as Merlyn the True."

"Merlyn?" said Vivian in disbelief. "The wizard? Garrison Arnold's Beasts and Battlements character?"

"The same," said Merlyn proudly. "Of course, I was me long before Garrison made a character based on me for his game—I've got a bit of history in England as well, but that's a story for another day." He took another long sip of his tea. "I've been keeping an eye on things since Garrison passed— to keep things in balance. Today, Arborem threatened that balance."

Vivian flopped back down on the couch, rubbing her eyes and temples. This was all too much. She thought her brain might explode, which, she thought, would be an unfortunate way to go with all she'd survived.

Merlyn rose slowly and headed back to the shelf he had been stocking.

"No offense, Mr. . . . uh . . . Merlyn," said Vivian. "But with your power, couldn't you tell it was Arborem when he came to your shop? When he bought me the *Book of Beasts*?"

"Oh, I knew right away there was something special about him, and so did Mort," replied Merlyn as he gestured to his bloodhound who now lay on the floor. "But Arborem's powers of deception—and otherwise—are great . . . they may even exceed my own."

Merlyn looked over his shoulder as the first rays of dawn began breaking through the shop window.

"You better be getting home—you father will be awake soon."

After a few swigs of tea, Vivian sluggishly pulled herself up from the couch and slowly hobbled through the store toward the front door.

"Your bike's outside and you'll want these as well," Merlyn said as he grabbed Vivian's guitar case from the behind the counter and handed it to her.

Her saber and B&B materials were inside, topped by a new booklet she hadn't seen before.

"What's this?" asked Vivian as she pulled out the unfamiliar book depicting a creepy, abandoned temple on the cover.

"Oh, that. That's another Garrison Arnold adventure—*The Sanctuary of Malevolence*. You might . . . need that someday."

"Thank you," Vivian said. She felt like she needed to say so much more to this man—this wizard—who had saved her life. But she hoped "thank you" was enough for now.

"Merry Christmas," replied Merlyn gaily. "Always happy to help the next generation. Oh, and Vivian, please try to stay out of trouble. I may not be there next time."

Vivian had never felt so tired and sore as she pedaled home through the freezing December air. All she wanted to do was get out of the wet clothes that were on the verge of freezing to her body and take a bath. The icy streets were covered in remnants of the Solstice Festival; confetti and discarded programs swirled in the wind.

When she arrived home, she decided to bring her bike up to the porch, instead of its usual precarious space on the lawn. This bike had gotten her through a lot lately, and maybe it could be rejuvenated with some new tires and a tune-up. She went to open the door only to find that it was already cracked open.

Vivian snapped back into high alert.

"Here we go again," she whispered.

She drew her saber and silently slipped inside. There, she

heard the sound of soft pacing coming from the living room. She tiptoed over and peered around the corner.

"Drusen!" she cried as she dropped her sword and charged into the room, startling the heavily bandaged warrior. "Drusen, you're alive," she added as she threw her arms around him while he stood awkwardly with his arms out to his sides.

Drusen slowly closed his arms around Vivian.

"I'm okay, Vivian," he said gruffly. "We're okay."

"We?"

"We're all okay," remarked a gentle voice from behind her.

It was Ms. Greenleaf. Vivian zipped across the floor and threw her arms around her favorite teacher, who had changed out of her dungeon rags into a sleek suit of silver-colored chain mail, and a silken green cloak. Like Drusen, she too was bruised about the face and her arms were covered in bandages.

"What are you doing here?" asked Vivian. "I mean, I'm thrilled you're here and all, but shouldn't you be wrangling monsters?"

"We're taking care of you the same way you took care of us," said Ms. Greenleaf softly. "Vivian, you risked everything to save us—to save this town, to save the world."

Vivian's father began to cough and rustle on the couch.

"Looks like your father is waking up," said Ms. Greenleaf. "We'd better go."

She gestured to Drusen, who nodded.

"See you at school?" asked Ms. Greenleaf.

"Absolutely," Vivian replied eagerly. "Ms. Greenleaf, Drusen, I don't know how I can ever thank you."

"No, Vivian, all the thanks go to you," answered Ms. Greenleaf as she turned to leave.

Drusen nodded and limped out of the house, but Ms. Greenleaf stopped at the door without turning around.

"Merry Christmas, Vivian."

Just then, Vivian heard her dad take a deep breath, and she turned to check on him. He was still stretched out on the couch but seemed to be waking up. When she turned back to Ms. Greenleaf, she was gone.

"Vivian," muttered Mr. Van Tassel as he rubbed his eyes and sat up. "Vivian, is that you?"

"Hey Dad." Vivian sat down beside him. "Another late night, huh?"

"I guess it was," he said shakily as he rubbed his temples. "I was so tired; I don't even remember anything after the festival . . . Look, Vivian, I'm really sorry—"

"It's okay, Dad—I know this job has really been a lot on you."

"No, I don't mean about last night—I mean yes, I'm sorry about last night—but no, I'm sorry about everything," he said as his eyes glazed over with tears.

"Dad, you're tired. We don't need to—"

"Moving here was a mistake," her dad interrupted, his

voice shaking. "I can see that now. After your mom died and I lost my job, I didn't know what to do. I thought the change of scenery would be good for us so I stuck with the plan we had made before . . . But I never asked you what *you* wanted—what *you* needed . . . I thought *I* knew best. What I now realize is that you didn't need a change of scenery; you needed a father."

"Dad . . . it's okay," Vivian said as she took his ink-stained hand. "I'm sorry too. And, believe it or not, I'm glad we came here."

Mr. Van Tassel looked shocked, but then a relieved smile formed on his face.

"You are so much like your mother," he said softly. "I miss her so much. I wish she could see the girl you're becoming; the girl you've become. She'd be so proud. . . ." He paused and took a shaky breath. "I love you, girly."

"I love you too, Dad," said Vivian as she leaned over and hugged her father tightly.

Mr. Van Tassel squeezed her back and rocked her for several moments before stopping abruptly.

"Vivy, you're soaking wet!"

Vivian pulled away, wiping her tears.

"Oh that, sorry." Her mind raced as she tried to come up with an explanation. "I, uh . . . went for a morning run."

"Well, you better go get ready," he said as he stood up from the couch. "We've got to finish—well, start really—our

Christmas shopping. That reminds me, did you hear the one about the thunderstorm on Christmas?"

Vivian crossed her arms and raised an eyebrow.

"They think it was caused by rain-deer?"

Vivian groaned. Her dad laughed, and Vivian realized how much she'd missed that sound.

38

A New Leaf

"SO, IN SUMMARY, the school that we stand in today is much more than meets the eye—like a Transformer," joked Vivian. In return she got blank and puzzled stares from her classmates.

She cleared her throat and continued.

"Anyway, it was once a sanitarium that housed individuals with a variety of mental health conditions, which were likely brought on by lead-contaminated water from local mining operations. The sanitarium closed in the 1920s and was abandoned for many years, becoming a favorite, spooky haunt of local Midnight Lake children until it was taken over by the city and converted to Murkwood Middle School in 1960. Thank you."

The classroom broke into polite applause, except for Amber Grausam, who sat scowling with her arms crossed, and Ms. Greenleaf, who clapped enthusiastically, even in spite of the bandages that still covered her arms and hands.

Vivian smiled and winked at her teacher as she began to pack up her foam core display.

BRRRIIIIINNNNGGGG!

Vivian's classmates packed their things and began clearing out even more quickly than usual, eager to begin their first weekend of the New Year.

"Have a wonderful weekend, everyone!" said Ms. Greenleaf as students rushed toward the door.

"Great job, Viv," commented Mary as she slung her backpack over her shoulder. She added a not-so-subtle wink.

Vivian chuckled.

"Thanks, Mary! See you tonight?"

"Wouldn't miss it!" Mary gave Vivian a wave and headed for the door. "Later, alligator."

Vivian smiled and waved back. Then, looking around the classroom, she realized that she and Ms. Greenleaf were the only ones left.

"Nice work," remarked Ms. Greenleaf. "That was really . . . creative. I especially liked the part about the lead in the water; that was a nice touch."

"Thanks, Ms. Greenleaf. Just imagine how they'd react if I told them the *real* story. So much for honest reporting." Vivian's eyes lit up as she remembered something. "Oh, I understand a 'congratulations' is in order. When do you start?"

"I already have," answered Ms. Greenleaf. "Since Mr. Thornwood 'skipped town'"—Ms. Greenleaf made air quotes with her fingers—"the school board said they needed me to start as principal right away, and I told them I would on one condition: that I keep teaching this class. After all, I wouldn't want history to fall into the wrong hands. . . ." Her voice trailed off and she smiled. "And speaking of Mr. Thornwood, SPECTOR has since filled his seat on the high council."

"With who?" Vivian held her breath.

Ms. Greenleaf's smile got even bigger.

"Drusen. The first in his line to ever serve on the council."

"Yes!" squealed Vivian as she bounced on her toes. "That's amazing news!"

"It couldn't be better," agreed Ms. Greenleaf, and she began gathering her things. "So, I guess I'll see you later?"

Vivian grabbed her bag and headed for the door.

"Yep. SPECTOR HQ, Sunday at seven," Vivian confirmed, tinkering with her mother's mythril necklace that dangled from her neck. "I'll be prepared to give a thorough report. I've even got exhibits!"

"You are your mother's daughter," said Ms. Greenleaf warmly. "I'm glad to see you wearing her necklace—she would've wanted you to have it."

Vivian looked down at the necklace and nodded. Wearing it finally felt right.

"Oh, and Vivian. You know I practically grew up in that house of yours and there's a couple more things I think your mother would want you to have. Take a closer look at the grandfather clock when you get a chance."

As Vivian packed up things at her locker, she could hear the shrill voices of Amber Grausam and her mean girls heading her way.

"Well, if it isn't Little Miss Vivian Van Tassel, the fork fencer and new Murkwood Middle School scholar."

"Hello Amber, Kelly, Madison," Vivian said coolly as the girls half circled her. "Any big plans for the weekend?"

Amber paused in confusion, but quickly recovered.

"Oh, you know, I thought I'd go to the spa with my *mom*; you know, do some fun *mother*-daughter stuff," she needled. "What about you?"

Vivian tensed up—Amber must have learned about her mom's death. Her temper began to flare. *Who teases someone about this?* Vivian wondered. *Could this girl be any more rotten?* But just then, her dad's words echoed in her ears: *"We only have to* deal *with them—they have to* be *them."* She then took a depth breath and gripped her mother's mythril necklace. A feeling of calm washed over her.

"The same," replied Vivian peacefully as she walked away, leaving Amber and her friends confused and speechless.

Outside, she unlocked her bicycle, now outfitted with new gleaming white tires, which she had begun to break in on her daily round trips to school. She zipped down the frozen Murkwood Hill and soon passed the museum, which displayed an updated sign out front: EXHIBIT NOW OPEN: MINING IN MIDNIGHT LAKE. Vivian chuckled as she flew by.

She sped down Main Street and looked around. At the park, there were little kids building snowmen with their parents; on the streets, hectic shoppers dodging in and out of stores. Coming up from the lake, she saw a plaid-adorned ice fisherman walking with the day's catch and nearly bumping into a well-dressed business executive, who was yelling into his phone while emerging from a coffee shop. There were dogs walking their freezing owners and retirees out for peaceful strolls. She smiled and rode on knowing that she had preserved their way of life. She had saved them, and herself in the process.

When she came upon the Catacombs Game Shop, she was reminded that she couldn't have done any of it alone. There at the front window stood Merlyn, waving as she passed Broad Street, his huge, droopy bloodhound snoozing at his feet.

A block later, on the library's frozen lawn, sat Drusen reading quietly. He seemed to be enjoying the freezing weather. He looked up and nodded stoically at Vivian as she rode by.

When she got home, she found her dad sitting in the dining room perusing the day's paper. The headline read: DISAPPEARANCES EXPLAINED! UNPLANNED VACATIONS THE CULPRIT by Troy Grausam. A much-smaller, secondary headline declared, ANIMAL ATTACKS DECLINE SHARPLY by Michael Van Tassel.

"Well, there goes Grausam again, hogging the headlines," muttered Mr. Van Tassel as he put the paper down on the table. "And there's no story—turns out the disappearances were just a bunch of poorly tracked vacations. Listen to this." He picked the paper back up and read. "According to Midnight Lake Mayor Brynn Greenbriar, it was all a 'big misunderstanding.' 'There was a glitch in the time-off request system. I was camping up in the north woods. Anyone that's been up there knows you can't get any phone reception—that's why I couldn't be reached.'"

"It's okay, Dad," said Vivian comfortingly. "You're the star reporter in my book."

"Thanks, Vivy," her dad said, smiling proudly. "Oh hey, I made you this for your game tonight," he continued as he handed her a crudely fabricated wooden dice tray.

A twenty-sided die rested in the velveteen center of the vaguely square tray.

"Thanks, Dad!" Vivian exclaimed. "I love it! Shall I give it a try?"

Her dad nodded and Vivian rolled the sapphire-colored die. The surface of the tray wasn't quite as flat as it appeared because the die seemed to get caught in some sort of divot and ended up landing between two numbers: twenty and two.

"Sorry, Vivy," her dad said sheepishly. "Looks like I'll need to fix that."

"Nope," replied Vivian cheerfully. "It's perfect the way

it is!" She pecked him on the cheek and went off to gather her Beasts & Battlements materials.

By seven o'clock, the misfits had arrived at her house. It was the first time they had been there. Vivian gave them a quick tour of her room and the first floor before ending at the dining room.

". . . And this is where we're playing tonight," she said as she finished the tour.

"Really great place," William said as the others nodded. "So much history; so much character."

"Thanks," Vivian replied, relieved her friends liked her house. She all at once realized she did too—even the portraits.

As everyone settled into seats at the table, Vivian didn't take her usual seat between Violet and Arturo. Instead, she circled to the head of the table and sat in the gamemaster's seat behind a dragon-adorned GM screen. Tonight, *she* was the gamemaster.

She glanced across at William, who now inhabited her usual space. He smiled and gave her an encouraging nod. Vivian took a deep breath, opened the book that Merlyn had most recently given her, and read:

"'You have been marching now for several hours along the rough mountain path. Finally you come up over a ridge, revealing a vast valley before you, anchored by a massive, blue lake. Meanwhile, dense forests and purple mountains rise high around you in all directions. As you descend into the valley, thin plumes of smoke rise from a collection of thatched-roofed wood, stone, and plaster dwellings far in the distance situated along the main road—Greystone at last!'"

The misfits played B&B late into the evening. Durin and Venna bickered; Snarfette skulked and sniveled; and William, now a player, added a new character to the mix: Cervantes, a swashbuckling swordsman.

"You round the corner and see the last of the raiding party cornered in a dead end. William, you recognize him as the one who murdered the mayor."

William's eyes lit up.

"I draw my sword and say, 'My name is Cervantes Alonso Quijano. You killed the mayor. Prepare to die,'" said William calmly.

Violet giggled; Arturo and Mary smiled.

"And that," announced Vivian, "is a good place to stop."

The misfits howled and applauded as Vivian wrapped her first session as gamemaster.

"Great job, Vivian," bellowed William. "You're a natural!"

"So fun, Vivian, thanks!" added Violet.

"That was just like *real life*," laughed Arturo, but the rest of the room went silent.

Vivian knew what was on everyone's mind: how close they had all come to losing everything that winter solstice evening. It was something they hadn't really talked about—no one had seemed ready. But Vivian felt it was time.

"You know, I can never thank you all enough for what you did," she began, trying to figure out how to make them understand how grateful she was.

"No need." Mary held up a hand. "That's just what friends do."

Vivian's voice caught in her throat. She smiled and nodded.

"And please do tell SPECTOR again we're really sorry about their door," Mary added. "Arturo here was convinced it wouldn't work without the whole bundle—"

"And it *did* work," insisted Arturo, adding in his best Durin voice, "I can't be responsible for shoddy elven construction— they should've hired the dwarves!"

The room erupted in laughter.

"Same time next week?" asked Vivian as the group filed out the door. "Maybe a return to the Tunnels of Terror?"

"Yep," replied William as he turned back on the front porch. "But let's make it a return to Greystone—*you're* the gamemaster now."

As Vivian waved her last goodbye and shut and locked the front door, her father, who had spent the evening upstairs, called down over the railing, "Hey Vivy, it's late. You going to bed soon?"

"Yep. Just a couple more things I need to do."

She quietly padded back into the dining room and packed up the remnants from the evening's game: sprawling papers, miniatures, maps, and books. She grabbed her backpack and sat back at the head of the table—the gamemaster's chair. She pulled out her beloved copy of *Harry Potter and the Sorcerer's Stone* and opened it. Her list filled the whole inside cover, Harry taking the advantage on each issue. She added a line at the bottom of the page—"Family and Friends"—and, for the first time since she had started the comparison chart, put a checkmark in her own column.

She closed the book, rose, and placed it on a bookshelf in her dad's office. With all that had happened, she didn't think she needed Harry anymore; she had exciting adventures of her own.

She sat quietly studying the mythril necklace that had once belonged to her mom. The house was still and the only sound was the soft ticking of a wall clock in the kitchen.

The clock, she thought excitedly. With all the evening's activity, she had almost forgotten about what Ms. Greenleaf had said.

Vivian walked into the living room and looked at the menacing, inoperative grandfather clock in the corner. It continued to show 11:59 p.m. She had never noticed before, but the lock was not shaped like a skeleton key, rather more like a shield. Fingers still on her necklace, Vivian realized that it was a similar shape. She removed the pendant and inserted it into the lock.

Click.

The clock hands advanced to midnight and the massive structure moved a couple of inches out from the wall; she quickly realized that the entire case had been set on a hinge, which swung open like a door. She opened the clock, which revealed a ladder descending into a narrow, dark shaft. A crest with a crossed sword and arrow in front of a glowing, eye-topped gate had been fixed on the wall above the ladder: it was the Silverthorn family crest.

Vivian's breath stuck in her throat. She had never gotten to say goodbye to her mom, but she now knew that she didn't need to. Her mother lived on inside her and always would.

She smiled and disappeared down the ladder into the darkness.

And somewhere, very far away, angry, bloodshot eyes reflected off a glowing crystal ball—eyes that waited; eyes that planned; eyes that watched her every move.

Prophecy of Thorns 1:8–10

Yet still a frightful vision remains
of Tree Lord's return, the world he gains
To finish work he once began
To cleanse all worlds of human span

He shall succeed except this claim
A girl who bears a special name
a silver thorn right in his side
If she returns, his plan shall die

She is the fourth, this one a daughter
Her power greater than woods, towns, or water
Should she succeed, a reign of peace
Should she fail, all things shall cease

–Fragments from the Codex Fey Historium

Acknowledgments

WORKING ON THIS book has been nothing short of a dream come true and it couldn't have been done without the love, support, and dedication of countless individuals. To my family (both immediate and extended) who loved, supported, inspired, and endured me throughout this process—my everlasting love and thanks! Next, to the to the people and organizations that made this book possible: Thank you to my incredible editor Kara Sargent, who believed in Vivian from the beginning and expertly guided me through a (sometimes perilous) editorial adventure to get this story to where it is today—my infinite gratitude! A huge thank you to all of the wonderful and talented folks at Aladdin / Simon & Schuster who helped make this dream a reality including Valerie Garfield, Anna Jarzab, Michelle Leo, Christina Pecorale, Kristin Gilson, Tiara Iandiorio, Olivia Ritchie, Sara Berko, Lisa Quach, Anna Elling, Gary Sunshine, Stacey Sakal, and the rest of the amazing team. Thanks to the brilliant cover artist Raymond Sebastien—if what's inside the book is half as good as what you've done outside, we're in great shape! A sincere thank you to my longtime literary agent (and friend) Jacques de Spoelberch, who helped me get this book in shape before placing it and continues to be a constant source of guidance and support. Thanks also to my friend and collaborator Jon Peterson, who provided invaluable feedback at key early stages of the manuscript. Also, a very special thank you to Gary Gygax and all the other RPG creators, designers, artists, and publishers who inspired me over the years. My deepest thanks also extend to you, the reader, who gave this story a chance—I hope it was as fun for you to read as it was for me to write. Last, but certainly not least, thank you God for Vivian and everything else!